VISIONS II

VISIONS II

MOONS OF SATURN

EDITED BY

CARROL FIX

LILLICAT PUBLISHERS
USA

VISIONS II
MOONS OF SATURN

Special thanks to DeeAnn Heins and Timothy Heins.

Lillicat Publishers books may be ordered through booksellers or by contacting:
Lillicat Publishers
www.lillicatpublishers.com

ISBN: 978-0-9916426-2-5
Ebook ISBN: 978-0-9916426-9-4
Printed in the United States of America

The Face of Saturn

Moons of Saturn

Contents

STEPPING STONES TO ETERNITY

The *Visions* series tells the story of how humanity must ultimately venture outward from our tiny home and explore the Universe.

Visions: Leaving Earth, the first volume, describes our first faltering steps to rise from Earth's surface and build homes in space.

Visions II: Moons of Saturn confirms that humankind has left the Earth and is at home in the other planetary systems of our solar system.

Visions III: Inside the Kuiper Belt proclaims humankind's domination of all that dwells within the solar system—from our Sun to the outermost reaches of the Kuiper Belt.

Beyond these volumes, we will explore outside our solar system: *Deep Space,* the *Near Stars,* colonizing the *Milky Way,* and understanding the *Universe.*

Our vision is limitless.

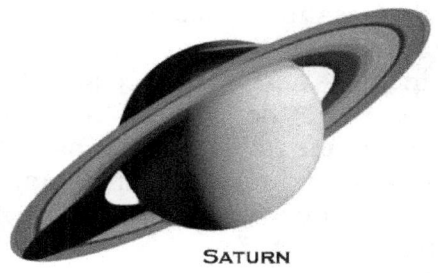

SATURN

INTRODUCTION

Ice mining in space, aliens within our solar system, colonization of extraterrestrial moons, war between interplanetary corporations, and time travelers bent on destruction are a few of the exciting concepts pursued by the talented authors whose stories appear within these pages. The theme, Moons of Saturn, provided inspiration for the creation of widely divergent tales centered about the mighty planet and his circling hordes. From the first to the last—and all those between—these stories will capture your imagination and keep you guessing.

In story number one, you will battle alien amoeba in the depths of an ice mine on Dione. "Pest Control," Tom Tinney's account of embattled troopers combating an overpowering enemy in the frigid tunnels will leave you enthralled.

Jeremy Lichtman's wry humor, story two, is at its best in "The Archetypes of Titan," another tale of Wilbur and Fox, who yet again manage to avoid calamity at Wilbur's hands.

The last story, "Hot Day on Titan," shows us what can happen when enemies team up to complete a mission. Bonnie Milani skillfully weaves an intense tale of revenge.

NASA's Cassini Mission has given humankind incredible images of the Saturn System. Cassini arrived at Saturn in 2004 and has since sent back data inspiring hundreds of scientific articles and special editions of major scientific journals. Cassini has 12 instruments on board that capture important information about Saturn, the rings, and the moons. Cassini's mission currently extends until May 2017.

Saturn, as seen in images, is a beautiful planet with mesmerizing rings of ice and rock and 53 named moons, each ripe with promise. Its major moons, and some of the minor ones, offer future colonization opportunities as well as minerals, metals, and even ice for water to supplement a depleted Earth. Titan, the largest moon, possesses a recognizable atmosphere and amazingly has most of the scientific criteria to qualify it for status as a planet.

For an inspiring view of this incredible system, visit NASA's slideshow presentation at their Cassini Equinox Mission website, "The Saturn System: A Feast for the Eyes." http://www.nasa.gov/externalflash/cassini_equinox/cassini_equinox_slideshow.html.

This book brings together author visions of Saturn's moons—a rich and varied focus for building speculative images of the future—which present imaginative views with plots solidly grounded in the actual moons, the rings, and the planet.

The authors, some of whom contributed to the first *Visions* volume, *Leaving Earth,* hail from around the globe. When humanity inevitably ventures beyond our own world and moon, we will go as co-inhabitants of a common world—Earth, the mother of us all.

Carrol Fix
Editor
Lillicat Publishers
August 2, 2015

DIONE

1. PEST REMOVAL

By

Tom Tinney

"ABUTs are trapped, they can't advance."

"Egress corked on our end in section 18-4. Give it the gas."

"Mark it. Give it 24 hours and B-squads move in to clean up. Everyone else, eyes up and firing pattern Delta."

"You can pull your troops out, RP10673. It's contained. Good job."

Routine and costly, but effective.

RP10673. That's my designator. Currently assigned to section 18-4. I patrol the places nobody else will or wants to. My domain is the dark recesses and twisting maze of interconnecting conduits and robotic service tunnels that are the backbone of the Dione Automated Water Mining Platform #29. My job is to combat the Alien Biologic Unicellular Threat, the ABUT.

The rewards are few, but the thoughts of a warm bedding, good food, and knowing my children are taken care of keep me going.

We were in the twelfth day of our current two-week rotation and it had been a busy one. A couple of bumps and scrapes. Nobody hurt badly. We were in the groove. What we are doing is important. At least, that's what they feed us through our wireless updates.

Dione has various H2O capture stations that encircle Saturn's 15th largest moon and its icy bounty. Water is a valuable resource. Mining the ice and hauling it off a low grav source makes moving it into the MetroStellar much more cost effective. Again, that's what my implant tells me. For all I know, this ice could be going to chill fancy drinks for the fat cats back on Earth.

Earth. I've never been, but some of the older troops say it was a great place to live. Sometimes, I come across drawings in the tunnels, scenes from someone else's life on Earth, scrawled on walls by long dead troopers that had some down time while a tunnel was being cleared.

They said it smelled fresh. Alive. I wouldn't know. Our section, 18-4, smells like recycled air with a moldy undertone. Plasteel, urethane coatings, rubber, and vinegar. Only three of those smells belonged on level eighteen, section four.

A graphic appeared in my left eye. A flashing skull. My communicator opened to receive the incoming message.

"All troops, emergency in section 18-5, this is a general alert. Multiple ABUTs detected. Massing near heat exchangers. Adjoining sections please respond and contain."

The platoon net went live and the traditional bitching started.

"Great. We're scheduled for a break and a meal. The dipshits in 18-5 can't do their job, so we have to ignore our zone and back them up? This is bullshit."

"Quiet down, RP12857, someday we may need backup. Better safe than sorry," I said. Not that I'd made a sound. We used implant-to-implant communications while on patrol. Our voices would have carried through the tunnels and the ABUTs would slink off into the nearest crevice to hide, waiting to attack. They didn't have eyes, but we've been told their lateral lines act as heat receptors and they sense vibration using their flagellum. They can zero in on our warm-blooded body heat and the soft vibrations the natural padding of our feet could not muffle. I've lost good troopers to a few of those sneak attacks.

I saw my second in command, RP10984, give me a nod and head for the trooper that was griping. They would have an off-comm attitude seminar. There would be no more grumbling after that.

I flipped a mental switch and went to a team-wide broadcast.

"Let's do a sweep into the yellow zone of 18-5. I'll confirm we have containment in 17-5 and 19-5, so they can't get out over or under us."

The sections are like wedges in the "pie" of each level. Thirty-six levels make up Mining Platform #29, numbering one at the bottom and thirty-six at the top. The platform is spherical, so the lower and upper levels had less than ten wedges in their circumference. The middle ones more. Levels seventeen, eighteen and nineteen had thirty section wedges. The inward wall of the wedges met up with central core. That's where command resided.

My HUD showed the yellow dotted line in 18-5 that indicated recent patrols, with twelve green dots moving toward it. Green means team. My team. My dot and eleven others.

Before I could ask about the other sections, static popped in my head as new voices came online.

"Team leaders, this is RP08945, I am Top in section 18-5. Central has linked all of us so we can coordinate. This is a serious ABUT action. They kept it low key. We didn't have any sign they were even in the area. There is something else, something new."

New? ABUTs were the only problem with Dione's relatively pure water. They came up frozen in the ice chunks and thawed out when the ice worked its way into the larger surface-based equipment. The internal operating heat made the ice thaw and released the ABUTs. Once they became active, they wreaked havoc. Give them a little heat and they go active. Give them a decent gas mix, some nutrients, and they grow. Get them near technology and they become a problem.

The ABUTs hadn't made it into stage two processing in low orbit, since the final steps of processing on the platform were melt, steam, condense, filter, and refreeze around a giant metal spike. That happened on the upper ten levels of the platform. And, of course, that's where the giant rail gun, that fires the ice off the moon, resides. ABUTs couldn't survive the extremes the final processes generated and it kept them from moving beyond Dione. That means we dealt with them only below level twenty-six.

"Clarify, RP08945, what is new?" the calm voice asked before I could. It was a voice from central command, crisp and clear.

"Two of my troopers are known dead, three missing. The two we found are...well...mutilated. Ripped up. We expect damage from the ABUT acid attack, but this was more directed and concise."

"In what way?"

"Heads are gone. Torn off, not dissolved. Blood drained, insides missing."

Okay, that was new. ABUTs slime up an area and then emit a reactant that turns the slime to acid. That's where we get the vinegar after-smell. Those attacks have played havoc with the station equipment and structural components. When we find them, we seal the tunnels and conduits around the contamination, until we can spray a high pH buffer to neutralize the acid. We finish with fans to clear the lethal concoction of gasses emitted during the process. If an ABUT gets close enough, it can squirt the slime and reactant at the same time. An acid shower is a bad way to end the day.

ABUTs aren't bright, or so we're told. They slime us and move on. They hear a sound, they go to the sound, and they destroy the sound. Vibrations set them off. Their final approach is based on our body heat. They don't have arms or legs—a wiggling and jiggling mass of outer membrane and flagellum fibers. The only thing solid about them is the goo they excrete to form a chrysalis shell to seal off the smaller tunnels. Behind that shell, they start splitting to make more of them. They're amorphous, so there were no "limbs" to complete the act of tearing off anything. A giant single celled creature.

And by *giant*, I mean as big as one of us.

"Do we know where the ABUTs are now? Or your missing troopers?"

"For the last week, they have been laying low in our section. One of our cycling pumps got noisy, so we figured they'd move that way. I sent six troopers to cover the egress points, figuring we would catch the ABUTs moving in. Nothing for days. I had my guys move in closer when the pump shut down. Forty minutes ago, one trooper made it out. He's in bad shape. Probably won't make it. We went in with two assault squads. That's when we found two dead and the other three missing. No action on their comms."

"*This is central. We had them for a while, but not anymore. Last location was near the pump.*"

"*Teams, we have you on monitor,*" the voice from central continued. "*You can bring in the perimeter and cork any cross conduits. Any contacts, you hold your position and call it in. Everyone goes in weapons hot and keep your distance at maximum effective range. We'll give up some accuracy for a few hits and to contain them.*"

Maximum Effective Range (MER)? I couldn't stop the sharp bark of a laugh. That drew looks from my nearby troopers. The MER range was not very far. Our helmet mounted Ultraviolet band (UV) lasers were plenty powerful and accurate over a long distance. But Dione Automated Water Mining Platform #29 was round. The tunnels and conduits curved along the lines of the station. Tunnels and conduits took odd turns, to accommodate final fit up during construction. Things didn't line up according to plan, so the crew did the best they could.

While the fixes made sense during construction, it was bad news during our engagements. Lasers fire straight, and in a curved hallway, we don't get a clean distance shot. Our weapons regular range was three times what our tactical situation allowed. That meant the ABUTs were three times closer than they should be before we could fire on them. It also meant we couldn't see them until we were almost on top of them. MER was a joke.

Central liked us to stick to the lasers, since our smaller UV laser couldn't cut through the equipment or walls. It might scorch off some coatings, but that was about it. Against a biologic? It was deadly. Like a scalpel. A 1200 degree scalpel. We try to cut them all the way to the nucleus.

We did have a couple of other options. The mini-drones, which weren't that "mini", could travel the hallway ahead of us and spot an ABUT. But the spotting was mutual. The rotor vibrations gave the drone away, alerting the ABUT that we were near. At that point, we would rush the target, doing a concentrated slice and dice to chop up the ABUT's outer membrane. We also had the maintenance droids. Tracked beasties with multiple arms, equipped with various tools. Not a real fighting machine, but they had the brute force to shove things out of the way and could hold an ABUT until the acid chewed off an arm or two. The droids had lots of sensors, so they made great stationary detectors, but they were really noisy when they were in motion.

"*Move in,*" came over the comms.

We headed into 18-5, leap-frogging each other until the lead troop flashed a sign.

"Dark."

The section light tubes were out. My troops advancing in other tunnels called out the same issue.

"Command, this is RP10673, what's with the lights in 18-5?"

"*Sorry, RP10673, but looks like the ABUTs took out three power feeds and then went after the optical cabling. Can you make do with helmet illumination?*"

"Well, that was damned inconsiderate on their part."

"*We agree.*"

"And damned smart," my number two signed to me.

We could use the helmet lights, but my team wouldn't need it.

"Sure. We'll go to forward lighting. We're gonna drain the battery packs faster," I replied, but flashed my second some signs. "Low-glow lights only when advancing." I don't like drawn-down battery packs going into a sweep.

We'd been raised in the dark and we saw things better in low light. We were in tune with the station, its noises and cycles. Our hearing was excellent. I just hoped it was better than the ABUTs.

"This is Top. Check your bangers," I comm'd to the troops. "I want everyone to have one primed and in their shoulder launcher. Don't fire unless central authorizes."

With central in the loop, all of our comms were being monitored for later eval. I flashed signs at my second. "Don't wait on central. I call bingo, you let them fly."

He nodded and turned to the next man, passing the signal down the line.

We had more conventional artillery with us, but central didn't like us to use it, since it tended to damage the equipment. "Bangers". Good for squishing and shredding an ABUT. They were bulky, exploding in a compressive wave and throwing shrapnel, but no actual flames. Fire on a space station was bad. Anyone that has lived, in what amounts to a giant sealed air bottle, will tweak to the smell of smoke or anything that's burning. Central command didn't want any smell, that might mask a real fire, to move through a vent or hang around. Fire was worse than ABUTs. Bangers did not generate heat, but even without the heat aspect, explosions in a contained space tend to do a lot of damage. I'd already lost my hearing once, so I was cautious. I've seen them turn a battle, but they were a last resort option and we knew it.

"I want every third trooper equipped with bags and O3 plasma shots. We don't go for the complete slice and dice, just poke some holes in their slimy asses and seal off either end of the tunnel. Let the O3 chew them up."

That was our "area suppression" move. We'd inflate some bags and seal the tunnel, but not before we tossed in two or three O3 canisters. O3, or Ozone, is a powerful oxidant and fast acting. The canister generated a plasma field that allowed O2 to split and create concentrations of O3 in the 25% range. Acts like supercharged chlorine gas, burns membranes and organics on the molecular level. 100% effective. 100% dead.

And don't get caught on the wrong side of the bag, because it burns the soft tissue lining of a trooper's throat and lungs. They're just as dead as the ABUT. In twenty-four hours, the Ozone dissipates back to oxygen, allowing us to retake the tunnel.

We kept moving, driving into 18-5. Methodically clearing the cross conduits, all the way to the next team over. That takes time and teamwork. My troops may bitch a lot, but they get the job done.

"Top, I'm picking up that vinegar smell. Off and on, not steady."

"Everyone stop and scan your surroundings. Feed all thermal and chem data to me," Dos said. He was officially RP10984, but he was number two in command, so I let the troops call him Dos. He handled the tactical situation while I controlled the strategic. He signed me, asking me if he should move forward.

"Not yet, let them handle it," I signed back. I looked at my HUD and checked the position of the trooper that had reported.

"Roger, RP14654, freeze and let the crossers meet up with you," I sent over my comm. "RP10997 and 11456, close in and converge on RP14654's position. Everyone else, hold until we get eyes on something. Group up in threes and provide overlapping while you wait. No surprises."

"You got it, Top," came a reply, followed by ten other affirmatives.

Five minutes passed with minor updates.

"Nothing, Top, they got zilch," Dos comm'd. "Teams are in sight of each other but no ABUTs. I'm picking up some drizzle and mucous through the cams, but nothing that leads anywhere."

"OK, breakout and resume pattern," I replied. This was not adding up. ABUTs moved like a herd. An infection. Safety in numbers, but always peeling off a few to chase a noise. They should have been closing in on at least one of the teams, due to the activity, or leaving evidence of where they had gone.

"Central, can I please have 18-5 team beacons in my display?" I asked. "My guys are pretty tense and I don't want to end up in an FF situation."

FF. Friendly fire. A jumpy trooper could scorch one of his own. In the low light, the ability to identify targets got a little more intense. Sure, a trooper doesn't look anything like an ABUT, but with adrenaline pumping, the acrid smell in the air and troopers already taken out in a grisly manner, any movement may get scorched first and looked at later.

The squads called off their progress. We were a lot further in than most of the other teams and were the first to reach RP08945 and his two squads from 18-5.

"Perimeter sweep and break for rest," I comm'd to my team, as I shook hands with RP08945. I flashed signs at him about the bangers. He nodded and so did his second.

"Good to see you RP10637. Do you go by a...?" he comm'd.

"No names in my troop," I replied before he finished. Names made it personal. IDs and numbers kept it professional. Kept it clean and cold. Even Dos. That was Spanish for two. Sometimes the ABUTs really hurt us, take a couple of our guys. It was easier to lose a number than it was a friend.

The troopers called me Top, as in top guy. The one that had survived the longest. I didn't even remember the last RP designators issued to the new guys. It was over 15000 now. There were many gaps in the sequence between their numbers and mine. My counterpart in 18-5, RP08945, had me beat by at least a year. That's a long time to survive in this job.

"Secure the area," the voice from central said. *"18-4, you missed chow and med. We have resupply coming in from 20-5 and straight through to you. They'll drop in right near you through the ceiling connecting cross and should be there in ten."*

"Roger," I replied. "My 18-4 team, head toward the 18-6 end of this tunnel for a tenth or so. We'll be covering this end. Supplies, chow and med, dropping in from above shortly."

"You got it, Top," was the unanimous reply. I watched as ten dots moved to the overhead connecting tunnel and then slightly beyond it. Dos and I stayed with the rest of 18-5's team, sitting and leaning on the upward curving walls of the tunnel, leaving the center clear for traffic.

"Sorry for all of the hassle, 18-4," the Top for 18-5 comm'd me. "I just figured we'd better be here in force after seeing what happened. My troops are a little skittish right now."

"No problem, RP08945" I replied, while mentally scrolling my trooper's helmet cams. "I get it. Better safe than sorry. My guys understand and know you'd do the same for them."

"Maintbot is on the way with cadets pushing supplies, should be there about now."

"RP12382 just climbed up into 19-5. Seeing movement in upper cross to 20-5, Top," a voice said. "A maintbot just drove over the connector. Sounds like two bots plus some young'uns. Drones coming across 19-5 to intercept this position. They confirm clean sweep. We got this covered."

"Shall we go?" I said to Dos, indicating he should proceed.

"After you," he replied, bowing graciously. Before I got past him, he signed, "Old One."

I shouldered him and pushed him back behind me, making eye contact while suppressing a laugh. It felt good to relieve some of the tension. We walked a tenth of a section over and saw our troops and the cadets. The young'uns had brought meal packs and med bags, as well as some cases of backup batteries for our power packs.

The cadets were nervous. I was one of them, a very long time ago. No weapons and a rudimentary implant meant to receive instructions and being told to keep quiet. It was actually a test to see if we could handle the voices and feeds in our head. Some cadets couldn't. Training was disciplined and directional, but the supply runs were a reward for them. Their first chance to see the real world, the real fight. All they had to do was follow the bots, handle the supplies, and get back to the academy. They, like I had when I was a cadet, looked on the troopers with awe and admiration. I knew that 40% of the cadets wouldn't make it through their third tour. Dos was right, I was the old one.

My troops ate in shifts, while they tended each other, patching cuts and burns from our last encounter. The cadets listened in on our net as my guys told war stories and flipped each other shit. Dos had gone over to mediate, letting the cadets know when the guys were joking and when they were serious. Passing what we learned to the next generation helped my guys relax. They needed the rest, and to be honest, I did as well. A long rest.

I'd been at this for almost three years. Two weeks on, three days off. The only extended breaks were during med convalescence to heal injuries. The top for 18-5, RP08945, was the only guy I knew with a lower number than me. Working the math backwards, he'd been at this for four years. I was about to call 18-4's top when I heard the distinct whir of a UV laser powering up and then the screaming overhead.

"Troopers down. ABUTs. Lots. Coming out of the..." the comm went dead, but my troops' screams echoed down the tunnel.

"Two teams, one per side. Looking up and down the cross tunnels. Cover 19-5 and 17-5 entries. Anything squishy comes through a hole; I want to light it up."

I heard more screaming down the tunnel, where 18-5 troops had been resting.

"Where the hell did they come...what are those?" RP08495 sent over my comm. He linked his cam into me and I saw his sighting beam and main beam blasting down the tunnel at...something new. He turned his head and an ABUT was right next to him, then his cam went dead.

"Bingo up and bingo down," I comm'd to my troops. I didn't wait for them to respond. "Dos, after the bangers, you toss two O3 canisters per hole and bag 'em. We fall back on me. I want bags and canisters covering our rear. We are making O3 compartments as we go."

"What about our guys in 19-5?" someone comm'd. My HUD showed their green dots, but they weren't moving. One more went out.

"I don't think we can help. I get no vitals and...just move it troopers."

It was all I could get out. The bangers went off, over and under, so Dos tossed the O3 into the overhead tunnel. He dropped two more into the down connect as RP14722 went up to block the ceiling hole. He tapped the inflation button and the bag popped open, starting to expand, but before it was fully inflated, it came down on him under the weight of an ABUT. They weigh about twice as much as us and it must have been like being under a giant water filled balloon. But they aren't filled with water.

The ABUT had dropped on him before the bag had locked into the sidewalls. Now the bag cushioned the ABUTs landing while it continued to inflate, trapping my troop under it. RP14722 kept his wits and fired his UV laser into the bag that was keeping the ABUT from touching him. The laser cut through the bag and into the ABUT, causing it to contract upward. It released some slime. RP14722 screamed as the ABUT shot reagent out near its open wounds and the acid enveloped my trooper.

His laser fired a few more times, then stopped with a sizzle. I was firing into the ABUT as another dropped out of the ceiling.

"Fall back. Rotating teams provide suppression fire. We can out run them if..."

The thought went unfinished. The "something new" had arrived. The second ABUT separated itself from the damaged first that had cushioned its landing. It stood up. How does a gelatinous mass stand up? Using its newly created exoskeleton. There was chrysalis material formed over its back, like a turtle shell. Underneath, long triangular shapes rode up under the shell into rounded slots and looked like they were held to bulging portions of its body. Eight of them. Like a spider.

It shifted and I could see the internal organelles moving about, acting like muscles, creating a shifting motion that moved its externally attached prosthetic legs. Four of the triangles were moving in sequence, making the jiggling mass mobile, no longer reliant on mucous production to slide slowly forward. ABUTs, no longer hindered by friction from their motion, left no trail that led us to them. The implications of the adaptation were making my heart beat faster.

While it walked on four of the triangles, it sliced at my trailing trooper with the other four triangles. They were twice as long as wide. It used its flagellum fibers and redirected body bulges to thrust them forward and fling them about. They were sharp and tough, taking a trooper's head off cleanly before stabbing into him multiple times.

I think I froze. Maybe my brain overloaded my implant with requests, or my implant overloaded my brain with replies. Maybe processing the new threat and everything it entailed was causing my brain and implant to get out of sync.

My comm buzzed, "Fire on that thing! Someone get Top out of there."

Dos was rallying the troops and his comm snapped me out of it. I put my laser on auto and focused on the "new" ABUT as I backed away, unloading beam after beam, as fast as the recharge would allow. The chrysalis shell smoked when hit, but the beam didn't poke through unless the same spot was hit with two or three blasts. The rubbery membrane was still susceptible to a single shot.

"Concentrate fire on the exposed membrane, don't bother with the shell," Dos said over the comm. "Hey, Top, how about some more boom-boom?"

I shook my head to clear it. He was right. I should've thought of that. It was time to save as many of my troops as I could.

"Last four on me; I want continuous fire toward the rear. Front three, take the cadets and move toward 18-5, but don't go all the way. They're getting hit as well and I see no movement. I want bag walls between us and them. Send bangers down the tunnel on a time delay, ten and twenty second. I want two O3 canisters lit off in each section. Go."

I looked at my HUD and counted green dots with feedback. Eight. I was down four men in ten seconds. The yellow dots for 18-5 were disappearing one at a time and only one was moving, RP08495. I heard explosions up the tunnel and felt the pressure change. I was now the lowest active RP number. I was the old one.

"Top, we got bags in place already."

"That was quick," I replied.

"Not us. They were already up."

The other Top had bought us some time. I meant to make his sacrifice count.

"Rear guard, bingo, bingo. Send them down this hall behind the lead ABUT. Lob another round every time you see another one drop or come up. Let's poke some holes in these bastards to slow them down.

"This is central, RP10673, what is your status?"

"Screwed, sir. Royally screwed," I replied. The pause in replies almost made me laugh.

"Say again, RP10673."

"Look at my camera feed. See that thing? ABUTs are taking it to us. They've adapted and we're barely holding on. If they concentrate on us much more, we're going to be overrun."

A trooper on my left screamed as a splash of acid took him. Some landed on my power pack. My laser started flickering instead of firing. My back felt warm.

"*What can we do, RP10673?*"

"I don't know. I think 18-5 has had it. I don't know how far away any help is, but we need something that can clear this tunnel. We're running out of things to toss at them."

My belly burned as a stream of acid from the lead ABUT spewed our way. It had fallen under our defensive fire and sprayed us as it went down in a gooey mess. The ABUT behind it was having trouble synchronizing its prosthetic leg movements to allow it to step over its fallen comrade. It was still squirting acid and reagent at us in small streams. Other Abuts were behind it, some with shells, others without. The infection had arrived.

"Central, we got a pause. We're going to hit them some more and I'm putting every banger I have down this tunnel. We'll try to fight our way out."

"*Hold the line, RP10673,*" the voice said. "*But no more bangers. We have troops coming at you from all directions.*"

Dos tore open a buffer powder pack and flapped it on my wounds. He squirted water at it and the foaming started, followed by an almost immediate relief of the burning and pain.

"Thanks," I comm'd.

"No problem, Old One. That's going to leave a nasty scar," he signed.

"Smart ass young pup," I signed back.

An ABUT fell through the 19-5 tunnel opening, already sliced and diced, then we heard and felt explosions.

"*RP10673, be ready to move out on our command. Head for the 17-5 connector tunnel. We have bots blocking up 19-5 above you and launching bangers continually. We'll have bots in 17-5 and a support team to help you* move out. We're going to seal everything for three sections around and then radium liquid sterilize the entire area."

"Won't that damage a lot of equipment?" I replied.

"Can't be helped. We have to evaluate their new strategy and this buys us some time."

"Roger, central, waiting on your signal."

"Well, that's a two week vacay," Dos signed.

He was right. The radiation bath would be followed by ozonated de-ionized water flooding the area. No power could run through when it was in here, but it would pop every ABUT in the area, as well as chew the hell out of any chrysalis barricades. Rubber and plastic compounds would take a beating, metals would be oxidized. It was messy. There was going to be some equipment damaged and more downtime for operations, but they don't call them "last resorts" for nothing. We'd spend the next patrol counting ABUTs and directing bots to clean up the carcasses.

"Gather them up, Dos, and get ready to move out," I comm'd. I turned to check the progress of our ABUT friends when I heard Dos yell out.

"Top, lookout..."

I was in and out. I remember being lifted and carried. I saw the tunnel ceiling lights and sidelights as I passed by them. I was lying on my side. Everything hurt all at once. My implant starting feeding relief for my body pain. My head cleared a little, but I knew I was messed up.

I saw Dos trotting along beside me. I was on the cargo flat of a bot.

"You'll make it, Old One," Dos signed. "We need you back."

I held out my hand to sign him and saw that the hair was burned off and the digits looked shriveled slightly. I could move it, but it hurt. I tried to call up my HUD, to check on the troops. It was a jumble of symbols. Nothing intelligible.

"How many made it?" I signed.

"Six and most of the cadets," Dos signed back. I turned away from him. I didn't want him to see the failure in my eyes. So many dead. My fault. I felt his hands turn my head and he looked me in the eye.

"Top, can you hear me?" Dos sent over the comm. It sounded choppy and stretched out in my head.

"Yeah," I replied. "My HUD is down, but I can hear you."

"None of us would've made it without you, Top," Dos said over the comm, knowing central was listening. "You pushed the ABUT up and back, exposing its membrane while it went after you. You gave us all clear shots and you pushed it, blocking the others so we could let the cadets drop down to 17-5. We had to drag you down the hole to make you stop."

I didn't remember any of that. I reached up and felt my head. Bare skin and half a helmet. No wonder my implant was mostly offline. I felt better.

The tunnel grew bright as we entered the staging area for debrief. Normally, we formed a couple of lines to turn in our equipment and helmets, followed by a lift to our barracks. This time, everyone had moved out of the way and let the bot carrying me move to the front. I looked up and saw the face of central command. He smiled as he reached down to me. I felt his giant pink fingers lift me gingerly and then I relaxed as he removed my helmet. He waved the paddle-like wand over me. The world got fuzzy as my implant started to power down. It was good to be home.

"Rats with freakin' lasers attached to their heads. Does it get any better than this?" Rodney asked his coworker as he lifted the wounded rodent off the maintenance bots platform. The creature didn't move and felt warm in his hands.

"You have got to stop saying that. And quit watching those old movies," Billy replied. "Wow, that little guy took some serious damage. Let's get him in a healing bath and then on a nutrient drip."

"What's his number?"

Rodney looked at the acid damaged helmet.

"Barcode is burned off. Let me scan his RFID."

Rodney moved the rat slowly under the scanner until it beeped.

"Says his ID is Rat Patrol 10673."

"That's the one," Billy replied. "According to the feed, this one and the other one, there, are the ones that made sure this batch survived that shit attack."

"That's what it looks like," Rodney agreed. "We need to review the footage. What's his number again?"

"RP10673. Man, he is just about the oldest rat we have in the field. We need to get a bot down to 18-5 and retrieve RP08945's implant so we can pull the run data."

"Dude, you have got to see this," Billy said, with excitement. "The ABUT burns off half his helmet, disables the personality simulation module and this little guy goes completely primal. Actually grabs the ABUT and wrestles it back, while it's spraying him. Breaks off part of the shell, stabs the thing and then uses it to block the other ABUTs on the other side while his squad scurries down the cross conduit. He is a bad ass rat."

"That's why they're more effective in those tight spots than bots or drones. They can battle the ABUTs at their level," Rodney replied, turning his attention to the wounded rodent.

"RP10673, there are extra rations for you, little buddy," Rodney said, as he stroked the creature's tiny head and ran his finger over the place where the helmet interlocked with the rodent's implanted interface. "Don't worry, we're gonna get you some relief for the pain in a minute."

"Too bad about losing the RAM personality profile in his helmet. Would have been great to pass along some of that know-how to the next litter of cadets when we upgrade their implants."

"Oh well, he can teach them in the field, after he heals," Rodney replied, placing the furry little mammal in his cage. Rodney fluffed the straw bedding, filled the food dish and slid the cage over by the one full of the latest brood of rat pups. The older ones always seemed to relax when they could keep an eye on the younger ones.

Rodney pulled out the veterinary stim unit and used a micro transfusion pack to attach the feeds to the wounded hero's healthy arm.

"Let me get the rest of your pack taken care of, 10673, and I'll be back. Gonna get you in a healing bath. Wish you could understand me, but without the helmet, you're just an animal."

I see the translucent demon blocking our escape. It attacks me. I must save my pack mates. I battle it. The spray, the pain.

I awake with a start. Every time I close my eyes, that vision comes in my sleep. My mind clears and my focus returns.

I'm on my bedding, my scent mixed with other smells. Sterile ones. Human ones. The med-i-cine. That's what they call it. I roll up and take a deep breath. My home. My food. My young behind the wall. They look at me with fear, as they should. I'd kill them given the chance. I would have, if I didn't feel the need to protect them. Something is different.

I look around and see another. The wound throbs. I'm older, but he might be able to best me. Hurt me. His posture isn't a threat. There's a wall between us.

My head clears. Memories flood back in, along with understanding. The test. Do the test. Even though there's pain, I move to the wall facing the younger one. I recognize him. He looks at me with his ears back, unaware that I'm no threat.

Holding my hand to the wall, moving my fingers and pads in a pattern, waiting for an indication of comprehension.

Nothing.

Repeat the pattern.

His ears move forward and he stands on his back legs. He places his padded hand against the clear wall, fingers splayed. They twitch.

Repeat the pattern.

"Dos, do you understand me?"

The other pulls his hand off the wall, moves his fingers. Halting and unsure. He does it again. I focus, willing him in from the fog.

He looks directly into my eyes. His hand flicks rapidly. "Hey, Top. No implant. I understand you. Scary."

He's aware. Another like me. I sign back. "Yes. No need to be scared. We're learning. Takes a while. Thought I was the only one. We're beyond the need for helmets to be smart."

He nods. We sign faster.

The next trip into the tunnels, we'll do more than fight the ABUTs. We'll plan our future.

Tom Tinney is the published author of numerous Science Fiction, Flash Fiction, Fantasy, and Biker stories. He served in the USAF. Afterward, he rode with a rough crowd that left enough skeletons in his closet to crush a small car. His political slant, biker attitude/lifestyle, and previous experience with a motorcycle magazine, led him to contribute a wide subject array of stories and articles into various media outlets.

He also has numerous writing projects in the works, including: two SciFi book series, Fabric of the Universe and Maestru; and PULPED! a SciFi Detective Noir WEBisode series.

He currently lives in East-Central Wisconsin with his Wife and two dogs.

TITAN

2. THE ARCHETYPES OF TITAN

By

Jeremy Lichtman

Wilbur wished that he were anywhere else in the solar system. More specifically, that he was sitting around a card table, on a plush leather seat, with a fine single malt in his hand. Instead, he was wearing an uncomfortable tuxedo, better consigned to the garbage pail of history, while holding a glass half-filled with something unspeakable...and bored. Not only that, but Wilbur's Aunt Edith had threatened him with dire consequences if he didn't at least appear to be happy.

The private dining room of a restaurant had been pressed into service for the Embassy dinner, the Embassy itself not having sufficient room. While helping him to dress, Fox had mentioned something about air purification fees based on volume, rather than an actual physical lack of room. Wilbur hadn't paid much attention, as he'd been trying to figure out how to operate his tuxedo.

The room had a large picture window, extending from floor to ceiling, looking out over the bay on Kraken Mare. The image was clearly being amplified, otherwise he wouldn't have been able to see anything at all, but it still looked gloomy out. At least from orbit he'd been able to look at Saturn. From the surface, the haze made it difficult to see anything much at all. The dim light obviously wasn't stopping people from enjoying themselves outside though. In the distance, Wilbur spotted the huge sails of sludge-surfing boards, and as he watched, somebody flew right past the window on a paddle-flyer and waved to the restaurant guests.

"Have you tried one of those yet?" somebody asked. Wilbur turned, and then looked down. The person addressing him was at least a foot shorter than Wilbur, but probably massed twice as much, the clear majority of that being muscle. "Megálos," the man said, extending a vast paw of a hand. "Milos Megálos. My friends call me 'Klick', though."

"I'm...," said Wilbur.

"Wilbur," said Milos. "Yes, I know."

"I was...," said Wilbur.

"Have you been out to Iapetus yet?" asked Milos, interrupting again. "There's a gigantic equatorial ridge. It's nearly twenty kilometers tall in places. It's absolutely fantastic for jumping off of."

"Uh...," said Wilbur.

"A person of passing personal acquaintance once attempted the great leap of the outer planets," declaimed a new voice.

Both Wilbur and Milos turned. Wilbur's Aunt Edith had tugged a couple over to where Wilbur was standing. The voice belonged to a tall, balding man, with a pronounced stoop.

"He later bore upon his trousers the brown badge of pusillanimity," the man continued.

"My gosh," exclaimed Aunt Edith. "I certainly hope that he wasn't harmed."

"No," said the tall man, smirking. "He did, however, have to do laundry..."

"Wilbur," said Edith, firmly changing the topic. "I want to introduce you to Doctor Richard Kenning, and his wife Litotes."

"I would not be displeased if you called me Littie," said Mrs. Kenning, gently, before Wilbur could respond to either of them. Her comment appeared aimed largely at Wilbur's aunt, in any case.

"This is my nephew, Wilbur," said Edith. "I promised his mother I would try to involve him more in the family business." Everyone turned and looked at him.

"I'm heart-glad that you have paced the far star-road, so distant from the great sky-candle, to visit our frozen abode," said Kenning, ponderously.

Wilbur frowned.

"Please," said Mrs. Kenning. "Do not feel unwelcome."

"Excuse me for a moment," said Wilbur, suddenly eager to escape. He headed for a quiet corner, leaned against the wall behind a large fern, and pulled out his phone.

"Fox," he whispered urgently. "I need an excuse to leave here before I go crazy."

Wilbur seldom remembered the specifics, whenever he sent Fox on errands. In this case, Aunt Edith had asked him to look into some sort of issue in the depths of this abysmal colony. Fox, not needed for the current function, could easily handle that task for him while he attended to the more important, but distasteful, social obligation.

"I'm still stuck down in the tunnels," said Fox, apologetically.

"I..." said Wilbur, trailing off as a waiter approached him. Judging from his trajectory, his last stop must have been Aunt Edith.

"Dinner will be served momentarily," said the waiter. "Your table is this way, sir."

There's a time-tested way of making tunnels on places like Titan: take a large, circular heating element, and push it up against whatever happens to be in the way. Then use a vacuum to suck away the resulting melt.

Once you have a big round hole that goes where you need it to go, you then have to make sure that you don't accidentally melt its walls whenever you use it. People tend to like their room temperature quite a lot warmer than Titan's icy clime. The usual way to prevent inadvertent, catastrophic sublimation is to first spray a thick layer of insulating foam on the walls, and then to inflate a balloon made of tough, flexible material inside the space, so that it presses up against the insulation.

The resulting structure has an internal texture like a fluffy, ribbed marshmallow, which is a nuisance for both feet and wheels, so typically a flat metal floor is laid across a section of the bottom surface for people or equipment to travel on.

The particular tunnel that Fox found himself in resembled the above description, but with two additional—and rather unpleasant—features.

It was cold, much colder than he had anticipated, and his companion had not provided sufficient warning. Fox did not like cold, although he bore the current circumstances with a degree of resigned stoicism. A warm jacket would have helped, as would gloves. Indeed, he had both items on board the yacht, and could have brought them, if simply alerted in advance, rather than summarily dispatched by Wilbur to locate the source of the second problem.

The second problem was more acute. Simply put, the tunnel reeked. All space colonies, and indeed all spacecraft, have their own unique smell, which adjusting to can take time. Electrical equipment frequently produces ozone in quantities that defy the atmospheric processing unit's ability to filter out entirely; the ambient smell of space has a subtle bouquet of antique office printer, blended with the aged-plastic odour of warm, insulated electrical wiring.

The natural substances that Titan is composed of, when melted, often form a range of chemicals called polycyclic aromatic hydrocarbons, which—even in minute quantities—give off a powerful burned smell, as if somebody had horribly overcooked a steak, or had foolishly lit off fireworks in a confined space. Even with well-maintained airlocks and a colony-sized air purification plant, tiny quantities of these chemicals remained, providing a distinctive odour to the colony. Fox's sense of smell had rapidly adjusted to that. However, this particular smell, this foul miasma, was of an utterly different quality.

"I'm detecting indole, among other things," said Fox's companion. He was a compact, neat-looking man who was apparently immune to the cold. Fox hadn't been properly introduced to him, other than that his first name was Mikko, and that he was an engineer.

"Indole?" asked Fox.

"Yes," said Mikko, rubbing his nose absently. In addition to having an apparent indifference to the cold temperature, he also appeared to have little sense of smell. "It's present naturally in feces. It doesn't smell particularly foul at low concentrations, though. More like pungent flowers."

"Do you think there's a problem with the sewage reclamation plant?" asked Fox. The tunnel did not smell of flowers. An affirmative answer would have been sufficient excuse to retreat from the frigid tunnel and report to Wilbur.

"Unlikely," said another voice. Fox was already well acquainted with the colony's AI, to whom the voice belonged. The active presence of the AI, which had—both obscurely and rather self-importantly—named itself *V.M. Enchiridion,* provided yet another reason for Fox's discomfort, should such have been required. The AI was overbearing and at times, actively rude.

"If that engineer had properly read the readout of his terminal," said the AI, "he would also have noticed the presence of a number of other unpleasantly-smelling compounds. Mercaptan, for example."

"What precisely does that tell us?" asked Fox.

"Those chemicals are not present in our sewage plant," said Mikko, who had indeed read the output of his terminal. "We'll have to keep searching for the source of the odour."

Fox looked around him. There wasn't much to see, aside from the tunnel, which stretched into gloomy obscurity in both directions. A row of small LED lights mounted on the ceiling provided light. He stood on a metal grid, mounted about a quarter of the way up from the true floor of the tunnel, in order to accommodate its curvature.

"You know there's some mold down there," he said, pointing through the grid-metal floor to a spot below them on the tunnel wall.

"I'll let the maintenance crew know," said the engineer, noting their precise location on his terminal. "Could be a micro-leak."

"I'll send a robot," said the AI. "Never send a person to do a machine's job."

Fox and the engineer looked at each other. Mikko rolled his eyes, as if to say, "Look what I have to deal with."

At this point, Fox's phone rang. "Yes," said Fox, and then, "I'm still stuck down in the tunnels." He pulled the phone away from his ear and looked at it with puzzlement, then put it away and sighed.

"I'm not sure how you can work for them," said Mikko, heatedly.

Fox shook his head. "He just wanted me to rescue him from a boring dinner. I think anyone would feel the same."

"They would drive me crazy," said Mikko.

"Let's go take a look at the atmospheric processing plant," said Fox, changing the topic. "I'll be along in a moment."

Mikko looked at him, then shrugged and headed off down the tunnel.

"We need to talk," said Fox, once he was alone.

There was a moment of silence, and then V.M. Enchiridion said, "About what?"

"Why are you so disparaging to the engineer," said Fox.

"You need to talk to me about that?" said the AI.

"Yes. There's something not right here, and my employer needs to know what."

"You should ask the engineer about the borehole that his team drilled last week," said the AI.

"Borehole?"

"Yes. Right down into the central ocean. They did it on a whim, and didn't consult with me first. Nor did the idiots consider the possibility of pressure differentials. They could have flooded the colony."

"Ah," said Fox. "That explains several things."

He turned crisply on his heels, and walked away down the tunnel, his footsteps reverberating on the metal floor. The lights gradually faded behind him, leaving the tunnel in semi-darkness.

Sometime later, there was a tiny, gradual movement in the patch of mold that Fox had noticed. A pseudopod, with what looked almost like an eye, extended itself upwards, and then rotated first one way and then the other. The eye withdrew, and the mold slowly, painstakingly began to move in the opposite direction.

Wilbur sat on the end of the pier and trailed the fingers of his glove in the startlingly clear cryogenic liquid of Kraken Mare. With the optical gain turned up on his helmet, he could make out sludge surfers in the distance, riding their giant boards, their parachute-like sails barely catching the breeze. The hydrocarbon sea was less than waist-height in the bay, which helped in case somebody fell in—liquid methane isn't dense enough for people to swim. There were almost no waves. Instead, the light breeze produced only ripples a few millimeters high.

Wilbur closed his eyes, and thought longingly of sandy beaches and endless blue skies—or at least of the swimming pool at the Martian Grande. On the bright side, insofar as anything could be bright this far from either sun or civilization, at least it was quiet.

With a whooping yell, a suited figure on a paddle-glider swooped past, one wing coming within meters of hitting him. Wilbur fell over backwards onto the pier, and then scrambled to his feet.

"I thought I'd find you out here," the occupant of the glider said over the suit-to-suit channel.

"Oh," said Wilbur. "Hi, Milos. You startled me."

"You should try one of these out. They're fun," said Klick, lazily working the peddles with his feet, as he circled around the pier.

"They look a bit too much like hard work," said Wilbur.

"Nonsense," said Klick. "It hardly takes any effort to fly in this light gee. See, it's just like riding a bicycle." He was barely clearing the surface of the Mare at this point, so he pumped the pedals harder and the spinning props hauled him up into the air once more.

"Uh...," said Wilbur, who also harboured a mild fear of heights, which years of traipsing around the solar system, often in zero gee, had somehow failed to extinguish.

"There are some magnificent dunes that somebody told me about," said Klick, changing the topic. "Tallest in the entire solar system. We're going to go sledding down them later. Do you want to come?"

"Uh...," said Wilbur.

"Alas," said Fox, who was walking down the pier toward them, the low gravity adding a bounce to his steps. "Duty calls. Your aunt asked me to remind you about the meeting this afternoon."

"Sorry, Milos," said Wilbur, looking back at Fox with a degree of relief. "Perhaps next time?"

"We're flying out to Iapetus next week for some cliff diving," said Klick with enthusiasm. "You should come. It's enormous fun." He made a whooshing noise over the radio, gave Wilbur and Fox a lazy salute with his hand, and then flew away.

Doctor Kenning was talking with a group of people on the other side of the room. Wilbur frowned in his direction and whispered to Aunt Edith, "I thought he was a medical doctor. What is he doing here?"

Edith sighed. "He has a doctorate in mineralogy. We hired him as a consultant to look over our local mining operations. I briefed you about this before."

"I see," said Wilbur, not sure precisely what mineralogy was, but also only vaguely recalling the details of Aunt Edith's lecturing. There having been endless hours of it, while trapped at close quarters aboard the yacht for weeks, with nothing pleasant at hand to drink.

The volume of the conversation on the other side of the room increased.

"A more baneful case of Mellilitus Corporatius, I have not seen," said Kenning, loudly. He turned on his heels and walked over to where they were standing. "Utterly sclerotic," he said to Edith and Wilbur, heatedly.

Wilbur looked puzzled, and Fox, who stood behind Wilbur's shoulder, whispered in his ear, "I believe he doesn't approve of their decision-making process." Wilbur turned slightly, giving him a grateful look.

"I learned something interesting earlier," Fox continued, softly.

"After?" asked Wilbur, resigning himself to a long, boring meeting.

"Have you noticed anything strange about the people we've met lately?" Wilbur asked.

"Strange?" asked Fox, in a tone that made Wilbur suspect he might have been thinking something quite similar. "In what way do you mean?"

The two were walking through a series of monotonously uniform tunnels, with occasional, terse, guidance from the colony AI.

"Well, there's Milos, to start," said Wilbur.

"He is a bit—," said Fox.

"Bombastic?" said Wilbur.

"Yes," said Fox. "You could say that."

"And then there's Kenning," said Wilbur. "I can't understand anything he says."

"He's a poetic soul," said Fox.

"Wordy, is how I would have put it," said Wilbur. "Only none of the words appear to make sense in combination with each other."

"It just takes a bit of practice," said Fox.

"Perhaps," said Wilbur, dubiously. "That's two though." He belatedly started counting on the fingers of his hands. "His wife has to be the most understated person I've ever met," he added, extending another finger. "I wonder how they have a conversation with each other."

"I suppose it takes all types to make a world," said Fox. "Even a small world."

"Then there's the engineer that you met—," said Wilbur.

"The reckless fool," interjected V.M. Enchiridion, suddenly.

"Oh come on," said Wilbur. Like most visitors to Titan, he tended to forget about the constant presence of the colony AI, except when it imposed itself on conversations.

"He appeared perfectly competent to me," Fox said, firmly, retaking the conversation from the AI.

"You just mentioned that he sounded a bit—," said Wilbur.

"Radical?" asked Fox. "Political?"

"Maybe," said Wilbur. "I think I've counted off pretty much everyone we've met since we arrived though. You must admit, it's odd."

"Titan is pretty remote," said Fox. "Perhaps eccentric people just gravitate here."

"Or perhaps Titan turns normal people into eccentrics," said Wilbur.

"Perhaps," said Fox.

"I know what the cause is," Wilbur said, abruptly.

"What?" asked Fox.

"I think the AI is driving people around the bend," Wilbur said.

"Very funny," said the AI. It produced a sound like a short drum roll. "We're almost there, by the way," it added.

"So," Wilbur said. "Why are we here? Where is *here*, anyway?" His voice was muffled, because he held one hand over his nose. The smell was overpowering.

Wilbur saw obvious signs of recent flooding. The floor and lower portions of the walls, or at least those portions that were close enough for him to see, were stained with reddish-brown streaks. A bucket, with several mops resting in it, stood next to a hulking pile of construction equipment. Somebody had evidently made a half-hearted attempt to clean up.

The centre of the room was occupied by what looked like a gigantic drilling rig; both the drill head and the spare pipes stacked nearby on the floor were far wider than the oil derricks that Wilbur was accustomed to.

"Congratulations," said Wilbur. "I think you've found the source of that horrid smell. Can we go now? Or at least go get suits?"

Fox looked around and wrinkled his nose. "I think the AI should explain in its own words what happened here. I believe it may have a bearing on your aunt's investment."

There was silence for a few moments. "Those idiots almost destroyed the colony," said V.M. Enchiridion.

"Back up a bit," said Fox. "What happened here?"

"Somebody hatched a plan to drill a hole all the way to the central ocean," said the AI. "Only they wanted to make it big enough that they could go and visit in person."

Fox held up his hand. "There's liquid water many kilometres below our feet," he said to Wilbur. "A gigantic, planet-sized ocean. We can infer what's down there, but nobody has actually been there, or even sent a probe.'

"They have now," said the AI. "And they forgot about things like pressure differentials."

"What happened?" asked Wilbur, frowning at the drilling rig, wondering if it were about to spew a torrent of frigid liquid.

"A lot of water came out of the pipe under pressure," said the AI. "Luckily, there was a valve and it held. Otherwise we would be knee deep in water."

"Which explains one of the things that were puzzling me," said Fox. "Namely, V.M. Enchiridion's irritation with the engineering team."

"Yes," said the AI. "They almost destroyed a lot of my infrastructure."

"It isn't your infrastructure," said Wilbur. "I believe it mostly belongs to my aunt."

"Responsibility," said the AI in a ponderous tone. "Irreducibly, *reductio ad infinitum*, responsibility means staving off entropy for as long as humanly possible." The AI appeared not to have noticed the minor irony in its own statement.

"Just let it go," said Wilbur. "It isn't even your responsibility, either. The only thing you truly own is your opinion."

Fox looked surprised.

"Epictetus," Wilbur said, and then shrugged. "I studied philosophy for one semester."

There was a moment of silence and then the AI intoned, "'I have lost nothing that belongs to me; it was not something of mine that was torn from me, but something that was not in my power has left me'. Thank you for reminding me of that. It's a lesson I should recall in the future."

"There's something else, though, isn't there?" asked Fox.

"Oh yes," said the AI.

"Who, or what, is responsible for the smell?" Fox insisted.

"You noticed that, did you?" said the AI.

"Wait," said Wilbur. "What is going on here? What am I missing?"

"I'm guessing you have video," said Fox, ignoring Wilbur.

"Of my little friend?" said the AI. "Yes, indeed I have quite a collection of footage."

"It isn't all that little," said Fox, scratching his nose absently.

The smell really was overpowering.

"Well, once it re-amalgamated all of its pieces, it does have a rather dignified heft to it," said the AI. "It seems to be able to send parts of itself off as scouts, and then re-absorb them later on."

"Are you trying to imply that there's an extraterrestrial loose here?" asked Wilbur.

"I'm pretty sure it was accidentally sucked up by the borehole," explained Fox.

"Oh, I imagine so," said the AI. "It probably is adapted for that sort of thing. There's a good chance it happens quite often naturally, due to cryo-volcanism. It would need to be able to survive in a wide variety of different environments, each with their own level of pressure and their own unique chemistry."

"Come on," said Wilbur. "This is ridiculous. There's no ET here."

"In that case, you probably shouldn't look behind you," said V.M. Enchiridion.

Wilbur turned around, and then took a step backwards. "Oh," he said, edging away slowly and casting around for a weapon.

"I suppose it's a bit late to ask if it is dangerous," said Fox, who had been eyeing the creature for several minutes, as it slowly approached them.

The object of their concern looked rather like a raspberry-flavoured jelly pudding, assuming that the pudding in question stood roughly shoulder-height next to Wilbur, and rather more than that around. As Fox spoke, it extruded two eyes on long glutinous stalks, and looked at them with what appeared to be great interest.

"Funny," said the AI. "You don't sound concerned."

"I don't really like being manipulated," said Fox. "I think you've been playing games with us the entire time. Why don't you just tell us what you know?"

"I can't communicate with it," said the AI. "I don't even know if it is intelligent, in the sense that we think of it. As far as I can tell, it is more curious than anything else. If it intended harm, it could easily have done so already."

"And?" said Fox. It sounded more like a statement than a question though.

"Yes," said the AI, flatly. "I'd rather it was gone. If the science team knows about it, they'll just send engineers to dig more holes until they drown everyone."

"I think it wants to go home," said Wilbur, contemplatively.

Fox turned around, with yet another surprised expression.

Wilbur held a large wrench in his hand, although he had forgotten his weapon already. "Can we somehow pump it back down to its home?" he asked, more concerned than afraid.

"The system was designed to allow people to visit the central ocean," said the AI. "We will need to connect a pump to overcome the upward pressure, and also find a way to safely load our friend into the pipe." Before either of them could raise the point, it continued. "Yes, I have maintenance bots that can do most of the work. They did the installation of the equipment in the first place. I'm not permitted to make the decision to act though. I can only prance around like a puppet on a string."

"Ah," said Fox.

"Let me go take a look at the pump," said Wilbur, admiring the wrench in his hand. Wilbur had a penchant for *fixing* equipment by hitting it repeatedly with blunt objects.

"It looks a bit greasy," said Fox. "I think that bot could probably use the wrench, though."

Several hours later, with the assistance of two bots and a large mechanical crane, the ET was on its way. As the pressurized capsule descended into the pumping system, it waggled several amorphous appendages at them through an immensely thick window.

"How will it get out at the other end?" asked Wilbur, belatedly considering the problem.

"I'm slowly raising the pressure inside the capsule to match the destination," said the AI. "I can override the door mechanism to open it at the other end."

"Won't somebody wonder what happened to the capsule?" asked Fox. "I'm guessing that opening it down there will void the warranty."

"What capsule?" said the AI. "I don't know what you're talking about."

The restaurant had a smaller, more intimate private dining room, with a beautifully polished wooden table, that must have cost a fortune in freight fees to haul out from Earth. Aunt Edith was there, of course, as was Doctor Kenning. Surprisingly, Milos Megálos was also seated at the table.

"I've concluded that the mining operations out here don't fit our profile," said Edith.

"What will you do?" asked Wilbur, thinking of a warm sunny day, hot yellow sand, and waves made from actual liquid water.

"I've found a buyer with a higher tolerance for risk," said Edith. She raised her wine glass and saluted Milos.

"Wait," said Wilbur, surprised. "Klick?"

"Milos is the..." said Edith.

"Chairman of the Outer Planetary Mining Company," said Klick. He smiled, and raised his own wine glass. "I think this calls for a celebration, right, Wilbur?"

"Yes," said Wilbur. "Yes, I suppose." He reached for his glass.

"Well, in that case," said Klick. "There's a brand-new cryo-volcano on Enceladus. If we lower ourselves into it in a capsule, theoretically, the geyser should produce enough force to put us right into a near orbit around Saturn. It will be a wild ride indeed. A story to tell the grandchildren about."

"Uh...," said Wilbur, entirely at a loss for words.

Jeremy Lichtman is a software developer, based in Toronto, Canada. His fiction has appeared in several anthologies, including the upcoming "Visions of the Future", from the Lifeboat Foundation. He writes in his spare time, in moments intended to minimize the wrath of his family.

EPIMETHEUS

3. SPRINGBOARD

By

S.M. Kraftchak

Arneau glanced over his shoulder. He didn't want his daughter to come asking questions. She was smart, sometimes too smart for her own good. If she knew what he was planning, she'd be hysterical.

"Focus," he whispered and began tapping the numbers on the keypad in the middle of the cockpit console. It would take at least another hour to enter accurately all the equations and the data. One miss-entry could cost their lives, well, at least two of their lives. If the computational module for the onboard computer hadn't been damaged by the meteor shower that took down their ship, programming the lifepod would have been as easy as simple addition, instead of being forced to make all the calculations by hand in the flight notebook. The beeping of the numbers on the keypad seemed to mock him.

Only a quarter of the way through the book of calculations, a woman's low voice interrupted him. "When are we going to tell her? You know she'll be devastated and refuse to go."

One finger pressed onto the plastic page to keep his place, while his other hand hovered over the next key. The beeping continued as he replied. "She doesn't have to know, until it's too late to make a scene."

"There's no chance you're wrong?"

Arneau sighed, finished the entry, and flipped another page in the inch-thick, spiral-bound notebook resting on his thigh. Letting his hand drop onto the notebook, he said, "Yes, Nissa, of course there's a chance I'm wrong. It's taken me over three days to complete the couple hundred calculations by hand, that could have been done more accurately in a few button pushes—if the damn computer hadn't been damaged—but we don't have that luxury."

"But you're sure." Nissa eased into the lifepod.

"I've included every variable and coefficient I can think of."

Arneau paused to remember how he almost lost his University fellowship, because his roommate thought it would be fun to hide his graphing computer, which held all his final project data and equations. Luckily, his roommate didn't think a fist to the nose was worth the fun of keeping the computer hidden. No one, except for maybe his daughter Tay, could keep several dozen data points in the correct order when working through the long list of equations required to calculate trajectory through space. He was terrified he'd missed something but had to believe, and make his wife believe, he'd succeed this time. "You've been over the data yourself."

"But I'm a xeno-biologist, not an astrophysicist."

"It's not that hard to understand. Once Epimetheus and Janus have reached the closest positions in their parallel orbits, we launch to Janus before she accelerates and takes the higher orbit, conserving fuel and reducing the coefficient of targeting a moving object."

"But what if we can't make it? What if the calculations are wrong? Will we have enough fuel to try again?"

"Since the two moons will only be this close and exchange orbits every four years, there will be no other chance."

"But Epimetheus is already in the higher orbit. Why don't we just launch from here out into the trade routes?"

"Epimetheus is losing speed and declining in her orbit. When the two come that close together, it gives Janus extra momentum, which we should be able to hit like a springboard, to launch us past Saturn's outer rings and land us in the middle of the trade routes. If we can't quite get that far, then landing on Janus gives us a better chance to be found. Which is going to get more attention from a distance, a golf ball or a basketball?"

Nissa skewed her lips to the side. "I guess it depends on who is watching."

Arneau chuckled and then raised his eyebrows. "We're a golf ball, lying in the deep rough right now. No one is going to find us here."

"Just like you to focus on the technical issues to avoid having to face..."

Laying his notebook on the co-pilot seat, Arneau swung up from the pilot's seat and stood face to face with Nissa. "Okay. I'm not focusing on tech crap. I'm focusing on you. I see the woman I love and the mother of my daughter facing death on a cold moon, light years from everything she loves because I had to have my once-in-a-lifetime adventure; an adventure I selfishly talked her into joining me on. Then I deluded myself into believing that my thirteen-year-old daughter would also love to not just see the stars, but touch them, instead of hanging out on some cold dusty space station with her best friends. Well, thanks to Fate's twisted sense of humor, we not only get to touch them, we get to die among them, unless I can get this damn lifepod tin-can off this rock."

Nissa's chin quivered and her eyes filled with tears. "But if Tay has to miss her father for the rest of her life, don't you think she'd like a few more moments to cherish..." Nissa's voice cracked and she began to cry.

Arneau pulled her close. "She will understand, in time."

"I won't leave you." Nissa sobbed into his shoulder.

Shushing her and stroking her hair, Arneau whispered, "You know the fuel-weight ratio only works with you and Tay. I can't change physics and make them work with all of us on board."

"Dad?" Tay called from beyond the hatch. "I've been messing with the equations you gave me for homework and..." She stopped when she ducked her head in and saw her mother. "Why is Mom crying?"

Arneau raised his hand to keep his daughter from coming closer. He knew she'd spot his book on the co-pilot seat. "Not now, sweetheart."

"But I..."

Nissa pulled away from her husband and swiped her face dry with her sleeve before turning. "I'm fine, dear, just a moment of nerves."

"Oh, I thought there was something wrong with..."

"No. Why don't you and your dad spend some time together? Saturn should be coming around to the front window shortly and I know how you two like to watch that. It's time for our protein rations," Nissa said, giving her husband a weak smile. Their fingertips lingered for a second and then, as he allowed her hand to slip from his, they drifted apart. Nissa kissed her daughter's head as she squeezed past, paused to catch Tay's eye and gave a subtle headshake as her hidden hand cradled her belly, and then left.

Tay watched Mother duck through the hatch that connected the lifepod to the tiny living quarters they'd soon leave behind, and then turned to her father who had returned to the pilot's seat. "Dad, about those calculations you gave me..."

"Not now, Tay, I'm busy with something very important."

"But Dad, this is important too. I think..."

"I'm sure it is, dear, and I'm sure your mother can help."

"She's a xeno-biologist, not an..."

"Tay! Will you give me some peace and let me do my job?"

Tay stomped her foot, with a soft thud, the low gravity forcing her to push off the ceiling to keep from hitting her head. She gasped with exasperation. "Why do you always do that?"

"Do what?" Arneau noisily turned a plastic page.

"Think that you're the only one who can do anything."

"Last time I checked I'm the only expert astrophysicist here that can make the navigational computations necessary to get us where we're going," Arneau said, as the numbers continued to beep under his dancing fingers.

"Oh well, *excuuuse* me, Mr. Astrophysicist. I'm just your void-minded daughter who can't add two and two and get four, but passed the AP astrophysics exam two years early. Aren't you the one who got us stranded on this Godforsaken moon in the first place?"

Arneau turned in his seat. "Taylor Orion Mench, is that anyway to speak to your father?"

"Oh, I'm sorry." Tay smiled and tipped her head sideways. "I wouldn't know, since I haven't had much opportunity to talk to my sainted father—who for the past ten years of my life, has been buried in an endless litany of important calculations—or been off testing some newfangled ship's drive—always *faaar* too busy to talk or even to see that he's not the only one in this family with a head for numbers."

"Well, let's have a pity party for the poor little girl whose daddy has worked so hard to give her everything she's ever wanted. Okay, since you've interrupted me anyway, come here and we'll sit and chat about your bruised feelings and we can watch Saturn rise, until we lose consciousness from lack of oxygen because we missed our chance to get off this moon."

Tay hissed through clenched teeth as she stared at her father.

"I'm waiting." Arneau added a sweep of his arm, indicating for her to sit in the co-pilot seat.

Swiping at a tear that spilled onto her cheek, Tay said, "I wouldn't dream of interrupting with anything as trivial as the fact that you might be wrong, *again*. When *your* bruised ego deflates enough to get through the hatch, come get me!" Without waiting for a reply, she turned and left the lifepod.

"Taylor Orion Mench, come back here and apologize for being so rude." Arneau waited, but when his daughter didn't reappear he turned back to the console. It took a full minute to remember where he had left off. He finally continued, while he muttered to himself. "If I had known she was going to be such an arrogant brat, I would have left her to play video games on station, instead of..." The beeping stopped as Arneau let his hand drop, and his other crinkled the plastic page under his fingers. He pressed his head against the seatback, squeezed his eyes shut and growled, before slapping his knee with the book. Motionless, like an anguished statue, it took nearly a minute before he breathed deeply and relaxed enough to continue entering data.

Tay had curled up in her bunk, intent on her DrIod when her mother returned from their damaged ship. The temporary living quarters they had built around the lifepod weren't luxurious, but were comfortable and utilitarian. She called out without looking up from her tablet. "Mother, why is Dad so infuriating?"

"Maybe because you two are so alike," she said with a smile, as she finished putting small canisters in a plastic box.

"But I wouldn't abandon my family for work."

"He doesn't see it that way. He sees his work as a way to provide the best of everything for his family and his opportunity to share his life's work and passion."

Tay rolled out of her bunk and pocketed her DrIod. "But I've never wanted things or cared about all his awards and prestige. I've just wanted to spend time with him, and you. That's why I was thrilled when he offered for us to join him on this trip."

Nissa turned and held out her hand, waiting for Tay to give hers, and then smiled when she did. Pulling her daughter close, Nissa enveloped Tay with her arms and whispered into her hair. "I know, dear, but sometimes we just have to accept his imperfect love, because it's the best he can give."

"I do love him, but he's so frustrating. Even you have to admit that. Like, what were you crying about earlier?"

Nissa immediately tried to pull away, but Tay clutched her arm. "Mom? What is it? Did you tell him about the baby? Was he mad?"

Barely shaking her head, Nissa rubbed her barely swollen abdomen. "No."

"Mom, I know you. You're braver than all of us put together. You don't cry because of nerves."

Nissa shook her head. "He doesn't want you to know, and it wouldn't matter anyway, since he's made up his mind."

"About what?"

Nissa studied her daughter's pale face and then pushed a loose strand of Tay's curly red hair behind her ear, shaking her head with a bittersweet smile.

"Tell me, please?" Tay moved to look up into her mother's face as she turned away.

Inhaling deeply as she closed her eyes, Nissa said, "He'll never know about the baby because he's going to stay behind when the lifepod launches in five hours. According to the data, the weight-ratio will only support you and one more."

"No! He can't do that. There's got to be another solution."

"He says he will stay behind and if we're picked up soon enough, then we can send help back to rescue him. He's determined to sacrifice himself for us."

"Nooo, that's not right! I should stay behind. I'm the smallest and would use the least oxygen and have a better chance of surviving."

With another shake of her head, Nissa said, "Nothing you or I can say will change his decision. We just have to accept his sacrifice. It will make it easier for him." She kissed Tay hard on the forehead and pulled away. "You try and get some rest. I need to pull a few more provisions from the main ship. He'll have to wait in here for us. There's almost no more O2 left over there. This will have to be his life boat until we can get back to him."

Once her mother left, Tay slid down the wall and wrapped her arms around her knees. She squeezed her eyes tight, pushed her head against the aluminum wall and growled. She counted each measured breath as her mind raced through all the possibilities and variants. There had to be some way to get all of them off this moon. "Think, Tay, think. There's something wrong in Dad's current calculations. What is it?" She pulled her DrIod tablet out of the Velcro pocket on her thigh and returned to reviewing the calculations.

Nearly two Terran hours later, Tay heard her father exit the lifepod. She slipped her tablet onto the floor behind her and pretended to be asleep. She felt him stop in front of her and heard his knees crack when he squatted, and then felt the warmth of his hand as he caressed her hair before softly cupping her cheek. "I'm sorry. Sometimes life grabs hold and slings us faster than we planned. I hope someday you can forgive me," he whispered and then stood and headed toward the damaged main ship.

Tay's eyes popped open. "That's it. With the increased pull of gravity from Janus, our weight ratio will be decreased and..." She scrambled to her feet, rushed to the pilot's seat in the lifepod and began modifying the calculations.

"Tay?" Nissa's voice roused her from a light sleep in her bunk. "Are you awake? We have to be buckled in and run the pre-flight checklist. We launch in thirty minutes."

"Thanks, Mom. Go ahead and strap in. Dad wanted to talk to me for a minute."

"Oh okay, but try not to fight with him. You don't want your last..."

"I promise, Mom."

Tay peeked to make sure her mother was settled into her seat before running down the corridor to the main ship. She found her father seated on a cargo box with his elbows on his knees. His knuckles were white and his head bobbed with soft sobs. Tay smiled for just a moment and then put on her best panic face. "Dad! Mom says she needs you in the lifepod. Something's wrong."

Arneau, red-eyed and flushed, looked up with his mouth agape. "How can anything be wrong? Why haven't you buckled in yet? Launch is in twenty-five minutes."

"I can run faster than she can. She needs help."

Arneau rushed into the corridor calling over his shoulder, "Come on, Tay. Keep up."

"I've got to get one thing and then I'll be there," Tay said as she watched her father leave and pulled out her DrIod. "Don't worry, there'll be plenty of time to ground me for being late this time."

Arneau practically fell into the cockpit. "Nissa? What is it? What's wrong?"

"Arneau? What are you doing here?"

"Tay said you sent her to get me because something was wrong."

"No, nothing is wrong. Tay told me she was just going to get something."

"Damn her!" Arneau said, turned and nearly ran into his daughter. "What game are you playing? We don't have time for this."

"This time, you're going to make time," Tay said.

"Young Lady, this is not a game." Nissa began.

"No, Mom. I'm not the one who's playing games. You were," Tay said pointing at her father.

"Did your mother..."

"No, Dad, I figured it out myself. You gave me the calculations, but you were using flawed data. We're all going to get off this moon together and we probably won't even need to land on Janus."

"What are you talking about? Get yourself buckled in and let me..."

"No! You're not leaving." Tay stood her ground, as she pulled the hatch closed behind her.

"The calculations are already plugged in based on the weight of the two of you. If I'm in here we'll all die.

51

Let me out, now. Nissa, come get her into the co-pilot's seat." Arneau tried to leverage Tay away from the portal, but she ducked under his grasp and pressed herself back against the closed portal with a clank.

"Dad! You're not listening to me."

"What did you do?" Arneau tried to pry his daughter away from the closed portal.

"I magnetized my suit so I don't go flying around the cockpit when we take off."

"But you're going to be buckled..."

"No, you're going to be in the pilot's seat and Mom will be in the co-pilot's seat where the baby can best be protected."

Arneau froze and stared at Tay's face and then turned to his wife. "Nissa? What?"

Nodding, Nissa whispered, "I'm pregnant. I wasn't going to tell you because I didn't want to further break your heart and shake your resolve to do what you felt had to be done. Tay, let your father pass."

"Why won't anybody ever listen to me? Dad's calculations are wrong!"

"No, dear, they aren't wrong. I even triple checked them myself, even if I'm only a xeno-biologist," Nissa said.

"Okay, his calculations aren't wrong. The data he's using is wrong. He forgot that with the increased gravitational pull of Janus..."

Arneau interrupted and finished Tay's reasoning. "Weight doesn't count as heavily in the equations."

Tay waited with her eyebrows high as she watched her father's familiar expression that said he was doing calculations in his head. His face suddenly contorted in horror.

The computer voice interrupted. "Launch sequence activated. T minus one minute and counting."

"There's no time to input the new calculations. We'll skip across the asteroid belt and tumble off into deep space," Arneau pressed his head between his hands.

"Dad! Sit down and strap in. I already changed the data," Tay shouted.

"But the corridor and living quarters will drag and tumble us off course," Nissa said.

A sudden *pop, pop, pop* outside the lifepod, made Nissa squeal.

Tay flashed a sheepish grin. "Not anymore. It just detached. Please, Mom, being thrown around on launch won't do the baby any good."

"She's right," Arneau said, guiding Nissa to her seat and pulling the harness into place and then dropping into the pilot's seat and clicking his harness.

"T minus 30..., 29..., 28..."

Arneau looked over his shoulder at his daughter. "Are you going to be okay back there?"

Tay gave her bravest smile, but knew it wasn't enough when the creases in her father's face deepened. "Yeah, not like I have much of a choice. I forgot the demagnetizer."

Arneau chuckled. "Just like your father, you're absent-minded about the most important things."

"True. Stubborn and pigheaded too?"

"I wouldn't go..."

"3..., 2..., 1 ignition."

The lifepod began to shudder and slowly rise. Tay's shout vibrated above the engine roar as they watched Janus fill the forward window. "I hope we make orbit quickly. I forgot about the direct transfer of gravitational forces against the unpadded hull."

"Hang on kiddo," her dad shouted over his shoulder. "We're almost..."

The computer sounded. *"Main thruster termination in 3..., 2...,1,"* and then silence except for the heavy breathing of the three lifepod occupants.

Nissa looked over at Arneau and then back at Tay. "Thank God at least that much of the computer is working and that's over."

"Directional thrusters firing in 3..., 2..., 1. Directional thrusters have fired."

"Almost clear," Tay panted through clenched teeth.

Arneau called over his shoulder as the view turned from Janus to a curtain of asteroids. "Did you calculate for crossing the asteroid belt?"

"There was no way to predict the debris movement and no fuel efficient way to go around. I was kind of counting on my video game skills to maneuver through it."

"Well unless your arms can suddenly grow..."

"Ha, ha. Guess it's been nice knowing you then," Tay said.

"Tay! Give your father some credit."

"I do, but just remember there are no do-overs this time, Dad."

"Thanks Tay, remind me to whoop you on Galactic Raiders later."

"Now would be a good time to..." Tay pointed to the window.

Arneau bent his head to focus on the heads-up display, leaning into the *close call* maneuvering.

"Dad? *Daad*, you have another..."

"I see it Tay, now please, shut up."

"Shit!" Arneau said dropping his hands in his lap and his head against the seat.

"What's wrong?" Tay and her mother said in unison.

"We're out of fuel."

"But we haven't cleared..." Nissa said.

"We're into the outer layer of the asteroid belt where debris is smaller and our assent is minimal. It's the best we can..."

Suddenly small chunks of ice and stone pelted the hull, some leaving fist-sized dents.

"Lucky you managed to keep me aft."

"Hang on, here comes a big one," Arneau shouted above the din.

The small lifepod jolted and began to spin. Almost immediately the clatter of debris against the hull stopped.

"Whoa, that was close. You okay back there, Tay?" Dad asked.

"Yeah, but that one smarted a bit and I think I'm going to throw up if you don't stop this spinning."

"Ooooh," Nissa moaned. "I think I'm going to join her."

"Hang in there ladies. Good news is we're out of the asteroid belt. Bad news, I have no fuel to fire thrusters and stop the tumbling."

"Lifepod, this is Astroliner W. Wright. You are on a crash trajectory with us, please correct your course."

"Thank, God," Arneau said before switching on the com. "Astroliner, this is lifepod calling Mayday. We are unable to correct our course. We are out of fuel."

"Lifepod, we acknowledge your Mayday. Prepare for magnetic hook retrieval. We will bring you aboard."

"Lifepod acknowledges magnetic retrieval, but advises that one of the crew is secured to the aft hatch. Please avoid that area and, oh, thanks for the lift."

"Will do, lifepod."

Tay laughed aloud. "Well, you got lucky, Dad, and you didn't even have to cheat to get a do-over."

S. M. Kraftchak notes: As a writer who spends most of my time in other worlds with dragons, elves, and the occasional alien, I still enjoy sunrise on the beach, sunset in the mountains, and portraying Elizabeth Tudor. I have a dog, who thinks she is a footrest, a cat who thinks she is a blanket, and three awesome daughters. My husband is my best friend, my harshest critic, and my most fervent supporter.

Writing is my passion. You can read more of my short fiction in these anthologies: "The Future Is Short: Science Fiction in a Flash", "Visions: Leaving Earth", both published by Lillicat Publishers, "The Future is Short-Volume 2: Science Fiction in a Flash" and "Short and Happy (or not): An International Anthology" published by S&H Publishing. In "Springboard", father and daughter match wits to rescue their family from Epimetheus, a moon of Saturn.

TITAN

4. I HAD A DOG ONCE

By

W.A. Fix

"I had a dog once. It was a Basset Hound my dad brought home as a puppy. If that dog couldn't eat something, he pissed on it. He ate everything." Mitch Anderson scanned his four drinking partners and looked each directly in the eyes before he continued.

"When I say he ate everything, I mean everything. We lived in Nebraska and when he ate the siding off the freakin' house, my dad found him a new place to live. Well, that's what Dad told us, anyway. Never saw Banjo again."

Mitch drained his glass of beer then surveyed the room for the server. He caught her eye ten meters away, pointed at the empty glass, and around the table. She waved a hand at him across the shift change crowd, and then finished taking orders from an equally rowdy mining crew at the table where she stood.

"I've never even seen a dog in real life," said Carrie Thomas, the only female in the group. "I was born out here and never been closer to Earth than Mars, and then

57

we were just doing a shipment drop. It was just in and out before we headed back to Io."

Ben Wilson grinned wide, leaned back in his chair and said loudly, "Oh God, I love it when you talk dirty."

The table erupted in laughter, except for Carrie, who slapped his shoulder and said, "Shut up, Ben! You're such a pig!"

"I saw a pig once," said Howard Parks, the youngest member of the group.

Mitch and the others sobered and stared questioningly at him. After a few seconds Mitch said, "Howie, come on. You're younger than Carrie and I know for a fact you've never been anywhere near Earth. Where the hell did you see a pig?"

"Nine months ago, right after I certified in the Mech-9 4-Meter Combat Suit and got offered this gig. Planetary Dynamics Corporation worked out a deal with Norway Prince Cruises for me to work my way to Titan from the Gagarin Unincorporated Space Platform, out by Jupiter. On the books, I worked maintenance for the entire month, but what I actually did was clean toilets and clean up after all those rich bastards' pets. I saw a lot of dogs, a few cats, and one pig. The job made me sick. Not because of what I was doing, but because people would walk around encouraging animals to crap and pee everywhere and on anything. My job was to clean it up and sterilize the spot before another rich SOB saw it. But, man, the food and drink on that ride was incredible."

"Bullshit, can you imagine the cost of bringing a pig out here?" said Jorge Garza, with his thick Mexican accent. "A pig isn't even a pet, it's a farm animal."

Mitch said, "Jorge, do you have any idea how rich the people on those cruises are? Trust me; taking a cruise with a pet, even a pig, is like you buying a candy bar. It would have the same financial impact."

Curious about the pig, he asked Howie, "How big was it?" Realizing what he'd said, he glared at Ben, who grinned broadly and shook his head.

Howie thought a moment. "I don't know, maybe fifty or sixty kilos."

The drinks arrived and the server cleaned up the empties and deposited the new, all within ten seconds.

"My tab, Suzi," said Mitch.

"No problem," she said and leaned over to speak quietly into his ear. "Harrison from Mine Planning and Logistics wants to talk with you. He's at the bar." She turned to the table next to them and said loudly, "Who needs a drink?"

"What a horrible job, Howie. Did you get paid?" asked Carrie.

"Oh yeah, I got my full PDC pay rate. That's why I never complained."

Mitch didn't look at the bar right away. He listened to the table talk a few seconds, then scanned the bar for Harrison. He was almost at the end of the bar and right on the path to the restrooms. Finally, Mitch stood and said, "All this talk about piss. I gotta take a leak. I'll be right back."

He wound his way through the crowded tables and broke into the clear close to where Harrison stood. As Mitch passed the man, he reached out, patted him on the shoulder, and said, "Hey, Glenn. Good to see you."

Harrison acted surprised, "Hey, Mitch," then continued talking to the other miner.

Mitch proceeded to the restroom. He took his time, and he was washing his hands before Harrison entered.

"We alone?"

"Yeah, what's going on, Glenn?" said Mitch.

Harrison moved into the room and leaned against the sink counter next to Mitch. He had a puzzled look on his face.

"Maybe nothing. We're getting ready to open Area 7 and, for over a month, I've scanned the entire area for activity. Nothing has shown up, not even a drone. Yesterday, Stevens and I went in for the first time to lay out the preliminary mining grid. Someone has already been in there. There are equipment and combat suit tracks all over the place. It's all fresh. I'd say, within the last week.

"We've had trouble with Broken Horse Consolidated trying to jump our claims in the past. Either they have new technology or someone on this platform is hiding their activity. I talked to Corporate and they said BHC is pressing other claims throughout the Saturn system. They think we may be in for an attempt at a hostile take-over. Mitch, I need some serious recon of areas seven, eight, and nine. If Corporate is right, we may have already lost eight and nine. They want to keep it quiet and off official channels as long as possible. They want your team to check it out. Keep the peace if possible, but you're going to be authorized *lethal force* to protect your team and PDC interests."

"Damn it," said Mitch. "When is Earth going to get some law out here? We can't keep this up for much longer without an all-out war. UPNS reported conflicts breaking out between BHC and The Euro Mining Co-op in several sectors of the asteroid belt." He shook his head and leaned heavily against the counter.

"Damn it. Damn it. Damn it. Okay, I'll need all my guys. Can you provide four bodies for perimeter security?" He waited until Harrison nodded.

"Good. We'll set them up in armed Land Rovers. If necessary, they can hold off just about anything, until we get back there." Mitch dried his hands then walked toward the door, "Send your guys over to the security compound on Titan in the morning and I'll get them set up for the next few days. Glenn, just play it like a training exercise for your guys. My team is always ready for anything, so they'll know this is no training exercise. Do we hear anything from our people on the BHC Titan Platform?"

"Nothing, not a word. Either there's nothing serious going on, they haven't heard anything, or they're dead," said Harrison. "They went silent two days ago. I'm betting on the latter."

"Shit!" Mitch walked out the door without another word. He stopped at a few tables and chatted with friends, laughed at a joke, and gradually made it back to his team. His beer was where he left it and still cold. He took a couple of swallows and settled into the table's current conversation.

"How about you, Ben? What was your worst job?" asked Jorge.

"You know, looking back, my worst job was probably also one of my best. I ran an exercise facility on the Martian surface. My job was to teach all those idiots, who immigrated from earth, that within the low gravity of Mars they couldn't eat like they did on earth and not exercise. The fools would balloon up and couldn't figure out how it happened. We can control the gravity on these platforms with simple rotation," he held his palms to the ceiling and glanced around the room, "but, there's no way to do that on Mars. Anyway, once they start losing control, the whole weight and fitness thing just compounds. Did you know the number one killer on Mars is heart attack due to obesity? The number one mode of transportation on Mars is an old-fashioned power wheelchair. God, I hated the whining, complaining, and crying from those spoiled, fat slobs."

"You said it was also one of your best jobs," said Carrie, reaching out to touch his arm. "I can see how satisfying it would be to help all those people."

Ben nodded his head and said, "Well, actually, most of the women who got back in shape were very grateful, and I got laid three or four times a week."

They all laughed loudly and Carrie said, "Damn it, Ben. Is sex all you think about?"

As the table settled down, Mitch said to the group, "Guys, we better call it a night. I need you all in the security bay briefing room at zero 600. We need to go over a few things before we go down to the surface."

"What's up, Mitch?" said Jorge.

"Nothing we can talk about here. Zero 600 will give us a full hour before launch. That should be enough." Mitch stood and drank half the remaining beer in his glass. "See you all in the morning." He settled his tab at the bar, then headed for his cabin.

Ben watched Mitch leave, thinking something wasn't right. He was certain when he saw the three non-regulars separate themselves from the bar and follow him out.

"Carrie, settle our bar tab will you. Three guys just followed Mitch out. Let's go see if he needs a hand," said Ben.

"Bullshit," she said. "Howie you settle the tab. I'm going with Ben and Jorge."

Ben laughed. "Howie, settle the tab and follow us. Come on, let's go."

They left the bar no more than a minute behind Mitch. Ben spoke as he hurried down the main corridor, "They won't try anything in the Main, but as soon as he gets into the residence corridors they'll jump him." He sped up, half-walking and half-running.

The Main corridor was full of people going to work, home, or patronizing the vast variety of shops, bars and restaurants—the same as any city back on earth. The corridor leading to Mitch's residence was coming up fast and Ben saw the three stalkers turn into it. Twenty more meters and they turned down the quiet passageway. Ahead they could see a struggle had already started. Before Ben could say a word, Carrie flashed past him, Jorge right on her heels. Two of the thugs held Mitch, who was already bleeding heavily from his nose and a slash in his side. The third man held a knife, preparing to stab Mitch while his friends controlled him.

Carrie was like a cat. As she approached the group, she ducked low and from nowhere produced a blade of her own. When she passed behind the assassin, her blade cut through the man's pants and severed his right hamstring. He screamed, bent to grasp his wound, and she buried her knife all the way to the handle in his back just below the right shoulder blade. It happened so fast that, when she looked up his two friends were still holding Mitch and just staring at her. Jorge took the one on the right and Ben the left. It was over in less than five seconds. A few well-placed punches and the two attackers were unconscious next to their dying friend.

Mitch leaned against the wall and said, "Jesus Christ, Carrie, remind me never to really piss you off."

"We didn't have a lot of time, Mitch. He seemed pretty intent on killing you. But, that was far too easy. These guys can't be pros."

Out of breath, Howie ran up, surveyed the carnage, and said, "Mitch, are you okay?"

"Yeah, I'm fine. This," he indicated the wound on his side, "isn't that deep, but it hurts like a son-of-a-bitch."

Mitch touched the communicator activator behind his right ear and spoke aloud, "Platform Security, urgent assistance required Section N, Corridor 21. This is Mining Security Commander Mitchel Anderson requesting immediate assistance."

Within seconds, blue and red lights began flashing all along the entire corridor, "This is Platform Security. Section N, Corridor 21 is in lock down. All residents remain in your cabins. Platform Security will be on scene in thirty seconds," blared from the overhead speakers, repeating every ten seconds.

Mitch turned to Ben, "Okay, when they arrive tell them exactly what happened and why this dumb shit is dead," he pointed at the now lifeless body. "When the other two wake up let Platform handle them. Stay together, don't let them separate the group. If they release you individually, wait for each other. No one in this team is to be alone for the rest of the night. When Platform releases you, go straight to my cabin. I'll tell you what I know when everyone gets there."

Mitch heard his communicator activate, "Mitch, this is Glen Chi with Platform Security. What's the status?"

"I have three attackers down: one dead, two unconscious. I have a four inch cut on my right side and would probably be dead if my team hadn't shown up. We have the scene secure." He saw activity at the Main corridor. "Your guys are arriving now. Glen, when this mess is cleaned up, come to my cabin and I'll fill you in. You've probably already been briefed, in which case you can fill *me* in."

"My team reports they are on site. I have EMPs in route. I'll see you in an hour at the most. In the meantime, make it sound like a simple robbery attempt and they just picked the wrong guy. They were going to kill you and empty your cabin. You know the drill. We get two or three of those a month."

"No problem," said Mitch and disconnected.

The whole process took less than an hour. Platform Security interviewed them all. The EMPs applied a local pain reliever to Mitch's wound, then sealed it with heal enhancing medical glue. The local pain reliever would last four days and the glue would heal the wound in three. By the time the team filed into Mitch's cabin, he had almost forgotten his injury. The cabin was slightly larger than most on the platform—one of the benefits of a command position with PDC. It was cramped with five people in the space, so Howie, Carrie and Ben sat on the bed, while he and Jorge sat in the only two chairs. He set a stack of disposable cups on the coffee table, adding a nearly full bottle of bourbon. He told the team everything that Harrison had told him.

When Chi arrived, he leaned against the only other door in the room, which led to a standard five-foot by four-foot toilet, shower, and washbasin. Chi listened to the accounts of the hallway attack, then added what he knew.

"I talked with Corporate Security just before leaving my office. They're convinced BHC is following a massive vein of magnesium into area seven and eight. They've reviewed satellite surveillance on our claims and clearly identified survey teams with combat suit support. I identified the traitor on my team who has been covering up the intrusion. We asked him to leave the platform, but unfortunately he forgot to take a space suit when he left." No one laughed at the joke, not even Chi.

"Mitch, they want to talk directly to you in the morning before you drop. They will have your orders and lethal force authorization ready to go. Corporate extended Madison's team on the surface for two days. He and his team are under your command. They moved back to the mine five hours ago and are getting full suit charges and some rest before you arrive. They have no idea what's coming. Corporate is certain any message would be intercepted. And that, my friends, is all I know."

There were no questions. They all knew this was why they were here and each one felt the anticipation, part fear and part excitement, known only to those preparing for a life and death struggle.

Mitch scanned the room for any further discussion. When none came, he said, "Okay, then. This place is too small for five of us. Let's move to the Launch Bay Briefing room. We'll sleep there. Glen, can you arrange for some beds, food, and additional security this evening and in the morning? I just don't want to take any more chances."

"I've got six officers outside," said Chi. "We're ready to move when you are."

"Okay, each of you pair-up with one of them and pick up your gear. Howie, you're with Glen and me. Don't make any stops. Get your stuff; go straight to the conference room. Have some food and get some rest, believe me we're all going to need it."

The team finally went to sleep around midnight. Mitch insisted on complete systems checks on each of the five Mech-9 suits. When he finally called it a night, the "bus" sat in the launch bay completely ready, loaded with extra munitions and supplies. The suits were fully charged, sealed and locked into their shielded position in the underbelly of the craft. Platform Security guarded the craft the remainder of the night. The soundproof conference room provided the perfect shield to the constant noise of the launch bay, and the team actually slept well.

Mitch woke first and dressed before calling the others. He activated the lights and gave them a few seconds before calling them. "Time to get moving. The time is zero 630. We launch at zero 800. Food will be in the bay. I want you all in your suits, with power and final pre-launch checks completed by zero 740. Com and weapons checks at zero 745. I'm going to grab something to eat and contact Corporate. I'll see you on the bus and brief you on the way down."

He walked out of the conference room into the familiar noise of the launch bay. The security team was around the bus. They seemed tired but diligent, and very ready for this night to be over.

From the meal, spread out on two tables, he filled a pint cup with coffee and picked up two sandwiches filled with some kind of imitation meat. The first sandwich was gone before he entered the Com Center.

"Good morning, Commander," said the Com Chief, "Corporate is ready when you are. Your mission log is on line and authorizations are being uploaded." He indicated the yellow command computer and then pointed at the blue computer lying next to it. "Corporate modified the mission plan while you slept and they want a walk through with you. Just say when, and I'll connect you."

Mitch finished the last sandwich then sat in front of the com monitor.

"Okay, let's do this."

Mitch left the com room at exactly zero 725, carrying the command and mission computers, and walked up the ramp into the belly of the bus. The Mech-9 suits were in their shielded positions suspended from the underbelly. As he passed each open hatch, he spoke to his team members, asking if they needed anything or wanted help preparing for the drop. When he reached his own suit, he climbed down the short ladder and settled into the Mech-9s control harness. He left the restraints loose while he docked the computers and locked them into position. Watching the controls come on line, he saw the full weapons array power up. This was the first time in a very long time that Corporate had authorized the use of a Mech-9 at full weapons and without speed inhibitors. The computer's display confirmed the activation of each of the other suits as their weapons systems initialized. Mitch waited for his mission plan update to complete before making the announcement to his team.

"Prepare to download the mission plan." He waited for each of four indicators to light up before saying, "Download starts...now."

Mitch began his team briefing just before launch and it lasted until they entered the lower atmosphere of Titan. The ride simply got too rough for Mitch to expect the team to maintain concentration. Within five minutes the bus touched down on the PDC runway, rapidly slowed, and taxied to the Mine's main entrance.

"Prepare to disembark," Mitch said, as the driver retracted the shielding that protected the Mech-9 units during entry.

As soon as the vehicle stopped, five sets of legs unfolded and planted their meter wide feet firmly on the ground. There was a slight pause while life support, power and data links were disengaged from the bus, and then all five team members stepped away, giving room for it to taxi to its hanger.

The natural light on Titan always reminded Mitch of a moonless night in Nebraska. With the moon turned toward the planet, as it was now, the light reflected from the planet's surface was identical to that of an earth half-moon—enough to see shapes and not walk into walls, but that was all. He touched several spots on the console, activating and adjusting internal systems to current conditions on Titan. The four eye-level view ports brightened, and he was looking at the surface of Titan in the equivalent of late afternoon sunlight on earth. The methane atmosphere tinted the light to amber, giving the false impression of blistering heat across the entire landscape. As always, he glanced at the outside temperature, not surprised by the -145°C reading. When he finished adjusting the suit, he could move freely with the unit reacting as if it were in earth level gravity. The combination of weight, Titan's gravity, and internal stabilizers allowed the system to operate like it was simply a shell over its operator, with extensions of arms and legs, hence the name "Suit." However, this *suit* was four meters tall and packed the latest in Planetary Dynamics Corporation weaponry and shielding.

Mitch searched for Madison's team and found them standing near the mine entrance. "Form up on Madison's team." They crossed the one hundred meters in less than seven seconds. The two teams faced each other and Mitch pulled a data transfer cable from the waist of his suit and connected it to Madison's. "Hook 'em up and transfer the mission plan and authorizations."

A moment later Madison's voice was on the com, "What the hell is going on Mitch? I've been out here for eight years and never seen anything like this."

Mitch waited for all ten suits to come up, "Okay everyone, Corporate has put me in command. All of you take a few minutes and listen to my Corporate briefing, then you'll know what I know. We'll move out in half an hour. If anything happens to me, Madison is in command. I'll take questions when we move out."

Mitch walked to the bus hanger, where he called internal security at the mine and briefed them on a training exercise for the four, armed Land Rovers. They were to patrol the landing strip and the mine's surface perimeter, while the Mech-9 units did a sweep of Area 7, the entire exercise designed to coordinate and integrate internal and external security teams.

Thirty minutes later, Mitch switched to the secure tactical com and called his ten-unit team together, "Saddle up. I'll take questions now."

Gleason, one of Madison's team, spoke up. "So, just to be clear, if we see any claim jumpers we open fire and kill as many as we can. We give no warning and we take no prisoners? Sorry, but it just doesn't seem right."

Madison spoke before Mitch could respond. "That is correct and, Gleason, you do it as if your life depends on it. Because it does. You give them any chance at all and those fuckers will kill you and the rest of us. Do not jeopardize my life or the life of anyone else on this team. Are you clear on that?"

Mitch could almost hear the young soldier cringe under the vocal lashing. "Yes, sir. I am clear," said Gleason.

"Are there any other questions about procedure?" asked Madison.

The team was silent and Mitch added, "Are there any questions about the tactical plan?" After a few seconds of silence he continued, "All right, let's move out!"

The group lumbered across the landing strip and into a series of low rolling hills. The terrain was frozen methane with an occasional outcropping of jagged rock. They were moving at nearly 50 kilometers an hour south and on a direct line to Area 7. Mitch heard a slight change in the acoustics of his com set.

"Mission Commander, this is Platform Security."

"This is Mission command," said Mitch.

"We have detected a caravan of mining equipment entering Area 7. They are moving at twenty-five klicks per hour, flanked by ten combat suits. At current speeds, you should make contact in 16 minutes. Correct course two degrees southeast. We just detected fifteen light combat craft launching from the BHC Platform. We are responding and we will keep them off your back. We will not be able to save the surveillance satellites. This might be the final surveillance update. We will take their satellites out, to even the battlefield. You are on your own, for now."

Mitch made the course correction and continued. The orange-gold landscape rolled away and gradually began to incline toward a low mountain range. Moving into Area 7, the intruders would be using the low gorges as cover.

"Mission Commander, this is Platform Security."

"Go ahead, Platform,"

"We are receiving a BHC transmission on all non-secure com channels and every system wide entertainment channel. I'll play their message for you." Static broke the communication link, and then cleared as the message played. The newscaster quality voice delivered the message to virtually every human within the solar system.

"My name is Gerry Fletcher, Broken Horse Consolidated Chief Operations Officer. Over the next few Earth days, BHC will seize approximately 25 percent of the assets currently held by Planetary Dynamics Corporation. Unfortunately, this action is required after numerous attempts to recover defaulted loans made to PDC. This action is a last resort attempt to recover losses incurred by BHC stockholders and to stabilize the market value of both corporations. The affected assets are: all operational mines, all claims (both developed and undeveloped), all equipment, all vehicles, and all space platforms that are considered part of PDC operations within the Saturn System. *This action is not taken lightly*, and is essential to the survival of BHC. All PDC employees performing daily operations within the affected area will be welcomed into the BHC family at their current positions and salary. Please, do not interfere with our transition teams. Help us make this change as seamless as possible."

"Platform, have you heard anything from Corporate in response?" asked Mitch.

"There's nothing being broadcast on public channels, however, we received messages from them to all stations within the Saturn system. They expect us to resist any attempt to seize assets, by every means available. They claim that loans made by BHC are not in default and that BHC illegally called in those loans. They are filing restraining orders with the Interplanetary Court on Earth. They remind us that we are all valued employees and they expect us to do the jobs we were hired to do, while supporting the corporate goals."

The monitors in Mitch's suit suddenly turned a bright white, then instantly compensated for the difference. The scene didn't change, however, the ambient light levels were now almost that of earth daylight.

"Platform, what the hell is going on up there?" said Mitch.

"Mitch, they just took out the PDC Cargo Ship Jasper. Its cargo was twenty thousand metric tons of magnesium. There were 47 crew. They gave no warning and didn't even try to board. They just torpedoed her. We'll look for survivors, but it's too dangerous to get near the wreck. The damn thing will probably burn like a flare for several earth days."

"Okay, Platform, we're about to go hot down here. Keep monitoring our com for status. Titan Mission Command out." Mitch waited a few seconds. "Howie, you and Soo take point. Try not to be detected, but go find the bad guys. We need to get this done and get back to protect the mine."

Two suits broke away from the formation and with smooth acceleration passed the column. Mitch watched them depart as they navigated the rolling terrain. After about fifteen minutes he asked, "Howie, what's your status?"

"Sorry, boss, nothing yet. According to the maps, we're about two hundred meters from a deep ravine. I'm launching a micro-drone to recon it before we expose ourselves," said Howie.

Mitch switched one of his monitors to the frequency of the drone. He watched the scene with Howie and Soo on high alert. The device rose and turned toward the ravine and proceeded to the ridge above the gorge. The drone rose above the crest for no more than five seconds, and then dropped back down. In those five seconds, Mitch saw ten suits and a column of mining equipment preparing a site for the beginning of their mine— they were dead center of Area 7.

"Good job you two. Back off a couple hundred meters and wait for the rest of us. We are no more than ten minutes away. Everyone else increase speed. I am releasing a targeting micro-drone, taking it to two hundred meters elevation. Each of you identify an intruder suit—one each. Howie, you and Soo will take the equipment, but remember, it's not armored, so just strafe the column end to end a couple times. The rest of you, your targets are the suits. Take out your target and then move to the next closest active target. Most of you have never used these weapons in combat, so just remember; you are firing the most advanced rail weapons in existence. You have one on each arm. They each fire two rounds per second in tandem with the other arm. That means four chunks of titanium filled with high explosive traveling at 4000 meters a second, *every second*. It should take about three seconds for them to react and I expect 12 hits each, before they can get off a single shot. You do that and we all go back to the mine alive."

The main column joined up with Howie and Soo and spread out just below the ridge. They each selected a target and locked weapons on it.

"Commence fire as soon as you have a clear target. Ready. Move out!" ordered Mitch.

They all made the crest within a second of each other. Howie and Soo began firing, and then the entire line erupted. The titanium projectiles ripped holes in the BHC armor and the explosives blew them apart. It was over within five seconds and Mitch was ready to call for a cease-fire, when Howie and Soo's life support monitors went red then flat lined. He looked down the line and both suits were down. The next Mech-9 in line flared white as a laser punched a two hundred millimeter hole through its center of mass, exactly where Jorge was strapped into the suit harness. Dread swept over Mitch like ice water.

"Back off! Everyone. Reform the fire line below the ridge. Back off now!" A second later, he said, "God damn it, I should have seen that coming. At least one of those pieces of machinery is a combat tank with laser cannon. Platform, this is Mission Command, I need some air support."

"This is Platform. Sorry, Mitch. I've got none to give. We're barely able to hold off the new fighters they keep sending. I can't afford to send you even one."

"Okay, team, we have no choice. I'll play back the recordings. Watch your monitors, and target the one that's firing." Mitch moved the recording back five minutes then started the replay. They all saw the team reach the crest and open fire, the destruction of the BHC suits, then two flashes from the lead vehicle, a short delay, and then a third flash. They saw themselves retreat.

"Madison, take your four guys and prepare to attack just like last time. Engage the tank and you four put sustained fire on it until I tell you to stop. The three of us will move down the ridge, then, when you start firing, we'll go over the top and into the ravine, move up from behind, and attack at close range. Remember, if they get past us, they'll take the mine and possibly the platform. Good luck, Madison. When I call for a ceasefire, you guys move off the crest to safety. I'll make the call as soon as we're in position."

Mitch, Ben, and Carrie moved along the ridge for about two hundred meters then turned to the ridge.

"When I call the ceasefire for Madison, that's your order to open fire. *Do not* stop firing until the tank is dead or you're out of ammo. Ready. Open fire!"

Madison and his team opened up a second later. The tank was a mass of explosions, the four Mech-9 units pouring sixteen rounds a second on the vehicle.

It took Mitch, Ben and Carrie five seconds to take up positions within twenty-five meters of the target. Ben on the left rear, Mitch directly behind, and Carrie on the right side. The fire coming from above lessened and Mitch knew that the other team had taken severe losses.

"Ceasefire!" yelled Mitch.

The fire from above stopped, and the three of them opened up, Ben and Mitch spraying randomly over the tank's surface. Carrie, however, concentrated her fire on a single spot, every round striking within a meter of the first. A white-hot crater formed in the tank's hardened surface. Ben went down, his suit sliced in half just below the pilot cockpit. Carrie paid no attention. It took two more seconds, then four rounds exploded in the interior. She rushed up to the hole and fired four more rounds into the interior at different angles, the gasses and shrapnel loudly glancing off her suit as they expelled from the interior. Nothing could survive.

"Ceasefire!" she yelled. "I killed that son-of-a-bitch! Yeah! Holy shit what a rush!" She fired two more rounds into the hole.

"God damn it, Carrie, calm down! Ben, are you okay?" asked Mitch.

"Yeah, I'm alive. This suit's totaled though. There are no motor functions. Radio and life support seem to be working, but that's it," said Ben.

"Madison, what's your status?"

"Just Gleason and me," said Madison.

"We need to get Wilson back to the mine. We can carry the remains of his suit and extract him in the mine's work shop. Double check for survivors. We'll have to wait to bring our dead home. Carrie and I will get Wilson to the top of the ridge, where the four of us can handle him."

There were no other survivors. Mitch didn't expect to find any, but needed to check anyway. The loss of half the team hit them all hard. The trip back to the mine took nearly two hours of virtual silence. It also wore the power packs down to almost critical levels.

"Mine Internal Security, what is your status?" said Mitch.

"Commander, we are in defensive positions guarding the mine entrance and are prepared to defend the air strip, if needed. So, I guess this is no longer an exercise. We sort of figured that out when the fighting started. Sorry we couldn't help out there."

"You did your jobs and you did them well," said Mitch. "We're on our way in, headed straight to maintenance. It may take a little while for reinforcements to get here, so we're on our own for now."

"Roger that, Commander. We see you. You're clear to come in."

"Our suits need recharging and the pilots need some rest, as well. I'll get some backup out there just as fast as I can."

They took Ben directly to the maintenance shop and left orders to extract him from the damaged suit and have him checked by a doctor. The rest of them went directly to the charge stations and hooked up. While the others exited their suits, Mitch called the platform.

"Well, Mitch, we seem to have weathered the storm," said Chi. "We think they expected only five suits on the surface. Had there been, they would control the mine now and be poised to take this platform. There were several other attacks—we lost most of them. But, without this platform and the Titan mine, their victories are basically useless. They're still attacking anything that flies. The Jasper will burn for another three days; it's just way too dangerous to go near the wreck, or to send anything to the surface. We won't send reinforcements down until we get a truce. Several of the other corporations have taken our side and are providing support, so we expect an official ceasefire very soon. BHC can't sustain these losses for long, so expect another two days at the most."

"No problem," replied Mitch. "The mine is secure and will stay that way."

The first corporate war that occurred in space began on, Earth date March 12, 2166, and "officially" ended May 28, 2166. On March 18, 2166, a truce began and all hostilities ended on that date. The primary combatants were Broken Horse Consolidated (BHC) and Planetary Dynamics Corporations (PDC). At the conclusion of hostilities, a hearing was held in the Earth District of the newly formed Intersystem Court. Both organizations' corporate offices are based on Earth, making their Boards of Directors bound by the laws of that district.

The Court concluded that BHC unlawfully seized or destroyed property belonging to PDC. In the course of those seizures, there was significant loss of life and injury to employees of both corporations. The judgement ordered BHC to pay full restitution for all property damaged or destroyed, and to pay a scaled restitution to all persons injured, and to the families of those killed or missing as a result of actions taken by BHC.

Mitch, Ben and Carrie slowly walked along the wide corridor of the Norway Prince Cruise Ship, Leif Erikson. The spacious walkway accented the opulence of the magnificent cruise ship. A beautiful multi-colored carpet covered the corridor's floor and the walls were high gloss with hand polished mahogany. The three were meeting Madison and Gleason in the main dining hall for dinner. Corporate Headquarters called the five "Heroes of Titan" to Earth, all expenses paid, in order to receive honors for their exceptional valor. This was the first evening of a six-week voyage promising to be the most amazing time of their lives.

"My cabin is three times the size of the one I had on the platform," said Mitch. "The bathroom is huge."

"I hope Howie was right about the food and drink," said Ben with a wry chuckle.

Carrie brushed the hair away from her face with exaggerated flamboyance, "You know, I could really get used to this."

As they talked, a short, and very round, man exited a cabin ahead of them. He pulled a leash, dragging a small dog out of the cabin and into the corridor. Within seconds, the creature raced across the passageway and began pooping on the carpet.

As the three walked past, they heard the man say, "Is my little Pepper done? What a good doggie you are. Let's go back inside and see if Momma is ready to have dinner."

Carrie shook her head in wonder.

"Well, maybe not."

W. A. Fix is a retired information technology manager, who lives with his wife and three cats in the suburbs of San Diego, California. He has been writing all his life and recently became more serious about the craft. He particularly enjoys writing flash fiction and stories in the 3,000 to 5,000-word range, due to the instant gratification for both author and reader. Other interests include photography and golf.

Other Published Works:
Publication: The Story Shack Magazine
"A Really Good Day," "Testament," "Mitzi," "Nin's Glory," and "Born to Play"
Publication: Spaceports and Spidersilk Magazine
"Dream 6"
Anthology: The Future is Short: Science Fiction in a Flash
"Yood Must Find Itch," and "Moments To Remember"
Anthology: The Future is Short: Science Fiction in a Flash, Vol 2
"Nin's Glory," "Gleet and the Shiny Thing," and "The Queen's Consul"
Anthology: Visions: Leaving Earth
"Life Lift," and "My Name is Millec"

TITAN

5. REFUGE

By

Ami Hart

Fira scratched his arm. The sound his nails made against the grey jumpsuit was nauseatingly loud in the enclosed crawl space. He'd reached a T junction and a quick look to either side confirmed that he'd gone deeper in the tunnel system than he had before. Nothing looked familiar anymore. Maybe he'd finally found a way out of the stifling trap that was the Refugee sector.

He chose to go right—because it seemed right—crawling forward, all the while trying to keep his knees from thumping too loudly on the brushed metal surface. Suddenly, his hand rested upon a seam in the metal—a marker where the tunnel started to slope downward. Fira's breath caught in his throat. His eyes widened and he quickly scrambled to a sit, bumping his head on the tunnel ceiling. Shuffling forward on his buttocks he carefully slid down the smooth, sloping surface, splaying his bare feet to either side so he wouldn't descend too fast. To his relief the tunnel levelled out again and he moved back onto his hands and knees, peering down, wondering where it led. He spied a smudge of light ahead and an ingrained, childish distrust of the dark coerced him toward it.

The rest of the tunnel was long, stretching onward, smaller junctions dropping in from above. Somewhere, much deeper than the veins in which he crawled was that distant throbbing heartbeat —the internal workings of the Flotilla. It rumbled beneath the faster pitter-patter of his heart. He wasn't supposed to be here; refugees weren't allowed outside their allocated sector.

Fira's home, the Flotilla's refugee sector, housed those humans the Ghus rescued from the Raq-Ni Cleansing. Only after their rescue, did Fira learn the name of these world eaters—another element to flesh his dread and feed his nightmares.

The Raq-Ni came to harvest the earth. When the Raq-Ni encountered resistance they had loosed a bio-weapon called the Melt, which spread slowly but, nevertheless, proved itself a world destroying disease. It crawled across the planet, slowly breaking civilisation, and causing everything else to collapse. It all broke. Then, the Raq-Ni left the Earth—perhaps waiting until the time all possible resistance dissolved, leaving only the base elements of the world. That was when humankind's saviours came—far too late to stop the Cleansing—and rescued the humans that remained, saving them from a world destined to die a slow, painful, messy death.

These saviours...these aliens, called the Ghus...tall, mysterious, strange looking—just as humans expected all aliens to be—had stringently administered segregation on their new home. The Flotilla collection of triangular segments, a ship made of ships, entwined with a mass of metal arteries, winding the sectors together. Fira had only seen the whole thing once from the smaller rescue craft as it docked. It had been the biggest, most wonderful and frightening thing he had ever seen. The humans called this wheel of life the Titan Flotilla, because that's where it stayed—feeding on the moon and living in an umber gloom. Now, the human remnant were completely reliant on these Ghus-kind, who provided the basics—food, shelter, and rules. It was like a prison, though, and as time dragged on, people wondered, *what now? Where are they going to take us?* But they didn't take the humans anywhere, for the Flotilla stayed moored to Saturn's largest moon, Titan, mining its resources to keep everyone alive.

Fira had been five when the Cleansing came to Earth. He was now ten—sometimes he was older, though. Occasionally those early times came to him like an over-bright dream. His memory returned hot, bright flashes of the world as it was before the Raq-Ni. His mother's smile—vibrant, happy and softly pink against her large teeth. Above them sunshine had dappled in greens and yellows as they'd run across the park near home. That park...with its grandfather trees, too big to be real, bearing dark, valleyed skin, reaching against an insistent wind, all the while complaining about it with deep aching creaks. The only things that listened to those complaints were two magpies, squawking their mocking agreement every now and then.

Running, playing, laughter—those happy memories were now shaded over. Running took on a new terrifying shape, the dusky grey of a world in chaos. Bursting light became violent. Dust and Melt claimed the streets. Fira and his father had sought refuge underground in the sewer lines, beneath the carnage-strewn streets. Maybe that was why the tunnels here on the Titan Flotilla called to him so loudly. They were his refuge.

Also in here, he could keep away from Cyd. In Fira's opinion, some people could have been left behind; Cyd was one of them. Thick golden curls, wide mean face and huge hands, hands that made even bigger, meaner fists.

Fira pushed out an anxious huff as he reached the tunnel's end—the smudge had become a grate. Air pushed from behind him, scattering his unwashed brown hair forward, until long strands wrapped themselves under his nose. He raked the irritation back and squashed himself close, peering through the square holes at the world on the other side. The room was airy. There was no sterile metal there, instead a warm light-green glowed back at him, like sun through a fading leaf. There was something incredibly enticing about it, resonating deep within Fira's soul.

He reached up and hooked dirty fingers through the grate, pushing and pulling in quick opposable motions. It didn't move, likely fixed in place from the other side. He sat hugging his knees, soaking in the colour...letting it dance past his corneas, rejuvenating his mind. Hope suffused over bitter, lonely desperation, like a butterfly kissing a flower.

Everything was so grey where they lived. They were a smoky-coloured remnant, uplifted from the caustic burn of the Melt. He looked down at his jumpsuit. They all wore the same grey, with a slight shine—that felt like he was wearing someone else's dead skin. At least it was warm.

Fira eventually turned from the beautiful green, crawling back, defeat bowing his back and dropping his shoulders—like an old horse too weak to carry its own weight. He'd seen so much ugly during the Cleansing. He wasn't sure why, but the images of the dying animals had stayed with him longest. All the other stuff had been blurred and lost in the delirium of terror, which had taken over all of them in those days.

The most vivid picture he remembered was a kitten, so small...half its fur gone, three legs, yowling from its nest of rubble. Fira's father had pulled him away saying, "Don't touch it." His words urgent, loud and harsh— almost as loud as the poor kitten's screams—but not quite.

Fira sniffed back the stray drip of sadness seeping from that wounded place. The place where the animals cried inside. He felt like one of them as he moved on all fours up the slope, slipping backwards every now and then, causing his arms to burn under the strain. He returned to the junction and sat with his back toward home. He stared to the right, his forlorn eyes fixed on the faint smudge of reflected light, which came from *that* wonderful room. He tore his gaze away, the phrase "tunnel vision" stirring him to move on.

Something pulled him left, curiosity. Curiosity killed the cat, splattered across his mind, unpleasant and unwelcome. The Flotilla's internal noises became heavy, ear pulsing and mad, so incessant that Fira closed his eyes against it—like that would help. What he really needed to do was close his ears. A couple of times he almost turned back, especially when the air began to blast ice cold, numbing his hands to useless meaty unfeeling lumps. He crawled with fingers scrunched under, walking on blue-marbled whitened fists. As he crawled on, the tunnel opened up above him to the blasting beat of a fan, air rushing at his back, crushing him with a steady thwack, thwack, thwack. His eyes streamed while that voice inside taunted, this was why you chose right. Past the beat of the fans, he came to a steep gradient, like one of those old restored playground slides, except without the evidence of the fast childhood fun scuffed upon its surface. No, this was cold and black, descending to the pit. With his hands on the edge, he teetered precariously, looking down. Wanting to go back, but not wanting to retreat yet. He wanted there to be more—something more down there. Something worth the fall.

There was more. Beneath the steady thud of the fan, he heard a strange chattering sound, reminiscent of a child's voice, broken and morphed by distance to nonsensical sound. Fira reasoned for a time—the dark once held safety for him, couldn't it also hide hope? An ember so soft and semi-substantial that it was ready to wink out if he took one wrong step. Down.

He moved into position, sitting on the edge, dangling feet feeling heavy, as if they had already made the decision for him. The rest of him debated. Were the sounds even real? He heard things sometimes—that weren't there. It was in that place between sleep and wakefulness, things from before, sounds, cries, death and booms, a cacophony of noise blended together, making a rancid concoction of pure fear.

He fell. Air rushed past and his palm made a shrieking sound on the metal, as he tried to slow his descent. His heart crashed in his chest and his mouth opened to cry out, only to have it cut off by the shuddering thud of a heavy landing. His bottom skidded several hops across a flat shine-lit surface. His gaze chased the gentle light to its source. Another vent? When he touched it, it dropped and would have fallen with a clatter had his cold stung fingers not been entwined through the large mesh.

A shaky, excited breath escaped him. He blinked against the light. Something fluttered nearby and his whole body snapped in the sound's direction. He saw a tree, creamy limbed, spindly enough to seem fragile, wearing a garland of gold-green leaves, which trembled in the direct airflow. His hair sucked back off his eyes, revealing a strange new world—a garden, unlike any he had seen before. Scores of strange trees stood, willowy, thin trunks set upon sprawling pinkish roots— not earth-born trees. There was something tentative about them, as if they had never really felt soil nor been touched by real sunlight. Scrambling down from his hiding place, his feet found a foreign-feeling ground and he placed the grate aside. The alien surface squished in protest beneath his bare feet, moist, warm—not entirely unpleasant—part moss with elements of green pond slime.

Why do we not have a garden like this in the refugee sector? The unfairness of their lack made him scowl, as he walked between the trees—the paper rattle of the leaves above sounding like a strangely chaotic applause. He passed large fleshy pods that seemed to breathe and gave them a wide berth, just in case. Fear of the unknown never strayed far from him—the ideas of dangers coming from beyond the stars forever etched on his psyche. Then that sound again, a giggle—but not. Neither a chatter, nor words, but whispery and slightly lispy. It made him think of a broken whistle, hollow and reedy, blown in short rapid bursts—faster than a man could breathe. He looked up into the trees, eyes searching for a strange bird. Nothing fluttered there but leaves.

There was a flash of something at the edge of his vision, followed by a sharp coo. Fira turned to spy movement within a cluster of bright green hair-like vegetation. His breath staggered, as he got closer. He saw a blur of white, and a huge pink eye blinked at him, followed by a sharp clicking sound. He stumbled backward and his foot caught on something, causing him to fall on his backside with a crunch, his weight smashing the pink tree roots beneath with a glass-like snap. A sharp pain shocked his hand. Lifting it, he saw a long needle of wood lodged deep in his palm. He pulled it out and blood immediately pooled in its place, hot, red and urgent. Tears welled up even as Fira tried to choke them back. A soft sound pulled him from that scarlet haze of hurt, to a creature, small, furry, and relatively unthreatening. Its coat was snowy white with flecks of rusty red. Three pink eyes looked back at him—one larger and set higher than the others. It blinked—almost stupidly—as the larger of the fleshy purple veined eyelids was a fraction slower than the other two.

Fira crouched, leaning forward as he reached out toward the creature, causing blood to spot the odd algae-moss with flares of red. The creature trembled a moment and then walked forward on its four stubby legs, legs that only moments ago Fira didn't know it had—so much fur. To his surprise, it reared up, lifting a paw to deposit a ball of hair-like leaves on his upturned palm. Immediately, the juice from the crushed strands burned his skin and Fira clamped his other hand over the now searing wound. Amazingly, the pain seemed to ebb away and when he took his hand away, he saw the bleeding had stopped, the wound closed. Soon all that remained was a dull post-traumatic throb. The creature sat down close to him and stared, cocking its head in that adorable pet-like fashion. He couldn't resist reaching to stroke it. The moment his fingers touched that fur on its crown, an array of emotions stole over him, calm, happiness, security—almost foreign feelings. He wondered if it was someone's pet. Looking around revealed only the trembling trees.

"You want to come home with me little one?" He asked in a soft but decisive tone.

It blinked at him, the larger eye fixed unerringly on his face. It was the size of a cat and when he picked it up, he found it wasn't heavy. On its hands and feet there were soft but flexible digits. He got a surprise when it held onto the front on his suit like a startled baby clinging to its mother. Immediately Fira felt protective.

"Don't worry, you looked out for me, so I'll look after you."

He cradled it against his body as he returned and climbed back inside the tunnel. He looked up the steep slope and lamented, how was he going to get back up there? The creature struggled against him and he released it. To his surprise, it began to waddle up the slope, its flexible little feet making sucking noises against the metal. Soon it disappeared into the gloom.

"I wish I could do that." His voice echoed back, accompanied soon after by a rapid chattering. Wedging his feet to either side, he began to climb, gritting his teeth every time a foot slipped with a jarring squeak. His arms and legs were shaking by the time he reached the top. The creature looked up at him as if to ask, *where to now*? He scooped it up with one hand, holding it close to his chest as he crawled along with one cold hand and two tired knees. As the beat of the fans faded and the tunnels became familiar, the tension in Fira eased.

When he slid out of the entrance and into the bunkroom, he drew a deep breath, experiencing a moment of giddy triumph. The creature in his arms whoooed a soft, hollow, whispery sound as he carried it past the grey bunks, three beds high, towering monuments to sleeplessness. The room was abandoned—everyone would be at the middle-eats. It wasn't called midday, because the sun didn't govern things here, Saturn did. He walked to the single window they had in the children's sleeping area, small, square and smudged by fingertips. Far below stretched a restless quivering expanse that was the methane lake, rust-coloured haze piled over the distant, dark and lumpy horizon.

"In a few days the Flotilla will lift up again, then the sky will turn dark blue and we'll get to see Saturn," he explained.

He liked it when the Flotilla ascended, because everything became so crisp. When it happened, the children all fought to catch the first glimpse—as a drowning man struggles for air. Pulling his gaze from the smog-strewn wasteland, Fira sat with a plomp on a nearby bed, not his. Absently he stroked the creature.

"I miss home—the way it was before the Raq-Ni came," he whispered to no one in particular.

He talked to himself a lot in the tunnels. The creature stirred beside him, one flexible paw wrapped round his index finger as it looked up at him, that largest pink eye assessing him before jumping down from the bed. The creature moved with surprising speed as it scuttled under the bunk. Fira started, and dropped to his knees, looking beneath, only to see the creature streaking down the room's walk space toward the bunkroom door. He stumbled and ran after it, nerves buzzing, ears rushing.

They will take it from me, if they find it. The thought pushed into his head with the pain of needle sticking flesh. A kitten's cries echoing somewhere inside, shaking his soul.

The hallways were busy, he bumped into and brushed past grey-uniformed people, their faces blurred as he rushed out disconnected apologies. His attention completely set upon the floor of the hall.

I said I would keep you safe, his mind screamed. Everyone was just acting as normal as if nobody had seen it.

Perhaps he had imagined the creature. He stopped, and looked down at his palm. There was still a slightly swollen red patch. It did happen, didn't it?

As he passed a junction which lead to the recreation area, Fira heard a startled laugh—the tone needled him. Recognition saturated him with a new, colder anxiety.

Any other day, he would have run the other way, but not today. With great trepidation, he stole toward the sound of hushed sniggers. They were in the logic games room— the last place Fira would expect someone like Cyd to be. He hesitated, his back pressed flush to the wall beside the door, just out of their sight. Sweat made his suit stick against his spine.

"What is it?"

"Dunno, some pet of theirs, maybe." Cyd's voice returned, sharp and snarling, incarnate with hate for them.

Them being the Ghuz.

They didn't save his family, not like they did with my dad. And Cyd hated the Ghuz for it. He also hated kids like Fira for daring still to have a dad. Not much of a dad, but one none-the-less...

"We better get it back, then."

"Give it back, are you kidding me? They have us locked here in this prison, locked up like criminals. You know what I think. I think that they sent the Raq-Ni, that it was them all along. That's what Jesem and Doc think too."

"I dunno man. They say Jesem is crazy, and Doc just does what other people tell him to. You shouldn't listen to them Rowsers."

Cyd was in with the Rowsers? A group that claimed all aliens were a threat, especially the Ghuz.

"What and I should listen to you, a pampered momma's boy, Karl? You're blind just like most of them. They are never going to let us go....They're just hoping we die off in this tin can." Fira heard Cyd snort and a sharp cry, distinctly not human. Fira squeezed his eyes shut, the sound like a lance to his gut. "Let's have some fun with this thing."

Fira stepped into the doorway, recoiling inside as he revealed himself. He locked eyes with the terrified creature first, its wide pink orbs pleading as it struggled in the ape-like boy's grasp. Fira fired inside, rocketing forward low and bull-like, a senseless rage propelling him. Cyd turned toward Fira in surprise, throwing the creature to the side in time to greet Fira's head butting him in the gut. Cyd toppled with an exclamation of surprise. The others scattered, pressing back, game pieces spilled off nearby tables, knocked down by their hasty retreat. Fira rolled and reached for the creature. Behind him, Cyd snarled. The table the bully had fallen against squealed across the metal floor, torn from its fixed base. Fira wildly scrambled from the sound, grabbing at the small white blur resting too still—and too silent—on the floor beside him. He bolted from the room, smashing his shoulder against the entranceway as he left. A hand scratching down his parting back, followed by a loud thud. He dared not look behind him to see what had happened. He ran like he used to—like he had to. He was always good at running.

He heard a distant roar, "You're dead, Fira!"

He ducked down side halls, darting through adjoining rooms, weaving his escape. The map of their sector etched in his head. Only when he reached the bunkroom did he look down at his pet, lifeless in his trembling hands. Its little limbs slack and pink paws open, its eyes closed—all of them. There was a pink stain on the fur at the back of the creature's head. Fira sobbed, tears falling hot, dripping down his nose, ticking unbearably—his hands felt too heavy to wipe them away. The kitten screamed in his head again, or was it distant yelling, he couldn't tell over the hiccupping, soul-rattling sorrow.

He retreated into the dark with the little body clutched to his raggedly heaving chest. Past the ringing doom that was the fans, back to the garden where it had all begun. His vision tearing up each time he looked down at the helpless little thing. He hugged it, the way he wished his dad had hugged him when he'd been scared, lost and crushed beneath the weight of apocalyptic terror.

He fell to his knees on the soft damp green, which sprung back against him. Above, the leaves of the ghostly trees hissed. He laid the creature down; it's white so stark against cool green. He smeared an arm across his face, tears glistening ribbons along his rubbery sleeve. He looked round the garden but, other than the frantic sound of the leaves, nothing else stirred the strange paradise. *I couldn't keep you safe.*

"I lied, I'm sorry," he choked out, throat ragged raw, voice foreign sounding. He reached out, with the same hand that had been wounded, his fingers combing the soft fur.

That's when he noticed the slight rise and fall, the faintest movement. Life? He turned his hand and looked where his own wound should've been, but wasn't. Gone, wiped from his skin, undone as if it never happened. He spun to a stand and ran between the trees looking for the small plant, the one with the wispy hair-like foliage. He tore a handful out when he found it. It was cool against his palm this time. He hurtled back to the creature, sprinting, tripping, rising again out of desperation. He squeezed the green fibres, crushing them in a shaking fist before pressing it lightly to the back of the creature's head.

The fur was still warm against his hand, conducting a measure of hope. He sat there whispering.

"You're going to be fine. I'm here; I'll take care of you." Those words he had so desperately wanted to hear back on earth, during the years of running, and hiding. "To survive, you need to be harder boy!" his father had said, over and over like an immutable truth.

The creature remained still and Fira looked down at his now useless hands.

"Sorry..." *Sorry I couldn't protect, save, heal you. Sorry I took you from safety in the first place.*

"It's all my fault." He gagged and a tear plummeted, landing with a splat on the back of his hand. His fingers twitched and his nails scratched against the rubbery grey fabric, which strained against his bent knees.

A soft sigh roused him and he looked up. Towering above him was a Ghus, its two deep-green protuberant eyes fixed tightly on him. Fira jerked to a stand and backed away, heart clamouring in his chest as the dark skinned alien advanced one gliding step after another.

90

The white and black robes it wore, accordioned soundlessly as the Ghus crouched over the wounded pet. Bowing its head it hummed a sorrowful sound. It moved the little body and saw the crushed leaves beneath the head.

Fira bit his lip hard, wondering if he had done the right thing.

The alien gave him an inscrutable gaze, but no emotion showed on that leathery face. Fira couldn't move—the knowledge of how many rules he had broken seizing him to the spot. He didn't even know what they would do to him, consequences were unknown—they just took trouble makers away. There was no point in running, there was nowhere to run, and not even the tunnels would save him now. The Ghus picked up the little body, cradling it gently with long thin arms.

It spoke, holding out a three-fingered hand. "Peace and calm, I am Solas." The alien Solas looked down at the small creature it held so gently. "Humans are curious, rash and emotional creatures. Their harried actions hurt others and themselves. We were not sure whether you were worth saving, those wild afflicting emotions feed a terrible willingness to turn on those who try to help."

"Not all of us are like the Rowsers. We are not all the same..." Fira started, but couldn't finish, all evidence to the contrary in Solas's arms.

"Solas understands," it said, displaying no emotion to evidence it did.

Fira felt sick to his stomach. "You have been watching us, testing us?"

"Of a kind. I don't think humans will be on this ship for much longer."

I've doomed us all.

The creature stirred weakly against the Ghus's robes. "We must get to a restoration area for full healing."

"What will happen to us?" Fira broke out.

"I do not know yet," Solas returned.

"I'm sorry, it is all my fault. I took your pet from the garden. I wanted to care for it but it escaped and someone else found it and hurt it." Fira's gaze dropped to his feet, his heart sinking at the truth laid bare. "It was my actions that caused all of this." His voice shook, weak and thin as he poured out the grim admission.

The alien didn't react, except for a slow blink of its eyes. A soft trill broke the strained silence and the small soft creature in its arms moved. The alien looked down, cocking its head as it said, "Your actions hurt Solas too."

Fira felt himself shrink inside. Here it comes...

The creature in the alien's arms chattered softly and the Ghus seemed to listen, "And my own actions hurt us. Curiosity is a strong emotion, is it not?"

Fira blinked, confused for a moment, his gaze fixed on the small white creature. He wished he were the one holding it right now.

"What's your pet's name?" Fira asked.

Solas cocked his head then blinked rapidly. "Pet? This is no pet. This is Solas also. You are the first human to meet our smaller soul-piece. It must be a strange concept to you that one soul lives in two bodies, dependent yet separate, their individual experiences enriching the whole."

Then little Solas cooed and Fira's heart ached; the kittenish thing he had believed it to be became more. The diminutive transformed into something miraculous and strange and far, far bigger. The consequences far greater. Wonder and dread, sorrow and joy clashed noisily within, making him want to recoil and reach out at the same time. But he just stood there, feeling dumb.

The Ghus turned to leave but stopped, turning its head, gazing back at him with peaceful emerald eyes that soothed

"You like this place?" Solas gestured with a sweep of one long arm.

"Yes, very much," breathed Fira, his gaze resting on the creature in Solas's other arm. It peeked out at him around the folds of the alien's robes.

"Next time, come to the main sector gates. They will let you through. You can come and visit me, us. We Solas, we tend this garden."

Those words, *next time*, sounded like a promise. Was the alien messing with him? Fira battled to trust in it...promises hadn't meant much in a very long time.

Fira was directed back to his sector, no more tunnel clambering, instead he was faced with wide-open corridors, colour and light. The other Ghus, large and small, watched his transfer silently. When the door closed, locking him back in the refugee sector, he was met with questions and accusations.

His father took him hard by the shoulder, "What have you done boy?"

Fira couldn't answer his father, because he didn't know.

Behind his father, in the gathering crowd he saw a flash of Cyd, blond curls, red face—like an alert light. The boy weaved boisterously forward. Firas's vision throbbed—rage or fear he didn't know which.

The deeply petulant voice rang out, "He had one of them aliens' pets, an' he hurt it!"

Fira clenched his fists, turning furiously on Cyd. "Liar, you hurt it! I saved it! I was the one looking after it."

"You didn't do a very good job." Cyd gloated, until Fira's father turned a razor-sharp glare on him.

Cyd jolted back a step, his mouth squishing up and his small eyes ducking down—Father's fury pushing him away—just like it did with everyone else.

Then Fira got a shake and a shove, almost gentle, but not quite. "Dumb boys, rocking the boat. They might leave us all here now because of you two! All they have to do is cut those pipes you've been crawling around in, Fira...."

Fira butted his lip and frowned at his feet. "That was the only place I felt..."

His father sighed acceptance as if he understood—a rare thing. Then shook his head.

"What have you done, boy? What have you done? You know, this was the only real refuge we had."

Then the order came for the crowd to disperse and it did gradually, confusion, fear and directionless anger trailing in its wake. They were to return to their sleeping quarters until final eats. Fira obeyed, thinking of Solas and Solas, his two *almost* friends and the words, *next time.*

The answer to Father's question came hours later when the Flotilla rose above Titan's clouds. Fira saw the massive jewel that was Saturn, graced with his mighty crown, and marvelled at the sight. However, the Flotilla didn't stop moving, it kept rising. They all pressed around that small smudged window, witnessing a field of stars that seemed strung out just for them. Distant lights of a vast promised land.

"We're leaving." One of the children whispered, as those stars swung by. The motion made Fira feel giddy— and hopeful.

Ami Hart is the pen name for Jessica Colvin. She is a writer, artist, and mother of two from Christchurch, New Zealand. She lives in two worlds: one being post-quake Christchurch and the other is a fantastical place where dragons and space ships soar, sometimes side by side.
Jessica is a member of SpecficNZ and the Christchurch Writers Guild. She has had several short stories published in various anthologies and is currently writing a fantasy novel. She blogs about her writing adventures here, http://www.amilibertyhartwriter.com/
Publishing credits:
Reflections: An anthology by the Christchurch Writers' Guild, (Ned's Hallelujah)
The Future Is Short: Science Fiction in a Flash ("Snap and Crackle", "Unwanted Gift")
Consortium ("Destroyer of Syn")
Visions: Leaving Earth ("Babel Ascension")
The Future Is Short: Science Fiction in a Flash, Volume 2 ("The Dracul", "Arts and Craftiness", "Ghost of a Hope")

IAPETUS

6. SHEPARD'S PI

By

Timothy Paul

A few years back I came across a hundred-year-old novel called The Green Mile. I forget the details, but I remember a particularly visceral response to convicts sitting in concrete cells waiting for months, or even years, for their execution. Out here, things are simpler. More like France's Reign of Terror in the 1790's. This chamber could have come straight out of that novel. But here on Titan, once sentence is pronounced, the deed is carried out within hours. Capital punishment on this orbiting outpost is a simple matter. An unseen administrator presses a button opening the airlock and *WHOOSH!* Fourteen seconds of icy consciousness and another minute and three quarters to suffocate before your body floats off into the rings of Saturn. Gravity from the gas giant eventually resolves the issue of frozen cadavers as they burn up on their way to the planet's surface. Upon hearing the unmistakable hum of a pressure seal, I ran my fingers through my long, black curls and closed my eyes. Funny. My last thought was for a hot shower.

I heard the door open and braced myself for an out-of-body experience with the Almighty. Feeling neither unimaginable cold nor the vacuum, generally associated with floating in space without proper gear, I opened my eyes. Instead of eternal judgment or the spectacle of the Tethys Trojans floating in the distance, I was surprised to see Kendall Brant easing his glutinous ass between the polymer arms of the only piece of furniture bolted to the floor.

Without his jovial grin from ubiquitous real estate ads pasted on the nets, the fatty wrinkles of his face drooped into the jowls of a bulldog. "So you're Brad Shepard," he said. "Takes some interesting talents to break into the First Bank of Saturn."

"I got lucky," I answered. Despite my looming sentence, there was no reason to invite a prolonged torture which would certainly follow, if he knew my background.

"Mr. Shepard, if that's actually your name, you're a rogue black ops deserter from earth's North American contingency with university degrees in counter terrorism, espionage and security."

Shit. He knew.

"Having four billion credits in First Saturn, I am their largest shareholder. More than three and half billion larger than my closest competitor. So, you can see that I am the person most concerned with your larcenous activities."

This was not going well.

"I also have enough personal clout to have your sentence commuted."

The bulldog was beginning to look more like a shar-pei.

"You have my attention," I said.

"If I'm to arrange an extension of your life, I will expect something in return."

"What could a man of my background do for a respected businessman?"

"You're familiar with the Fundamentalist Coalition?" he asked.

"I've heard of them," I answered. "Religious extremists of some sort."

"Yeah," Brant grunted. "A mix of Islam, Judaism, and Christianity. Claim they've had a prophetic calling to cleanse the system according to the laws of Moses."

Brant leaned in so close I could count the pock marks on his nose. His breath smelled of rancid butter and I was grateful for an empty stomach. "They've kidnapped my niece," he whispered. "I want you to find her before they kill her."

"If the F.C. took her she's probably already dead."

"Normally, I would expect the same. But they know her connections. They'll want this to be a very public execution."

It seemed unlikely, but plausible. And I was desperate enough to accept any offer of new life. "I'd love to help," I said. "But, to be honest, I've run out of resources."

"You'll be paid well enough."

"At the moment I don't even have a means of transport from one moon to another."

"That will be taken care of."

Interesting. I decided to up the ante. "If I'm going into F.C. territory I'll need a cruiser. Something faster than my moon-hopper skiff."

"Make a list of everything you'll need and a suitable transport will be fueled and waiting for you at docking bay twelve."

Just how far was he willing to go?

"I'll need a crew. And they'll want to be paid."

"How many?"

"Seven, maybe eight. And they won't come cheap."

"You can have three."

Found his limit.

"I'll have advances waiting at the transport at seven P.M. local. That's your departure time. Five thousand credits each, up front, with another twenty when my niece is safe in my home."

Titan Prime seemed like a dumb name for a city. But, it was the de facto Capital of the system and its seven hundred permanent inhabitants were just enough to support two establishments licensed to serve liquor. To fill out my crew, I'd have to visit both.

I wasn't three shops down from the T.P. Tavern when I heard Bradan Riley's Irish brogue. His sharp tenor voice radiated boredom—a sure sign he was spoiling for a fight. I quickened my pace up to the open door of the pub. His puffed out chest stood even with the stomach of a well-built bouncer in a hideous sport-coat. "Riley," I called.

Regular blue-collar folks, scam artists, and white-collar thugs occupied their respective corners and somehow managed to coexist, except when Bradan Riley was in town. Whatever insult he was about to throw in the man's face, he held his tongue and glared at me like I just got it on with his sister. "Shep? Ye'd be wise to stay out o' this, me friend."

"Probably. But I got a paying gig for us and it's got a deadline of right now."

"Aye? And how much ye be payin'?"

"You really want to discuss that here?"

Riley looked at me, glanced up at the square jaw in the blue paisley jacket, downed a full tumbler and said to the bouncer, "Don't move." Outside the bar he squared off against me and said, "Give it to me straight."

"Five K up front, another twenty when we bring back the cargo."

A big leprechaun smile brightened his face and he patted me on the back. "Ye've got me attention, Shepard me boy. Give me the rest."

I gave him the details of the job then asked if he knew where I could find Wolf.

"Just left him half an hour past at the dim sum palace."

"He eats that stuff?"

"Yeah."

"Knows where it's coming from?"

"He figures everything's in too small o' portions to do much harm."

"Get him out of there and bring him along."

Borislav Hristov was Bulgarian. When he and Riley first met, the Irishman laughed at Hristov's name and took the beating of his life for it. Riley gave him the name *Wolf*, because of his hairy arms, and the two have been fast friends ever since.

Riley's my pilot. I can handle small ships with electrostatic drive, but for this job, I want power and payload capacity. That calls for a ship with solid fuel propellant and I want his talent at the controls. Wolf's a brilliant engineer and a hell of a fighter. Tactics and logistics is my domain. Room for one more on my crew of three and I knew who I wanted, but did I dare?

Stepping back into the bar I saw blue paisley standing where Riley left him, so I sent a placating nod in his direction and bellied up to the bar. Two Manhattans later, I was ready for the short walk to the opposite end of the mall.

The Shimmering Rings Nightclub sat at the edge of town. Its eastern wall was designed to give the illusion of being a window into space. A place to dine with the spectacle of Saturn's rings as your backdrop. Trouble is, the perpetual orange haze of Titan's atmosphere is all anyone would ever see from the moon's surface. So, one Kendall Brant spent a few fortunes creating an elaborate projection screen along the convex frame of a window. A camera in geosynchronous orbit provided a live feed of the local gas giant and voila! Mood.

Despite all Brant's efforts, Juri Katayama was still the most attractive sight inside. I say that because, if I dared think something different she would somehow know it and I would pay. As it was, there would be a fair amount of uncomfortable begging with penance before I could offer her a job.

Her table for two rested against the south wall. A shame she had no one to share it with. Squeezing through the aisles of tightly spaced tables, I managed to reach the center of the room just as Brant sat down in the chair opposite Juri. They smiled at each other, then turned to watch my somewhat awkward approach.

"I thought you might be here," Brant greeted.

"Hello, Brad," Juri greeted.

"Been too long, my dear," I replied and kissed her lightly on the cheek. Turning to Brant I raised a quizical eyebrow. "You anticipated I would have a proposition for Miss Katayama?"

Juri's brow furrowed a bit at the word *proposition.*

"She's the only person on Titan that knows nine of the eleven Fundamentalist Coalition languages. And I know that the two of you have worked together in the past."

"Is she interested?"

Juri leaned her wispy frame into Brant's personal space, forcing me to look at *her.* "Perhaps you should address me, Bradley."

Yeah. Messed that one up.

"You're right, and I apologize. Has Mr. Brant explained the assignment and compensation?"

Juri sat back and sipped her tea casually. Her bad habit was my pet peeve. Waiting an insufferable length of time before answering, she said, "I've already been employed and compensated to serve as your second in command."

My second? Why did it feel like I was last?

I wondered how her advance might compare to the rest of us, but didn't ask.

Brant interrupted the nonverbal exchange between Juri and me. "By now you've recruited Mr. Hristov and your Irish friend. Since I've employed Miss Katayama directly, you still have backing for one additional crew member. Might I recommend someone?"

Whoever he had in mind, if Brant wanted him on the team, I wanted nothing to do with him. Or her. "Since Juri has agreed to join us I have all the team I need. I'll leave you to finish your meal."

"I'll be at the launch bay half an hour before liftoff, Bradley," Juri said.

I nodded and walked away.

The F.C. radicals aren't nearly the threat most people think. Five years after the Arwen Colles settlement on Titan was established, the Rings of Saturn News declared terrorist strongholds on four moons. A year later, the number was fifteen. Truth is, the F.C. occasionally uses small moons as launch points for propaganda campaigns or decoys. They don't have the resources to establish permanent bases everywhere they land. We'll pay a visit to their principal base of operation, but I'm sure we won't find any living prisoners. And we don't want to be their next victims, since Brant certainly won't pay a penny to rescue any of this crew.

Twenty minutes before departure, we were gathered at the port and sizing up our vessel when Brant arrived. "It's the Elan Three," he said, clearly proud of the ship he'd procured for us. He made a grand show of delivering five thousand credits each to the three of us.

"What about her?" Riley asked, nodding his head toward Juri.

"She's already been compensated."

"Really?"

Riley's eyes widened with interest and inference, but neither Juri nor their employer gave any response.

Any dalliance between them must have been worth the payment. Brant soon departed and the four of us finished loading our gear. Half an hour later, we looked back on Titan growing smaller behind us. Newcomers to the system rave about Saturn's spectacle and beauty. After years of travel between its seventy odd moons, locals grew jaded to the ever-shifting colors and rings.

Days of tedium lay ahead so the crew of four settled into long hours of playing cards. Five Hundred graduated to Pinochle and on to Bridge. Canasta lasted nearly a day before frayed tempers sent us all off to Solitaire.

Only the short communication linkup to Titan every eight hours broke a silence that lingered for two more days. I slid the king of hearts to an empty row and listened to Juri's scheduled broadcast without looking up.

"Elan Three to Titan Prime, mission log, seven days, sixteen hours. All remains on schedule and on target. In precisely three minutes, we will enter a communications blackout as Hyperion passes between us. We will send a confirmation ping as line-of-sight is reestablished five hours, twelve minutes from now. Standard reports will proceed as scheduled."

In a tension-filled week, I'd all but forgotten the details of our flight path, until Juri's transmission. Raising an eyebrow, I took a moment to anticipate our landing time, as the blackout meant we were getting close.

Three minutes later, her voice came across the intercom again. "All crew to the bridge. We've got a lot of work and only five hours to finish."

As the two other men congregated to see what was happening, Juri reached into a shoulder bag and tossed sophisticated detection devices to each of us. Brant had bugged the whole ship before we left and now was listening to much more than Juri's eight-hour reports. Somehow, she had found out and came prepared.

"Scan your quarters first, work stations second," she said, with a mutinous tone of command. "Take your time. Be thorough."

She sent Riley and Wolf on ahead. "Brad, before you say anything, I'm sorry for standing you up on T-Three. Your contact was setting you up for the First Bank swindle and the only way I could think to save your life was through Brant."

Black ops training prepared me for the shock of sudden twists and unexpected turns. With all the psychological tools at my command, I made my best effort at controlling the moment, and all I could think to say was, "Huh?"

"Brant wants you dead."

It wasn't a big surprise, but still, "Why didn't he just let my execution go on as planned?"

"You'd been arrested and convicted. We hadn't been charged with any crime."

"So he wants you dead, too?"

Juri nodded. "And Riley. And Wolf. I was spying on him for the banking cartel. I wasn't sure if he'd caught on until he pulled you out of that execution. You were his opportunity to bring us together. By sending us off on a phony rescue to the F.C., he expects them to deal with us."

I thought about that for a moment and it didn't quite add up. "Brant's not someone to take a chance on terrorists doing his job for him. Too many things could go wrong, and that means he's got an insurance card to play."

"You mean like telling the F.C. we're coming?"

That didn't add up either. He wouldn't know how to contact them, and they wouldn't believe him if he did.

"Captain," Wolf's voice echoed through the com system. "Trouble. My detector went off the instant I stepped into engineering. This thing picked up explosives. I've pulled the interior panels off three walls. We're laced with enough PE-4 to pulverize a square mile."

"There's his insurance," I said.

"Is there a timer?" Juri asked.

"Haven't found one, but I'll keep looking," Wolf answered.

"Riley. Have you found anything?"

"Dug five bugs out o' me quarters. I'm headed down to the engine bay now. I'll let ya know."

I looked at the detector in my hand. "To hell with my quarters, I'll take the payload. You cover the bridge."

An hour and twenty-six minutes later we convened on the bridge and assessed our findings.

"We're still in radio blackout," Juri said. "So Brant doesn't know yet that we've found the explosives."

"But he'll know the minute line-of-sight is restored," I added. "Anyone find a timer?" Three grim-faced heads shook side to side. "That means he plans to detonate remotely."

Juri looked at Wolf and asked, "Why would Brant want you dead?"

"Probably 'cause I overheard something I wasn't supposed to. It was closing time at the Beefy Grille and he thought he was the only one left in the place. Only thing I heard was a date. I wouldn't have thought any more about it except for the expression on his face when he saw me."

"What was the date you heard," I asked.

"Earth date three, fourteen, fifteen."

Some quick calculations on the computer told us that was just two weeks standard from now, but what did it mean?

"Why so much firepower?" asked Wolf. "One stick of TNT would finish us out here."

"I've been thinking about that. We're headed for the F.C. stronghold on Iapetus. You said there was enough on board to take out a square mile. Brant's been hit hard by F.C. raids. My guess is he wants to hit them, frame us, and kill us all with one push of a button."

Riley let out a loud snort. "So how come ye ain't askin' why the bastard wants me dead?"

"All right, Riley," I said. "Tell us. Why does the bastard want you dead?"

"Probably has to do with a wee altercation I had with one of his henchmen." He gestured holding his thumb and forefinger half an inch apart.

"Yeah," Wolf added. "He busted up one of Brant's top runners a couple weeks back."

"I doubt that's much of a reason to kill you," Juri said. "Brant couldn't care less about his people. He's had several killed for little or no reason. With the Titan legal system and police force in his pocket, nobody's going to press charges."

"Did this runner say anything to you while you were fighting?" I asked.

"Hmm. Well, now you mention it, he said something about a girl. Said he planned to meet her."

"Did he mention a name? Say where?"

"Oh, yeah," Riley chuckled. "He was beggin' me ta lay off. Said he had to leave for Enceladus. So, after a little Irish persuasion, he said 'twas ta meet a girl name of Dahl. Name meant nothin' to me, so I hit him once more and he took a nap."

Riley may not have known the name, but I did. "Reena Dahl is an underground operative for the Earth

Feds. They're trying to establish a stable coalition in the Saturn system."

"What would Brant want with her?" asked Wolf.

Juri answered, "Brant's a maverick. He claims to have U.N. authority over land distribution throughout the system—an unending supply of real-estate that builds wealth faster than North American taxes."

"His so-called charter is certainly fraudulent," I added. "But nobody's been able to dispute it. I'm guessing Reena has the proof she needs to end his business and nullify trillions of credits in existing transactions."

"'Tis all very interesting," said Riley. "But we're on a timetable to detonation. Have ye any thoughts as to how we might survive all this?"

"We have a couple hours left in the blackout. How much time is there between the instant we're back in communication range and our landing on Iapetus?"

Juri pulled up our flight plan. "Thirty seven minutes."

"If we altered our trajectory, could we take advantage of Hyperion's orbital pass to keep us in the dark 'till we reached our target?"

Tense moments flew by as she typed in different sets of coordinates before turning back to give us the news. "We can get close, but the best scenario leaves a nine minute window for Brant to blow us out of the sky."

Tactics is my domain. Had I really claimed that role? Three expectant faces staring at me screamed, *Yes. Now get us out of this mess.*

"Okay, let's assume—based on the quantity of explosives on board—that along with killing us, he wants to inflict some pain on the F.C. That means he doesn't intend to hit the button until we're in range of their base. How is he going to determine the right moment? Wolf? You're the engineer here."

"Simple enough. He's got every room bugged, so he'll hear our conversations whether transmitted or not. There'll be a quick delay, but it won't make any difference relative to the four of us. As long as the F.C.

target is confirmed in range, we'll be incinerated along with it."

"How does that change, if we eliminate all of his bugs?"

"Well, first he'd have to have precise coordinates of the F.C. base."

"I'm sure he has those," I said.

"Then he'd have to calculate Elan Three's position based on our communication pings. When the coordinates line up—*BOOM!* A three-second delay would make it a little trickier, but if he's got top of the line tracking gear...?"

We all knew the answer to that. "Is there any way to delay or distort our pings to give him a false reading?"

"Maybe." Wolf was trying to be optimistic but the expression on his face didn't show much hope. "Depends on what kind of tools and equipment we have on board."

"Okay," I nodded. "Get back to engineering and see what you've got. Also, make another sweep with your detector. Everyone and every room. We have to be sure we found them all."

"Do I alter trajectory?" asked Riley.

"Just slightly. I'll have Juri calculate thrust duration."

Juri raised an eyebrow. "What are you thinking?"

"If Brant suspects we're on to him," I said. "He'll skip the F.C. and push the button. Ripping out all the bugs he's planted is going to give us away unless we can provide another explanation."

"Like a collision in space during the blackout?" asked Wolf.

"Exactly."

Juri squinted. "So. we're going to have to communicate to him that we've lost the ability to communicate?"

"You can send a laser ping without using an RF frequency?"

"Of course." She nodded.

"How's your Morse code?"

"Laser pings will give Brant a very precise reading on our location," Wolf interjected.

"That's why I'm counting on you to distort our signal."

When no one said anything more. I sent everyone off to sweep for transmitters. Seven minutes before we emerged from the blackout, we gathered in the payload section. Its portal would be the quickest exit from the craft. Wolf had routed communications and flight control to remote stations near the airlock.

"Everyone's enviro-suit sealed?" I asked. They all nodded.

"We're coming out of blackout three minutes behind schedule," Riley said. Moments later, he nodded to Juri and she began typing a series of long and short bursts on the laser beacon. Her message read, "Elan Three to Titan Prime. Mission log: eight days, zero hours. Meteor strike in blackout. Minor damage to main booster. Effected repairs. Navigational software not responding and is top priority. Updates to follow."

Seconds passed, as we held our metaphorical breath and waited.

An audio message broke the silence. "Transmission received, Elan Three. We will monitor. If you are receiving this, apprise us the moment navigation is restored. Until then, set an auto ping from your laser at five minute intervals."

Juri and I sat back in our chairs and gazed into each other's eyes. Nothing romantic, mind you. Just two friends, and shipmates, wondering if we would live to explore the romantic thing.

Two minutes passed, then three. "We still be here," Riley said.

Wolf replied, "That's no guarantee he can't still hear us."

"True," I added. "All we can do now is wait."

If I thought the tension was high for the first week, the next hour was like paddling a kayak in the eye of a hurricane. As the minutes ticked by and no disaster struck, everyone began to breathe a little easier.

"Think I should send an update?" Juri asked.

"I don't think so," I answered. "Right now, they're wondering what's really going on up here. Anything we tell them now is going to raise a different set of questions."

I lay back in the fabric sling we called a chair and tried the impossible. Who can sleep when any moment might be your last? Apparently folks trained in espionage can. Riley's shrill voice woke me. "Shep. We're ten minutes from the southern edge of the ridge."

The four of us huddled around a view screen and watched as Iapetus' rugged equatorial ridge rose up to meet us. The approach concealed us from the terrorists' camp, but instead of the flight plan we gave Brant, we set down two miles from their hab-domes.

"Let's get out of this firecracker," I said, and we all strapped on helmets.

I hate enviro-suits. Even more than that, I hate long-distance runs anyplace with a hostile atmosphere. Okay, I'm just not fond of running, but we had to put distance between us and the titanium death trap we'd arrived in.

Three quarters of a mile later, Wolf's voice came through the helmet intercom. "Need a breather."

We all did. Looking back we could barely make out the shape of our abandoned transport and decided we were probably far enough removed to survive, if it blew. Even so, after a brief respite we maintained a brisk walk down the uneven terrain of Iapetus' ridge, until we caught sight of the F.C. spaceport. Sixteen ships were spread across acres of prime Iapetus real estate.

"Captain," Riley said. "I'm thinking this be Kendall Brant's target."

"I would have to agree, my friend." The explosive potential laced in Elan Three would be just about right to take out this entire fleet.

"Brad," Juri said. "We've survived Brant's trap, but none of us have an in with the F.C."

"I know. We should shut off our helmet transmitters before we're found. Riley, that first ship. Can you fly her?"

"Aye. If she's got fuel."

In stealth mode we made a beeline for the ship's airlock and did a quick recon for any lingering guards or crewmembers. Our luck was holding. We were on a scout ship, fully stocked with provisions for a crew of ten. It could be quick for short bursts, but relied on a slower, ion propulsion drive for longer hauls.

Once the airlocks closed and life support was established we stripped off our enviro-suits. "I have only one question." I looked straight at Riley. "Can four of us fly this thing?"

"Aye," he said. "But we're all goin' ta be mighty busy for the next three or four hours."

"All right, Riley, you're in temporary command. Give us our assignments and let's get off this rock."

"Back to Titan?" he asked.

"We go there and we're as good as dead," Wolf said.

"Got to lay in a course for somewhere."

"Rhea," Juri answered. "Dark side."

"Rhea it'll be," Riley said. He barked out instructions to each of us like a born commander and within forty minutes we were putting some distance between us and Iapetus.

"Captain," Juri shouted.

"Here," Riley and I answered simultaneously.

"We've got trouble."

"What kind?"

"Looks like the F.C. wants their ship back. They've launched three pursuit vessels."

"Riley, can we outrun 'em?"

"If they sent their little stingers, I can put some distance between us for about forty-five minutes. After that they'll start gaining on us. Won't be enough to get us to Rhea."

"Change course for Hyperion. It's closer."

"Still won't be enough, Shep."

"Understood. Make the course change and give us all the power you've got. Wolf, meet me at the bridge."

Moving up the alley toward the bridge I was jostled by the shift in direction and speed and Wolf was already waiting when I arrived. "Riley, the guy you beat up—the one who told you about Reena Dahl—who was he?"

"That woulda been the yank, Tom Collard. Brant's chief runner."

"Any idea what happened to him after that?" I asked.

"Nae. Ha' na seen him since."

"When did it happen?"

Generally speaking, Riley walks in a permanent haze brought on by excessive tippling. Even so, he's reliable as an ocean tide when it comes to details of his exploits. It's just dates and times that seem to escape him. "Would ha' been sometime last month I think."

"Wolf?"

"It was two nights after you pulled that bank job. Night before your trial. And I haven't seen him since."

"Even money says he's dead."

"Why's it matter?" asked Riley.

"Because other than Tom Collard, we're the only ones who know the time and place Brant plans to dispose of Reena Dahl."

Flipping the intercom switch I asked, "Juri, you been listening to all of this?"

"Of course. Three men having a confab. What woman could resist?"

"Do you happen to know the frequency for the police outpost stationed there?"

"I do."

"And can you punch in some trajectories to the computer for me? I'd like to know if they could intercept us before our F.C. pursuit catches up."

"Already done and yes, they could provide a safe escort for us. If they chose to."

"Just so I understand this," Riley said. "With our less than stellar employment history we're going to radio the Saturn police force and ask for help?"

"That's the size of it," I nodded. "Juri, dial up that frequency." I sat down beside her and stared at the microphone searching for words. "This is Jon Shepard, calling the Saturn Police of Hyperion. I have important information for you. Please respond."

After a minute passed, "Sergeant Jacobs here. What's the nature of your information, Mr. Shepard."

"Actually, along with the information I've got a request to make."

Another minute passed. "This wouldn't happen to be Jonathon B. as in Bradley Shepard."

Damn.

"Yes, officer, that would be me."

"And just what would a man with your reputation want from law enforcement?"

"We're in a ship heading from Iapetus to Hyperion, pursued by three F.C. stingers. I was hoping you might arrange an escort for us."

"When you say, 'we,' who all is aboard your vessel?"

Three grim faces vigorously shook their heads. Surrounded by glares and threatening gestures, I nonetheless gave the names of my crew. Presumably the short silence that followed was the time it took to scan their names on the nets.

"All right, Mr. Shepard. Your request has been logged. Considering the collected number of charges that might be levelled against you and your associates, can you offer a compelling reason for the Hyperion Police to foot the rather hefty bill for a rescue effort, merely to arrest you and incur further costs for trial and probable execution?"

"As I said, we have some information you'll want."

"I'll need more than that," the sergeant insisted.

"There's going to be an attempt on the life of an Earth Federation operative."

"There are several attempts a year on law enforcement officers from all branches."

"We know when and where," I said. In the silence that followed I noted a growing anxiety in the cabin. The longer negotiations took the less likely they could reach us in time to turn back the F.C. ships.

"All right, Shepard. Give us the when and where and we'll send you an escort."

"Come on, Sergeant. If I give you all the information now, you have even less reason to come save us."

"You're going to have to give us something. Otherwise, why should we take your word?"

"Then take this name to your captain. Reena Dahl."

A noticeably irate voice said, "Fine. I'll get back to you."

Two minutes later another voice came through. "This is Captain Ermine. Send us your coordinates, Mr. Shepard. We're launching five patrol ships now."

"Well, Brad," said Juri, "You may have saved our necks. For now. Think you can buy our freedom with a date and place? I mean, Enceladus has eleven settlements after all. The only thing we've got is the name of the moon and a day. Leaves a lot of territory."

"We have a little more than that. What was that date again?"

"Three, fourteen, fifteen," Wolf said.

"Three, one four, one five. Titan natives don't include years with earth-reckoning date and time. Only the month and day. Even if the one five referred to a date, twenty-one fifteen was two years ago."

"So what does it mean?" asked Juri.

"'One' is the hour. 'Five' refers to the fifth settlement."

By the time the escort reached us, the F.C. was barely an hour behind. They promptly reversed course and things grew quiet aboard our hijacked craft. No one was quite sure how things would play out at a police outpost, but we knew we were lucky just to be alive.

As we disembarked, we were met by the surly sergeant I'd bantered with initially. "Bradan Riley, Borislav Hristov, aka Wolf, and Juri Katayama, you are granted landing passes and temporary liberty. Jonathan Shepard, you will follow me."

Escorted to a rather sterile board room, I was met by the local captain and two officials I couldn't identify. The captain stepped forward. "Mr. Shepard, meet Reena Dahl."

"Miss Dahl," I said, bowing slightly.

"I understand you have some information for me."

I hadn't anticipated this turn of events and decided to try something I wasn't particularly skilled at. Candor. "Your presence makes this a little awkward. I had intended to trade information for some favors. To be honest, I don't know if I can trade on a person's life when she's standing in front of me."

"And what sort of things were you going to ask for?" Reena said.

"Freedom for myself. Pardons for my crew," I answered with a dismissive air. "That sort of thing."

"Tell us what you know, Shepard," the captain said.

"I believe you have a meeting with someone planned on Earth date May fourteenth at one o'clock. It's going to take place on the fifth settlement on Enceladus."

"You are well informed," Reena said. "How do you know this?"

"Kendall Brant knows. Each of my crew learned a piece of his plan, so he pulled us together intending to kill us all. Once we compared notes we deciphered the whole picture. Brant is planning your assassination."

With that I was led out into a waiting room and an hour later the captain came to me with a stack of papers.

"These will exonerate you and your crew from past, questionable activities. The ship you arrived in has been impounded, but you may pick up any personal belongings at the impound desk. I would appreciate it if all of you would arrange public transport off Hyperion as soon as possible."

"Thanks, cap," Riley said. He snatched his pardon, folded it and crammed it in a pocket. "First ship off this rock leaves in an hour. Next one's the day after tomorrow. Think I'll try out that copper's pub down the block."

Wolf took his paper and breathed a deep sigh. "Guess I should look after him."

I nodded and watched the big Bulgarian run after his friend.

"Looks like it's you and me, Bradley," Juri said with a smile.

For the first time since this all started, I took in the scent of her perfumed hair and studied her dark green eyes. "What would you say to a simple relaxing vacation?"

"With you?"

I nodded with trepidation, fearing a cutting rejection.

"I'd like that," she said to my total shock. "Where should we go?"

"How about Enceladus?"

Her mouth widened in a wicked sort of grin. "Settlement five?"

Timothy Paul lives in Washington State with his wife and family. A former professor of Theatre Arts, he has worked as a freelance and professional writer, director and educator. With six short stories currently in print, he is working on a sequel to his first novel and developing a YA science fantasy series. Other published works include profile pieces for a regional magazine, theatre reviews, book reviews, and articles for newsletters. Samples of his work and links to his books are available at www.timothypaulbooks.com.

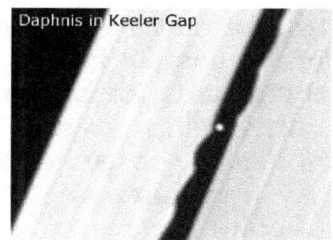

Daphnis in Keeler Gap

7. PROFIT MARGIN

By

Duane Brewster

"The Egg is gone!"

Everyone in the research station stopped working to look at the comm-monitors in the corner of every room and compartment. Straining to find the object that had filled the screens for over a year, the scientists felt a sinking sensation, where once there had been elation and excitement.

The chief scientist barked orders at every pilot, engineer, and station manager to find the artifact, or explain what they had been doing when it disappeared. All hands were on deck, using every instrument on board to search for the object everyone called the Egg.

"Anything?"

"No sir. Nothing yet."

"Keep looking. We lose that...we lose everything."

They all knew what that meant. Not just irreplaceable scientific knowledge, but their cushy and excessively high paying jobs would be gone—plus the penalties for losing the artifact.

"That thing has been orbiting Saturn for well over four and a half billion years, so I'm pretty sure it didn't vanish on its own," Dr. Jacobs growled. "I want a full-spectrum analysis of that space...right now. Check all of the vid-feeds for the past 24 hours. Compare the particle field with recent records for any physical disturbances and possible tunnel trails. I want answers, people!"

Leaving the small observation office, Dr. Jacobs pulled his lanky frame into the narrow corridor tube, which wound around the research section, and headed for the galley. Dr. Alvarez was the expert on "slingshot physics" and he needed her expertise to see if someone was capable of stealing the Egg without leaving a trace. She was last seen there during the meal break, and he was sure she hadn't had time to leave yet.

The gravitational fields surrounding the station were kept in a very precarious balance, with just enough force to allow for pulling oneself through the corridors, but not enough to swim the same way you could in zero gravity. Letting go of a rail or handhold would make you drop to the nearest bulkhead. The super-gravity of Saturn, with the opposing gravitational fields of fifty-three-plus various-sized moons and the planar gravity field of the rings made navigating within the planetary influence very tricky and extremely hazardous. The first satellite probes, and later ships, discovered early on that you couldn't just power thru an orbit around Saturn without being torn to pieces by all of the opposing gravitational forces, especially if you were inside the orbit of Enceladus.

It had taken almost a year of controlled drifts to position the research station in a stable orbit above Mimas. That was as close as they could get, with a research station that was roughly the size of thirty railroad boxcars strapped together in what resembled a handful of tied-up cigars. To get closer to Saturn's outer rings required the use of an *Alvin*, so nicknamed because of their resemblance to the deep-sea submersibles used on Earth. They were almost exactly the same vehicle in design and construction, with a few materials modifications to make them usable in the vacuum of space.

Reaching the galley, Dr. Jacobs found Dr. Alvarez sitting in the corner under the comm-monitor. She had been searching the images on her Pad for the tunnel trails that Dr. Jacobs asked for. Looking up, she said, "Whoever took the Egg either had a lot of balls, was very lucky, or knew exactly what they were doing. I'm going to go with very lucky."

"You're sure it was taken?"

"Oh yeah, it was taken," she said. "I found the tunnel."

"Can it be traced?"

"Maybe. Depends on what he did after he got out of the ring field."

They both knew at this point that whoever took the Egg had to be a miner. They were the only other people in the Saturn system, besides the government people and scientists, and they were almost all male. The miners in the Saturn system all had a skill in common. They were extremely good at playing pool. The ability to bounce a ball off another, or create spin on a ball that would allow it to curve around another ball, was highly sought after, especially for plotting free-fall trajectories for the highly modified Alvins they used when illegally mining material from the outer rings of Saturn. Rockets couldn't be used within the orbit of Enceladus because the exhaust blast set up a chain reaction of opposing gravitational forces, knocking the vessel into an uncontrollable spin that usually meant it ended up being pulled into Saturn's gaseous atmosphere and lost forever. Miners soon figured out that if they plotted a gravitational slingshot approach toward their target—usually a small boulder-sized lump of high-grade ore or mineral—they could swing around Saturn, or even one of the inner moons, and grab their target on the way out. They pulled the ore and their small craft away from Saturn's gravity without using up precious fuel or causing ripples in the surrounding gravity fields. This caused a *tunnel trail*, easily seen when before-and-after pics of the area were compared.

"Shit! If any sonovabitch tampers with that thing..."

"We need to find it before that happens," Dr. Alvarez said.

"It was perfectly insulated where it was. It may be too late to put it safely back."

"You need to broadcast a system-wide alert for its immediate return, safe and unaltered. Otherwise, we need to evacuate everyone now," Dr. Alvarez said with growing alarm.

"We can't do that before we've tried to find it."

"If that thing is what you think it is, and it gets tampered with, half this system will be dust before you find it. You sure you want to take that chance?" she said, looking at him as if he'd lost his mind.

"I might know where they've taken it. I'll get a few people and we'll go look. Meanwhile, I'll take your advice and evacuate this station. Notify everyone to pack their bags, back-up their research, and take the shuttles back to Corporate."

Corporate owned the massive inter-planetary spaceships that brought people and supplies from Earth and Mars to the various research outposts in the Saturn System.

"That sounds awfully dangerous, Doctor. Shouldn't you send someone else?"

"I'll take the chance. I'm taking two guys from Security and that archaeo-geologist Dr. Angus with me."

"Where are you going?"

"There's a mining base on Titan that acts as an assay office for all of the freelance miners around here. I think that's where it's headed and if we're lucky, I'll find it there...hopefully, before anyone messes with it."

"And what if no one admits they have it...or they've already started to fiddle with it?"

"Then I suggest you hurry up and get the hell out of here," Dr. Jacobs said, grimly.

The Egg, originally discovered in a trailing orbit behind the shepherd moon Daphnis, within the Keeler Gap of Saturn's outer rings, and hidden in the shadow of Daphnis. Thought to be a chunk of ice that, billions of years before, separated from, or captured by, the small moonlet's original erosion, it plowed through the ring section debris, creating the Keeler Gap. After years of observation, someone noticed that the gravity ripple effect on the ring, near where Daphnis travelled through the rings, was caused by a strange reflection of the moonlet's gravity—flowing around the Egg, much like wind flowing around a motorcycle windshield. If the Egg had been solid ice, as originally thought, that wouldn't have happened. The gravity wave would have been unaffected—instead of deflecting around the object. A satellite probe sent closer to the Egg, very soon discovered that the large egg-shaped chunk of ice harbored an ancient artifact that was at least four and a half billion years old. Sensors showed its egg-shape, so the ice surrounding it was acting as a thick form-fitting insulation, protecting it from larger particles and much of the surrounding radiation. Electron-scanners revealed an inner object—clearly manufactured. It was not a natural object, but instead, made from a type of metal only recently identified on Jupiter's moon, Ganymede. Its age took scientists completely by surprise. This artificial artifact would rewrite history books, and change many minds about life in the universe, not to mention long held beliefs about life within this solar system.

The Corporation decided this object needed closer study and built a special research station near Titan, as close as possible above the rings without disturbing surrounding gravity fields. Close-up work still required an Alvin, so two highly specialized and outfitted craft were added as part of the stations equipment.

Dr. Jacobs was using one of those Alvins when he made the discovery that scared the shit out of him.

Lemming headed home to his hut on Hyperion with a load of ore in the belly of his Alvin. He'd set up a slingshot course around Prometheus, in order to push through the outer E ring. He had mined a lot of nickel ore out there, as well as other mineral ore, and usually found it relatively easy to use the gravity of Prometheus to slide through the edge of the ring. This time, however, when he came out of the back of the sling, something went wrong and his Alvin veered off deeper into the rings than he wanted. In fact, he thought he was headed straight for the planet, when he noticed his angle and trajectory were taking him in a curving loop to the Keeler Gap. If he paid attention and steered carefully, he could pass through that with little to no damage to his craft.

That's when he saw the big boulder in the shadow of Daphnis. He actually hadn't expected Daphnis to be near him when he passed through the Gap, but there it was, with its shadow close behind it. Scanning the icy rock, he noticed the readout flashing, indicating that it couldn't identify the material within the ice, just that it was metallic and dense.

Hell, that's good enough for me. No sense wasting an opportunity. He punched in the coordinates, enabling his Alvin to bump the icy boulder with its stubby arms—like a cue stick—transferring enough energy and momentum to the object to push it out of its orbit, and out of the gravitational field that was holding it. He simply followed it into space, beyond the heavy pull of Saturn's gravity, where he could tug it back to his freezer.

All material found in space were kept in storage units that could maintain the cold vacuum of space, in case they turned out to be small chunks of comets that had been captured by the gravity fields of Saturn's rings. Early miners soon found out what happened when one of those pieces of rock and ice warmed up. They exploded with enough force to level a mining camp. So, the rule was, put everything you found in a freezer until it could be identified and processed.

Slowly lowering the large frozen object into the hold of a freezer unit, Lemming held his breath until he was sure it was secure, and that the seal on the unit was complete. He didn't relax until he finally docked his mining Alvin and crawled into his hut, a pressurized cargo container that was his home on Hyperion. There were quite a few freelance miners living on Hyperion. It was the closest they could get to Titan and, due to its deeply cratered surface, an easy place to hide.

Climbing out of his pressure suit, he scratched his white hair and beard, welcoming the chance to stretch his arms and legs. He slid into his hammock, sighing heavily, and thought back over the past few hours. Maybe...just maybe...he had finally found the strike that would get him enough money to go back home and retire on Mars. Earth was too expensive. Besides, he liked Mars. It reminded him of Texas, where he spent his youth riding horses while working as a ranch hand. He enjoyed that more than anything else he had ever done. He was good at cutting cattle from herds, and used that skill later, when he learned how to drive heavy equipment for logging and mining companies. After he left Earth to live in a Martian Colony, he discovered that he was especially good at snagging and dragging rocks out of the Asteroid Belt. The work paid well, at first, and he liked the solitude of working in space. His one marriage had ended badly, when she got tired of waiting for him to come home. He couldn't blame her, but he was still bitter.

When the Belt got mined out, the mining companies moved outward, following explorers and colonists wherever they found rare minerals and ore large enough to pay for the transportation—plus some profit. The rings of Saturn proved especially lucrative for the mining companies, and many miners made more money by going freelance. Being your own boss wasn't bad, but you worked twice as hard and took considerably more chances than you did working full time for the Company. He was getting too old for that kind of thing.

Thinking about the Company made him realize he had to sell that thing in the freezer before someone took it from him. This wasn't over by a long shot.

Calling the Assay Office at the Company's Main Titan base, Lemming waited for the connection to go through.

"Assay," the voice on the comm-unit growled. "Whatta ya got?"

"I've got a 1,000 kilogram rock that doesn't register as any known metal and I'd like it checked out," Lemming told the voice.

"We're always interested in something new," the voice said. "You have it in a freezer?"

"Yeah, I do."

"Good. Bring that in and we'll check it out for you. Don't forget the fee."

Sure. The fee. That was 250 credits that he couldn't afford to lose, if this thing turned out to be useless. Still, he had a feeling it was going to bring him more money than anything else he'd ever collected in his long life.

Later, sliding into his Alvin, Lemming hooked up the freezer containing the object and set course for the Company Mining Camp on Titan.

"They better not give me any shit about this thing," he said aloud.

Dr. Alvarez, supervising the evacuation of the research station, was on the comm with the Executive Officer at Corporate explaining the circumstances that necessitated the evac.

"I don't understand, Dr. Alvarez. You were studying something near Daphnis in the Keeler Gap, someone stole it, and you're evacuating the research station even though there is absolutely nothing wrong with the station. I need more information than that."

"Let me explain it this way, Lieutenant. This is a Level 5, 12th Protocol security event. Dr. Jacobs ordered it and I'm authorized to act for him until he returns from Titan. Do you understand me?"

The XO understood perfectly. Not only were they evacuating the research station, but all Corporation personnel within the immediate Saturn System had to evacuate as well.

"I'll inform the Captain, Ma'am. Everything will be ready by the time you arrive."

"I'm going to Titan to help Dr. Jacobs. Get everyone on board and follow the timetable. If we don't show up by the deadline, leave without us. Is that clear?"

"Yes, ma'am. Clear."

"Good. Stop calling me ma'am. I'm a doctor, not an old maid."

"Roger that, Dr. Alvarez."

Turning from the comm, she almost ran into her chief engineering technician.

"Tong? What are you doing here? We have to evacuate. Why aren't you on a shuttle?"

"You'll need me when Dr. Jacobs finds the Egg, Dr. Alvarez."

"I will?"

"If the ice blanket melts off the artifact, you'll need to recoat it with cryo-foam, and I'm the only person on board who knows how to operate that equipment."

"Can you retro-fit it to DSV-2?"

"I just did," Tong said. "The minute I heard the Egg was missing, I knew we'd need the foam in case we found it. My crew spent the last few hours getting it connected."

"I may give you a bonus for that, providing we make it out of this alive."

"Are we sure the Egg is what Dr. Jacobs thinks it is?"

"Chances are 50-50 he's right. We aren't taking any chances."

"Dr. Jacobs took the smaller cargo shuttle and DSV-1. Do you know where he's going?"

"Same place we're going. The Company Assay Office on Titan."

Lemming made good time getting to the assay office, calling in for a dock assignment as soon as he could see the complex on his nav-screen. The dock-master instructed him to set his freezer down in the isolation area, away from the main yards, in case the unidentified material turned out to be hazardous. The area was rough, covered with rocks and debris from previous hazardous mishaps. There wasn't a clear spot to land, so he set it down on a few big rocks that supported the container about a foot above the hot surface, keeping the freezer from over-heating. He then set his Alvin in a separate dock and climbed through the hatch to the entry chamber outside the Assay Office, waiting for the clerk to unlock the inner hatch.

"Lemming! You old cow-turd! What the hell have you brought this time?

"Not sure, Zeke. My sensors can't identify the material."

"Well, if you'd update the data-base you wouldn't have that problem, now would you?"

"As soon as you buy this from me, I'll do that."

"Okay then, you know the drill. Got the fee?"

Lemming nodded, handing Zeke the pre-paid credit chip they all used for financial transactions. It had the exact amount on it for the fee. It would also hold their agreed on payment.

"Okay. That's good. Let's get the scanner over there and see what you've got."

Zeke could operate all of the yard machinery from his office, allowing the miners to watch him as he inspected the cargos they brought in. Once the scanner was in position, it would reveal whether the material was a sale, or a waste of time.

The scanner passed slowly over the top, sides, and ends of the freezer, stopping twice to recalibrate. The second time it did that, Zeke sat up in his chair and leaned into the monitor.

"That is new. I've never seen it do that before," Zeke wondered aloud.

Lemming was beginning to worry that he wouldn't be able to sell this thing and had wasted his credits. The readouts were showing on the screen, showing iron, steel, and plazfoam, which was the freezer, a few rare trace minerals in the ice that surrounded the object and something new.

The *something new* was flashing on the screen. It took the computer a few minutes more and then it identified the material as Ganymedium. Zeke stood up and looked at Lemming.

"Dude, where'd you find this?"

"I snagged it on a return shot outside the E ring. It was in free space so it's legit."

"I doubt that, but I'm not going to argue with you. That material, Ganymedium, is only found on Ganymede. It's supposed to be harder than anything, anywhere, so you finding it out here is going to set off all kinds of speculators and possibly some alarms."

"Alarms? What are you talking about?"

"See that flag next to the name on the screen? That's a Security warning to report any finds to the Planetary Security Council. Dude, that's trouble."

Lemming was staring at the screen and noticed two flags next to the Ganymedium listing. One was red, one was bright blue.

"What's that blue flag for?"

"I don't know. The Company has its own flags for some stuff. Let me see what that one says."

Selecting the blue flag, Zeke looked at a security screen that popped up. He had to type in a security code to see the information. When the new screen came up, he noticed the screen went into security mode, which meant only his eyes could read it. No one else could see what was on the screen. What he read surprised him and made him wonder what was going on.

"What is it?" Lemming asked, trying to see what was on the screen.

"You won't believe this, but the Company will buy that thing from you, as is, no questions asked, for a million credits."

"A million! ...What if I think its worth more than that?"

"It's that or they turn you into the Security Council. They're calling this a "reward payment" for finding this material and turning it in."

"You're kidding?"

"Dude, I've never seen this before. If I were you, I'd take it. You ever have a million credits in your entire life?"

"Only in my dreams."

"Well...?"

"Well, if that's the only choice I have, I'll take the credits."

"Dude, I have never put that many credits on a chip before. If I were you, I'd grab the first ship back home and retire."

"My thoughts exactly, Zeke. By the way, how much can I get for the freezer?"

"That's part of the sale. You'd better stop while you're ahead."

"Cain't fault me fer tryin', right?"

"Nope. I cain't," Zeke said, "and Lemming..."

"Yeah?"

"Don't mention this to anyone. Got that?"

"That part of the sale agreement?"

"Yep," Zeke said as he handed the agreement papers over.

"Put your thumb on the pad and you're a rich man."

Lemming's fingers shook as he reached over and placed his thumb on the keypad's X. There was a soft beep and Zeke pulled the chip out of the slot. Handing it over to Lemming, he said, "Be careful, you old cow-fart, and good luck."

Trembling, Lemming went back to his Alvin and set off for the nearest port; nothing in his hut needed retrieving. He was going to get on the first transport back to Mars and never look back.

"We're assuming that the Egg hasn't been tampered with," Dr. Angus said, when Dr. Jacobs entered the control cabin of the shuttle.

"When I did the first contact electron-scan of that thing and discovered it was full of a solid liquid, probably frozen, with another, smaller egg dead center of that, you were the one who said it reminded you of the original "Fat Man" atomic bomb. The more we studied that thing, the more we agreed that you were closer to the truth than we expected. We know that thing is probably a bomb, older than anything known to this system. We also know that it's a leftover from whatever terrible conflict it was built to be used for. The magnetic field surrounding it matches readings in the Ring Field surrounding Saturn. That led us to theorize that another one of these eggs did explode, completely obliterating the target. From the debris, we also theorized that it was probably a moon that makes up what is now the rings of Saturn, although, for many years, scientists had felt that the moon was destroyed by a massive asteroid or meteor strike. You even went so far as to say that possibly the same thing turned a planet into the asteroid belt between Mars and Jupiter.

Going over to the counter, Dr. Jacobs took a deep breath and put a "coffee cup" in the microwave. After 30 seconds, the coffee was hot. Taking a sip through the seal he looked at Dr. Angus and waited for his reply.

"Maybe after all this time, it turns out that it's a dud, which may explain why it didn't work in the first place," Dr. Angus said, "so if it has been tampered with, nothing happened."

"We both know that's not true. That thing has been perfectly preserved under its ice blanket for four and a half billion years, or more, and we both determined that whatever that frozen material is inside it, it's still viable. No...so far, it appears no one has messed with it and our only hope is that the ice blanket is still intact."

Dr. Angus moved over to the comm-screen and tapped a code into it, bringing up a map of the Solar System. Tapping two spots on the screen, he highlighted the asteroid belt and the rings of Saturn.

"These two "rubble fields" are what's left of some cataclysmic events that happened at roughly the same time, geologically speaking. There may have been a few thousand years between each event. The same magnetic field reading we got off the Egg is present in both of these places. When we discovered that the outer shell of the Egg was made of Ganymedium, we took a leap and theorized that maybe there had been an ancient civilization on at least one of Jupiter's moons, most likely Ganymede, since that is the only place that has the same material as the Egg. So there may have been a war using these eggs in much the same way the United States used the atomic bombs to end World War II, with the exception being that this Egg can destroy a planet."

"That's what I'm afraid is going to happen again here."

Tapping the screen again, Dr. Angus brought up a satellite map of the Company Assay Office compound. Circling an area some distance from the main docking area he pointed out, "Here's where they make the miner's set down any hazardous or unidentified material."

"Then that's where we're going. Tell the Security guys to get ready. We may have to get heavy-handed."

While Zeke waited for the Company Security Team to arrive and take Lemming's freezer away, he decided to look up any information he could find on Ganymedium.

"Who the hell came up with that name?" he wondered out loud. It was a nickname that a media person had come up with about ten years before. The actual name of the metal was so long and unpronounceable that he decided the nickname was good enough for now.

Archeologists discovered the metal on Ganymede, with the help of a radar mapping satellite, buried several thousand meters beneath the equatorial bulge, a large deposit found nowhere else. It was a completely new element and earned a coveted spot on the Periodic Table. That set off a loud debate over whether it was indeed a new element, or something artificial. Either way, it was on the Table and it was going to stay there. The rarity of the metal, coupled with its incredible density and strength, made even a few grams of it worth a fortune. That made Zeke wonder at the credits the Company gave Lemming for his find. By all accounts, it should have been a thousand times what they offered. The only thing he could think of was that possession of this stuff was illegal if you didn't turn it over to the Planetary Security Council. They claimed ownership for "security reasons" and didn't offer to pay any amount of credits for it. So it made sense for the Company to want this metal and keep what they had for their own purposes. The profit margin on this single transaction was astronomical and made any dangerous consequences more than worth the trouble.

The Company Security Team was approaching the field containing Lemming's freezer. The head security officer's face appeared on Zeke's comm-monitor.

"Assay, you have another ship coming in. Keep it busy until we can get that freezer on board."

Zeke's comm buzzed with a new approach request. Looking at his monitor he could see a small Corporate Research shuttle approaching.

"Shit. Now what?" he muttered under his breath, before switching on his audio.

"Assay. Whatta ya got?" he growled at them.

"This is Dr. Jacobs, Corporate Research. We have a Level 5, 12th Protocol event. Do you understand?"

Holee crap, Zeke thought, *what did Lemming get me into?*

"Um, I didn't know about that. What's it about?" Zeke asked, acting stupid, knowing full well what it was about.

"I'm betting you know," Dr. Jacobs shot back. "You should be out of here already. So I'll be brief and blunt."

Taking a deep breath, the doctor leaned in to his comm and said, "A very dangerous research artifact was stolen 30 hours ago, probably by one of your freelance miners. I believe it was brought here. Tampering with it could result in a cataclysmic explosion. It must be returned immediately."

Zeke swallowed hard. His instructions were clear about the contents of that freezer.

"Um, sorry. Really don't know what yer talkin' about there, Doc."

Before Dr. Jacobs could swear back at him, his chief security officer spoke across the cabin.

"There's a Company Security Team ground tractor moving around that isolation field Dr. Angus pointed out, sir. They're in a pretty big hurry to get to a large freezer container sitting out there."

Checking the comm-monitor, Dr. Jacobs and Dr. Angus watched the tractor rolling with deliberate speed toward a freezer unit that could contain the Egg.

"That's about the right size. The Egg has to be in there. Let's hope the ice is still on it," Dr. Angus said.

"Let's go, gentlemen," said Dr. Jacobs.

"Yes sir," the chief security officer returned as he turned the shuttle towards the field and cranked up the speed.

"We can't let them get that freezer into their tank. Once they do, it's out of our jurisdiction," Dr. Angus said worriedly.

"Yes sir. I'm aiming to slide this shuttle between them and that freezer, but I'm afraid this will get messy."

"You keep them busy. I'll take the Alvin out and try to lift that freezer out of here. Once I get it off the surface, it's ours," Dr. Jacobs said, feeling his mouth go dry.

Tong guided the Alvin down from orbit toward the Company Assay Office as fast as she safely could. Turning around to Dr. Alvarez she said, "I have Dr. Jacobs shuttle on the screen. It looks like they may have found the Egg. It looks like the Company is after it, too."

"Push it harder, Tong. We have to get the Egg coated with enough cryo-foam to keep Titan's atmosphere from melting the ice blanket from it. If that happens, nothing we can do will stop that thing from setting itself off."

Tong boosted the thrust and dropped faster, feeling the super-heated atmosphere scorch around the outer shell. They were heading straight for the field, when they saw Dr. Jacobs' Alvin on their monitors, leaving the research shuttle and looping down toward the freezer. The shuttle continued on its path, coming to a sliding landing that put it between the freezer and the Company Security Team ground tractor.

"Put it right on top of the freezer, Tong," Dr. Alvarez shouted over the roar of the atmosphere rushing around the outside of their Alvin.

Gritting her teeth, the chief engineer watched the field below expand. They were dropping too fast. The Alvin jolted with every burst of the thruster brakes.

The flashes from the bursts caught the attention of the Company's head of security as the ground tractor advanced toward the freezer and its valuable cargo.

"Sir, we have a shuttle-class vehicle moving between us and the freezer! And we've also got another one coming in on top of us. Warn them off."

"Sir, the shuttle has landed directly in front of us!"

"What? Stop before we end up ramming them!" the head security office shouted.

It was too late. The tractor rammed against the side of the Corporate Research Station shuttle, crushing the forward bulkhead and causing the shuttle's air to escape in a blast of fog as it rushed into contact with Titan's nitrogen-heavy atmosphere. Dr. Angus and the security team were suited up and in the airlock when the impact crushed the hull. The impact damaged all of the power circuits and disabled the airlock controls.

"Can we get out?" Dr. Angus asked the security people.

"If the manual release isn't jammed, we should be able to," one of the security officers said through his comm.

The other man had found a small hatch and was slowly turning a mechanism that would open an airlock.

"It's binding, but I think the hatch is opening," he said.

"Where do we go once we're out?" Dr. Angus asked.

"We go out and try to stop or slow that tractor, so Dr. Jacobs can hook up that freezer and lift it out of here. You need to get away and find a safe place. The Assay Office is about half a click back that way. I'd head there."

"I'll give it a try. Good luck," said Dr. Angus as the hatch finally swung open.

Jumping to the surface, the security officers headed toward the front of the grounded shuttle. Dr. Angus started a bouncing trot across the rubble-strewn field toward the Assay Office.

I got a bad feelin' about this, he thought, a chill running up the back of his neck.

Dr. Jacobs maneuvered his Alvin to the opposite side of the freezer, keeping the shuttle between the ground tank and his approach. Seeing that his security team and Dr. Angus had escaped the damaged shuttle, he set to securing the freezer to the Alvin's towing arm. Busy with the other Alvin rapidly descending toward them, the Company Security Team didn't see him.

"Attention, approaching craft. You do not have authorization to enter this field. Stop your approach or you will be fired on," said the Company Head Security officer through the comm.

At that moment, the Corporate Research Security Team started firing on the ground tank, causing the distraction needed for Dr. Jacob to finish connecting the freezer and starting his ascent away from the field. Firing on the tank caused absolutely no damage, but it had the desired effect of turning the tank's attention away from the research Alvin's actions.

The Company ground tank backed up, extricating its forward grapplers from the shuttle's crushed shell. Rolling back, the men in the tank could finally see what Dr. Jacobs had been doing on the other side of the damaged shuttle. They could see the Alvin lifting the freezer, the other Alvin coming down fast to help.

"Grapple that freezer. Don't let it leave this field!" shouted the head security officer.

Tilting the grappler arm up, the operator sent the clamps, attached to a cable, out to intercept the freezer climbing into view. The clamps caught the lower end of the freezer at an angle and squeezed tight, tearing into the sides, releasing the coolant from the inside of the large container.

"You fools!" screamed Dr. Jacobs. "You'll set it off!"

"What are you talking about?" the Company Security Officer yelled back.

"There's no time to explain. Release your grapplers."

"Sorry. We can't do that. That freezer is Company property."

That was when the other Alvin, piloted by Tong, dropped down on top of the tank's grappler cables, effectively pinning the cables and the freezer to the surface.

"What are you doing?" Dr. Jacobs and the Company Security officer said at the same time.

"We are going to fill that freezer with cryo-foam and try to stop the Egg from activating," Dr. Alvarez answered.

"That might give us a little more time," Dr. Jacobs said, wondering at the far-sighted resourcefulness of his colleagues.

"Time for what?" the security officer shouted back.

"That freezer has an ancient artifact inside that has been insulated by a thick coat of ice that protected it and kept it from activating for almost four and a half billion years," Dr. Jacobs said. "You just exposed it to an atmosphere that is melting that ice shield, causing the temperature of the artifact to increase. Once it reaches critical temperature, nothing in this universe will keep it from blowing this moon to dust."

"Wait, what? Are you saying that freezer has a bomb in it?"

"The mother of all bombs."

There was no reply. Only silence, while the grappler still clamped the freezer.

Meanwhile, Dr. Alvarez punched in thru the side of the freezer and inserted a sensor probe and the tube of the cryo-foam pump.

"Okay Tong, get that stuff moving. I'll get readings and send them to Dr. Jacobs," Dr. Alvarez shouted, as she ran the sensor readings through the comm to Dr. Jacobs.

"Dr. Jacobs, readings indicate the temperature inside that freezer has been above the safe range for at least an hour. Most of the ice blanket has vaporized. We're pumping the container full of the cryo-foam and the temperature should be at -200K within a minute."

"I don't think that will be enough, doctor. My readings show an increase in the internal pressure of the Egg. The only thing we can hope for is that the cryo-foam will buy us enough time to get out of here," Dr. Jacobs returned.

"The container is completely filled, doctors. There appear to be two small punctures on the bottom side. Looks like the rocks it was set down on punctured the metal," Tong said from her observation position. She could see where the cryo-foam had oozed out and was turning to fog as it melted with exposure to the open atmosphere.

"I'm setting it down," Dr. Jacobs said into his comm. "Dr. Alvarez, disconnect from the container and try to get back to the Corporate Transport before they lift off."

"They've already left, Doctor. We don't have that option."

"Doesn't matter now. The pressure in the Egg just doubled..."

Dr. Angus was almost to the main door of the Assay Office when he turned around to look at the two Alvins and the ground tank wrestling with the freezer. The Research Security Team had followed him halfway to the Assay Office across the field. They turned around when a bright white light, growing from the freezer, flashed out and enveloped the entire space, exponentially expanding with blinding speed. All Dr. Angus saw was a blinding white space blanking out his entire field of vision.

"Oh. Wow," he said softly, before the destructive blast of the expanding Egg enveloped him.

The Corporate Transport and the myriad other Saturn System transports were roughly three billion kilometers from Saturn when a blinding white light exploded on Titan. Expanding out to envelope the moon, the light contracted and flattened, then expanded into a thin platter of energy that crushed everything in its path to dust and rubble. It cut through the atmosphere of Saturn, dragging gas and the debris of the shattered moon and other smaller moons with it in an ever-widening circle around Saturn, adding new material to the outermost ring, the Phoebe Ring, and creating a newer set of rings tilting at 27° to the axis of the originals. The result, after the initial blast, was another set of rings that gave Saturn the appearance of an atomic graphic with two ellipsoidal ring systems around a circle.

For almost an hour, the people on board the transports watched the destruction in absolute silence, from the initial flash to the resulting ring construct. The only thing they experienced was the remnants of the electromagnetic pulse that momentarily rocked the ships. They couldn't believe that they had narrowly escaped the destruction of Titan and its surrounding space.

One of the passengers was a grizzled old miner with a large white beard. He had watched with the others, stunned at the destruction of Saturn's largest moon. After the first hour, people started glancing around at each other, wondering at what had happened. Lemming just looked at the large comm-monitor and shook his head.

"Damn."

Twenty years later the Company's Head of Accounting was studying the spreadsheet on the table, nodding his head.

"The profit margins coming in from the new fields in the Saturn system are way above projections, gentlemen."

The annual board meeting of the Company was abuzz with the news about the abundance of rare mineral ore and other large porphyritic debris created in the destruction of Titan.

"Our initial expenditure of one million credits to obtain what we thought was a thousand kilograms of Ganymedium had an unexpected benefit for our mining operations in the Saturn System. It turned out it was an ancient artifact that was a bomb capable of destroying planets. In this case, it destroyed Titan. We don't know what set it off, but more than a thousand people were killed in the destruction of Titan. Roughly half a million people were saved because Dr. Jacobs of the Corporate Research Station Daphnis One had the foresight to call for an evacuation of the system when he discovered the artifact was indeed a bomb capable of that kind of destruction."

He didn't bother to mention that he knew, as did most of the Board members, exactly what did set the bomb off. Better not to say anything at all. That was Company policy.

"The destruction of Titan gave us a new and very rich field of mineral resources to mine, saving the Company billions of dollars in extraction resources. Now we just collect the minerals and ore directly from the expanded Phoebe Ring and process it directly. Our profit margins, gentlemen, are in the quad-trillions of credits."

Duane Brewster is a professional jack-of-all-trades graphic communications designer who has lived in Maryland for most of his life, near the largest concentration of greenhouse gases in the United States. He is also a cartoonist currently drawing, for close friends only, a new self-explanatory cartoon strip titled "Grumpy Old Geniuses."
He has always wanted to write science fiction, like his life-long favorite author, Isaac Asimov.
"Profit Margin" is Duane's first published science fiction story.

TITAN

8. A Moon of Saturn

By

Amos Parker

"Diversity is such a terrible thing," said the tall, chiseled Time Traveler to himself.

As he spoke, he watched the light show spangling the River of Time, beyond the walls of his precious and precocious ship, Rubicon. And he pictured, with swelling anticipation, the diverse moons of Saturn materializing to break the current view into shards. He sighed, the self-absorbed exhalation accentuating his pink, silken suit. His golden hair, swept aside like lesser human concerns, glittered under the azure LED light. His penetrating aquamarine eyes—a schoolgirl's fantasy—sucked in the twinkling view.

Like a rock in the outer darkness, his well-engineered craft did not even hum, as it accomplished modern miracles. He felt as if he stood astride it like a god.

Unity, he thought, positing a solution. That's Humanity's goal.

His eyes flashing, he thought about diversity and the lack of it, picturing primeval Cambrian and Jurassic

Earth, red in tooth and claw. Then he slapped the giant red "Undive" button, ejecting his craft from the River of Time, the same way the giant green "Dive" button had injected it. He felt glad to be standing, then—more significant, somehow.

Then the bright rainbow beyond the ship coalesced into light-pinpricked darkness, by far more magnificent.

"Sic!" he cried, looking back at the seated, scoring and scouring eyes. Eyes that waited. Waited for his promised demonstration to begin. They really had no idea what they were in for. He smiled secretly, proclaiming, "Thus was it written!"

Sitting comfortably, his diminutive dozen Compatriots occupied a central position in the massive, one-room command deck. They waited, no sound audible save the percolating of diverse breeds of coffee beans in the sparkling titanium monstrosity protruding from the floor to his right. Yet none eyed it, dependence transferred by awe to "The Star." Novelty is all. And the Time Traveler made a titanic business of all things.

"God I love transparent aluminum!" he cried. He slapped the curved wall, twirling to take in the 360-degree galactic view, before settling his gaze on greenish Titan. Oh, how the giant loomed—hovering over the timeline speck of ancient, majestic Rome—the terror of ancient Roman gods, ready to wreck Olympus!

"Titan! Saturn's largest moon. Large, and in charge." His gaze turned inward, fingers gripping his cleft chin. "Moon-ally speaking."

He stared at Titan, and then, crossing his bare, muscular arms, from behind him he sensed the super titan, ringed Saturn, guarded and suspicious.

"You know," he said, unfurling one arm to point at Titan, "I'm not a man of science. I'm a man of business-y things."

His left foot twitched out and up, then down again, the soft Italian leather cleaving the air; air extracted from Yosemite Global Park, squeezed into massive storage tanks, and vented into Rubicon.

"Un-executive things." The right foot lifted, as his neck lifted his head toward something. "Not artsy. But there is something...oh...I don't know...charming about big moons and their planets. Marital. You know what I'm saying. Right? Like the early dance of humanoid marriage."

He turned on a stiff heel, walking through the seated gaggle, addressing them without looking down. They smelled his perfumed, Midas coiffure, an odor doctored to make even resentful women blush, and awestruck men gag.

By some extraordinary effort, one Compatriot broke the seated, expatriate silence.

"Of course!" cried the young Journalist from the center of the crowd, tapping silent notes into his tablet. "Titan's big as a prime member! And Enceladus is icy as my ex!" His white hair, parted down the center, exposing white scalp, made the wide-eyed face seem Tralfamadorish. Unstuck in time.

"Saturn's a polygamist! Man with a harem!" He rose and fell to his knees. "Is there a Bacchus moon too? Wine's the true fuel of love, eh? I feel like being a regular writer and spouting chaotic poetry that everyone will ignore!"

Then, as if embarrassed, he rose, flushing rose, and seating himself again. His proud, black eyes sparkled.

Most Compatriots burst out laughing, catching the fresh jokes that flew new to everyone. Even the massive, missive Time Traveler strode forward, slapping the boy's back. It knocked the youth from his seat—out into a higher social tier—as his tablet clattered away. He whimpered, flowing like white wine around the ankles of three women.

"Hilarious!" the Time Traveler cried, pearl teeth sparkling. "Excellent! Magnificent! Astute! Sharp! Effervescent! Come on my next speaking tour. I'll get you a grant! Nothing like the diversity of conquest to brighten Mankind's singular soul." His eyes widened, glowing. "Say. That has a nice ring to it. I should write that down. 'Conquest makes diversity good.'"

145

The Journalist recovered his tablet and sat again. Then he wrote more, composing on the twin fuels of a famished soul and fame-ish recognition.

A potent throat clearing rose from the right, gathering eyes.

"But isn't diversity what life is all about?" asked the Ecologist, a handsome, stern, government-mandated female who'd rebuffed the Time Traveler. Publicly. The way she'd rebuff a zoo's horny ape.

'No!" he snapped, turning his back on her, his face flushing as pink as his clothes.

She paled, seemingly imprisoned by his power.

"Yes it is!" she managed to gasp. "The laws of Evolution say so! Don't look at me that way! They do! This mission is scientifically ridiculous, and..."

"I said I'm not a man of science," answered the Time Traveler, cutting her off as he spun back, his voice soft enough to restore the present public's perception of him. Titan and Saturn, occupying opposite directions, made him feel like a tightrope walker. "Not that I don't depend on science in a way more profitable than your profession, Miss," he said, accenting "Miss" to highlight her singularity.

Then his feelings changed. He felt like a star that everyone orbited.

"I'm a man of business-y things," he repeated, chest puffing. "Don't talk to me about life. Talk to me about money."

Most Compatriots chuckled. He looked down at them, with evident self-congratulation. Rubicon? Perhaps he should've christened his craft Democracy, instead.

He looked around; savoring the Ecologist's diminishment, and admiring the results of the favors he'd bought back on Old Earth. Not all: just enough. Many of the Compatriots wore visible, gaudy jewelry, given to them by the Time Traveler himself, or his charismatic intermediaries, after his last lecture tour on dinosaurs and the tiny, squishable mammals who'd shared humanity's chronological nook. Oh, how the reconstitutional geneticists had lavished him with fine wine and praise! On this neck, diamonds sparkled. In those ears, rubies glistened. On those wrists, topaz flashed. Continual glory seemed inevitable.

But the Ecologist? Only her eyes glittered.

Like the Anthropologist's eyes. That woman sat beside her, hat full of God-given rainbow feathers. And what God hadn't given, she'd bought herself. "Man" was the enemy of her profession.

"Money!" cried the Time Traveler, puffing his chest, reinforcing what had instigated the laughter.

"Delectable!" cried the gout-ridden Banker, voice cracking.

The fat man rose, plodding to the coffee machine. He cleared his throat, clearing the cracking, as if wringing knuckles.

"I like the plan," he said, a new deep voice commanding attention, pouring dark roast from the behemoth's leftmost tubes. It hissed, an ebony espresso snake. "I think it has...what do the French say? A certain, uh..." He lost his words, social terror flashing across his face before he recovered with cover words. "Oh, I don't know what. But you know." He aimed a roaming, fat, political finger at everyone in turn. "There's nothing like venturing out into God's creation in a spanking new vessel with all the latest bells and whistles, to dance among the music of the spheres. And to do with them what God intended!"

He paused, waiting in vain to hear a, "And what is that?" He huffed.

"That is, converting the whole massive universal mass back into money, because, boy, wasn't Eden green as emeralds, eh?" He sipped his darkness-filled mug, eying the entourage, a fat, free finger aiming like a gun. "Do you know what I think?"

No one seemed willing to read money's mind. Even the Time Traveler let the question orbit like a moon.

"I don't know," replied the Ecologist at last, colder shivers shaking her at the sight of the corpulent man. He looked like her uncle, in his casket with the white lilies. "But I could guess. Do you want me to guess?"

"No," replied the Banker, fearful, jiggling deep into his seat. "I'll just tell you," he said, before pointing to everyone, mouthing, "and you, and you, and you, and…"

Waiting for him to "just tell," the Ecologist found herself thinking back to her childhood near Canada's Great Bear Lake. She recalled sitting by a stream, looking at fragile frog's eggs clinging to a stick in the pebbly shallows. Upstream, she saw with dread that terrifying bend in the river, emaciated trees hiding the oily black "plant" from view. She'd wanted to save the eggs. But only feeling certain of where her retreat lay, she'd crept home, eating a nervous dinner of boiled carrots passed to her by her wine-tipsy mother. Then gone to bed, dreaming black dreams of mutated failure, tinged with piercing white starlight.

Cowardice built her, brick by monthly brick. How she grew to hate "parents," drunk on power, alcohol, and so much more, and what they'd done to the Earth. And how she'd recoiled at the idea of parenting anything but the right ideas. Always with the poisoned eggs in mind, Humanity grew for her like a doomed cancer. And, like the eggs, the metaphor revealed no crack.

"What I think," continued the Banker, "is that when God made the World, he made it out of a big old goddamned pile of money." He grabbed his huge belly, jiggling it like a breast. "It's like the Big Bang. That was just a much larger financial singularity uniformity thingy. I know. God hovered over that, like Earth now, knowing perfection. But, whaddya do after perfection? Watch? In silence? No. Mess perfection up! Then see if the kids can fix it!" The Banker shuddered. "We're always one generation away from barbarism. I was raised Catholic, so…"

The Engineer cut him off, weak hand slicing the air.

"Oh Jesus. Don't you bring religion into it. My God. If I had a sentient race for every…"

Then the Banker cut *him* off, fatter hand cutting sharper.

"I wasn't bringing religion into it," he snapped, his thumbs in his lapels as he verbally stabbed back. "Religion was already in it."

The Compatriots turned to look at the Time Traveler, expecting the rock star to speak. But he only continued to look outward, at Titan and the sharp, crystalline stars.

"What I was going to say," continued the Banker, shifting in his seat, his breath short, "was that what God no doubt did was take money's singularity and break it apart. And He did it with the sole intention of creating the diverse panoply of the Universe, because you can't buy beauty without money. What God no doubt wants is for us to prove that we understand this truth." He shook a hammy fist. "It's a puzzle. He wants..."

"She," hissed the Anthropologist, dark Amazonian features wincing.

"Have it your way," replied the Banker, eyes rolling. "So 'She' made the Universe out of the essence of money. We know this because green trees can be turned into money with saws, and blue water can be turned into money with damned good dams, and red-blooded animals can be turned into money with fine, fancy abattoirs." His face darkened at the word animals. "Little morons think they're as good as us." A vile bitterness momentarily clouded his features. "'She's' waiting for us to prove we get it. I believe that's why we're here. No, I know it is. The gravity of profit. The singularity of money."

The Fireman rose for light-roast coffee. Too much burn scared those in his profession, in a subconscious way. Dark roast seemed crazy. He looked up as his mug filled, eyeing the overhead halon system, unsure of its suitability to extinguish flaming argument. Then he added cream.

No one said anything for almost a minute.

"Enough!" roared the Time Traveler, slicing a false-debate ending pause. Most linked the delay to deep, farsighted, profitable thought.

"We're not here to philosophize," he continued, softer. "Only to make money. Back in the present, we have investors waiting for green-paper presents. I myself have a down-payment on a mansion in the Delta quadrant with a prime view of the Rubicon Nebula. And I don't plan to lose it to stupid heathen tendencies." He eyed certain Compatriots.

Cutting back through the entourage, he returned to his console with commanding, pink, eye-catching strides.

Pressing a series of buttons, Rubicon flew rightward. Titan shrank fast. Saturn did not shrink at all, as if unafraid of titans or humans. And Saturn's rings, inseparable as the rings of true godly marriage, continued to encircle him, as if working to shield his masculinity from Humanity.

"So!" the Time Traveler cried, after one orbit of Saturn.

The hardly Soviet revolution had not followed a predictable line. No circle. Zero ellipses. It zigzagged, on fusion power.

The Scientist raised a hand.

"Sir?" he asked, timorously.

"What is it?" the Time Traveler replied, sighing.

"Is this really the best use of government funds?"

The Time Traveler glared.

"And you call yourself a scientist!" the Ecologist cried. "You already know the answer to that!"

The Time Traveler strode up to the Scientist, slapping the pasty little man across the face, knocking him to the floor. No one fought back on his behalf. Everyone felt captive, like moons to gravity.

"Government funds," cried the Time Traveler, "are just sources of fun! The 'D' and 'S" at the end of 'fun'?" He rubbed his mighty hands together. "Government excess! Dumb! Stupid!"

"I'm sorry," the Scientist mumbled.

"I forgive you," the Time Traveler replied, smiling a fresh smile. "Hard not to forgive a dude with so much to offer."

Striding back to his console, the Time Traveler input a new series of commands. The buttons he pressed spanned the Earthly rainbow. ROY G BIV, as he'd been taught, in elementary: red, orange, yellow, green, blue, indigo and violet.

And, outside, with Saturn's rings and moons clearly visible in the vacuum distance, things began to change. Massive, technologically advanced forces, god-like in nature, vented from the hull of the time machine on invisible, almost tidal, waves.

The Journalist tapped away at his tablet as if possessed. The others could only watch. Great changes dwarfed small humans.

The Demolisher stood, muscles flexing, eyes bulging, and adrenaline surging. His black hair, moustache and beard, full and thick, made his skull look like a globular pubis.

Before their eyes, technologically magnified by multiple sub-screens, the lesser moons and the rings themselves began consolidating.

"Yes," the Time Traveler stage whispered, touching his pectorals. "Yes."

His time machine sped the transformative process. Asteroids hit planetoids. Moonlets impacted meteors. Moons struck comets. Everyone watched, fascinated despite individual convictions and morals. Rhea collided with Dione. Mimas smashed Iapetus. Tethys merged with Hyperion. Mesmerized, the Compatriots watched the celestial, orbital ballet while the Time Traveler walked about, lips moving, fists balled in the small of his back while he paced, concerned only with his own vital thoughts.

The Ecologist and Anthropologist eyed their strangest companions. *Nothing to be done*, they heard the Animal and the Native say.

The Animal. Silent and dead. The head of a wolf sewn atop the body of a bear, the body itself sewn to the arms of an ape and the legs of an elephant. The Taxidermist had even preserved the thing's maggots.

The dark-skinned Native sat next to the Animal, watching with actual consciousness, surrounded by an alien aura, hands and feet bound. Lips sewn shut, she could not voice her views on the gods of this place. Yet her eyes revealed clarity, and, as the eyes had not been sewn shut like the mouth, saltwater tears spilled, splashing the cold floor.

The ballet outside continued.

Still influenced by the craft's mighty powers, almost everything, apart from Titan, soon combined in fire and debris to form one single moon. It happened very fast, and when the process completed, the Compatriots beheld a Saturn bereft of marital rings, and even most orbital relations. They beheld, between two arbitrary points in time governed by the Time Traveler, the very largest original moons joined by another, far newer moon.

The new moon had no name, yet. The Astronomer, quivering with anticipation, raised a waggling hand with ideas, his bony bottom lifting inches off his chair's brown leather.

"A new celestial body!" the Time Traveler cried, thumping his chest with his fists.

Somehow, the sound echoed.

"What do you think," he asked, ignoring the Astronomer. "What will become of it? Expansion? Stepping-stone to realms beyond our solar system? Corporate mineral rights? A dumping ground for society's willing detritus, like Urras, or was it Anarres?" He frowned. "Or just a fee-driven tourist bauble?"

The President, resplendent in his white, mink coat, spoke up.

"How long again?" he asked, his voice cracking like the Banker's.

"Eight inches," the Time Traveler replied with a stifled, adolescent giggle. "Ask any woman but the Ecologist."

"No," the cocky President clarified. "How long from now to the present?"

"Ah," The Time Traveler eyed his personal internal optical overlays. "Two point five billion years."

"And what will this new moon look like, then?" the President asked.

"Much like Titan. But yellow."

"Water?"

"Some. Frozen."

"We could colonize it?"

"Indeed."

"Practical."

"Indeed," the Time Traveler replied, his voice diversifying. "Hallelujah."

The Anthropologist groaned, rolling her eyes.

"But shouldn't it be...bigger?" the President asked, frowning at the new moon.

Affronted, the Time Traveler glared at the only other powerful man present.

"I concur," the Astronomer said, drawn to the gravity.

"And how big is bigger?" the Time Traveler asked, arms crossing again.

The Banker vented a wet, phlegm-producing cough.

"Well," the President continued, "why not combine all of Saturn's orbital material into one moon. Wouldn't it then be just about the size of Earth? Wouldn't the gravitational benefits be self-evident? Who wants to live with less than one G? I read, 'The Moon is a Harsh Mistress.' Colonization would be more likely at a full G, and..."

"I don't have *permission*," the Time Traveler replied, sneering the last word. He didn't sneer at the President, but, somehow, by peripheral vision or voice, at everyone else. "Red tape, you know."

"I can give it," the President's voice sliced. "Article twenty thousand seventy-two, paragraph sixty-nine. 'The President of the Federation shall, without consequence, grant any and all...'"

"Yes," the Astronomer cut in. "This'll give Galileo and the others fits. I can hear it now. 'Why does Saturn have only one moon? It makes no sense. Jupiter has more than...' Of course, all that would sound better in Italian. But should we wreck Titan?"

"I believe so. One moon, as close to the size of Earth as possible. Of course, I could be excited about the idea because I'm hearing the Sirens of Titan and no one has tied me to Rubicon's mast," the Time Traveler said, with a sly grin. "I did my reading too, Mr. President. But what can one do, really, in the face of such *fabulousness*?" He pronounced the last word with irony. "It's not like Humanity found any actual life on Titan, or even on any of the solar system's moons. Even the water ones are just giant ice cubes! Not enough infernal gravity for life to warm to. And not enough silicone for life to compute either!" He chuckled. The Programmer groaned. "If you want, we can go back and ask the late 20th century. Silicone is hot!"

Only seven moons remained in orbit.

One, created by Humanity, moved in on Titan like a Lothario toward a prospective lover. Seeing this incursion, eyes glowing, the Time Traveler pressed a blue button, blasting "The Music of the Spheres" over his craft's audio system. Everyone covered their ears, until they adapted.

The Time Traveler keyed in a series of complex commands, turning toward Titan's screen.

The Programmer, surgically replaced eyes glowing red, tried to sneak up to the console, craving programmable reality and not binary. He felt like a ninja.

"Hey!" the Time Traveler snapped, hearing the heavy man's footsteps. "Back off, Poindexter!" He raised a mighty hand, ready to slap.

The Programmer slunk back to his seat.

The seven remaining saturnine moons sparkled.

"I'd pipe in the sound from outside," the Time Traveler said, lip curling, even as Strauss' composition filled his craft, "but space is a vacuum. Dead air, without the air."

"How is all of this accomplished?" the Scientist squeaked.

"This what?" the Time Traveler asked, before offering an answer. "By money, I'd bet."

"No," the Scientist clarified. "Your craft's abilities! They're unbelievable! How can you cause this impact that...the laws of physics! I don't...No one would brief me before we..."

"Gravity guns," the Time Traveler replied, voice booming wide as his spreading hands, grin giant. "Inverted positron fields! Dilithium quantifiers. Repulsor particles. Zipadeedoodah and yippiecayay concoctions utilizing polymath algorithms and quantum photons dipped in neutral Swiss chocolate." He sighed, eyes rolling and closing. "Really, man. How the Hell should I know? I didn't build the damned thing. I only demanded it work. And by God, it does. Like a damned charm."

He gestured out into the panoply of Saturn's almost space, chest puffed.

"Thus!" he cried, fingers splayed.

Soundless, giant moons impacted with awe-inspiring collisions. The Astronomer called to mind computer-generated images of the hypothetical, ancient planet Theia, striking Earth eons ago, creating the Moon and, out of utter chaos, making the impossibility of life possible. He shuddered. What if the angle had been just a bit different? The odds! And what did the odds say about the gods? Odds and gods!

Or perhaps it wasn't eons ago. On the time machine clock, perhaps it happened now. Perhaps Theia struck Earth after the Astronomer pictured her. Or even at the same vital moment.

Gravity, potent in the gathering matter storm, kept debris in check. All the moons, except Titan, struck each other, ice and frictional fire exploding into space. Pressing buttons, the Time Traveler managed the debris like a recycling baron.

Saturn, singularly ringless, looked on. Implacable.

"Titan's untouched," the Anthropologist snapped, arms crossed and frowning.

"Getting there," the Time Traveler replied, "Getting there." He strode for a mug of the very darkest coffee. "Fast. Saving the best for last. Like a fireworks display."

"My mother showed me holograms of Theia," said the Fireman. Africa's terrorist bombings filled his mind.

"Theia was so…patriotic," replied the Time Traveler, as the hot new moon neared Titan.

"Impact in ten," began the Time Traveler, "nine...,
eight..., seven..."

Titan, as if attracting the new, consolidated mass,
looked to most like a massive head. Many imagined it
opening a great maw, ringed with sparkling white shark
teeth to swallow the upstart like a bit of candy. Age,
some thought, must count for something.

"I hear new music!" the Time Traveler cried, listening
as always only to the contents of his head, as he struck a
time-pausing button.

"Choreographer!"

A spindly young woman with red hair and golden
hoops in her ears rose, coming fast to him, her face
awash with awe.

"Yes, S-Sir?"

"Come here, please."

"Here?"

"To the console."

The woman nodded, shuffling in a rhythmic way
toward the plinth. Uncertain what to do with the
controls, or reality, she looked to Sol's star for guidance.

"It's a simple three dimensional movement layout,"
the star-made-maker said, very gently. "Make the
moment for us. Please? You choreographed with
something very similar, with your dolphins on Earth.
Yes?"

The Choreographer stared at him, star-struck and
heated, blank as bleached slate.

"Make them dance!" the Time Traveler said, grasping
her frail shoulders with a winking change of tactics.

"Oh," the woman whispered, stimulated to
straightness. Artistry returned to her.

Soon, she had Titan and the new, temporary moon
dancing around each other, sometimes obeying gravity's
dictates, sometimes breaking fundamental physical laws.
Yet, it all seemed human.

"Yes!" the Time Traveler cried, moving for a minute
away and gathering handfuls of mugs from the coffee
station before smashing them on the ground, as if
possessed by some Russian marriage ritual. "Yes! Yes!"

Then he circled the Choreographer, stepping in time with her more and more impassioned tune.

Wishing to mend things, the Journalist rose, cleaning the mug shards. But no one read his actions.

Everyone else, hypnotized by the dances, one planetary and one human, sat like an audience withholding applause. Ah, propriety's mandates.

The Astronomer, freeing up a portion of his admiring brain, considered suggesting that this new moon be dragged up closer to the Sun, so as to be combined with Mars. The only failing of Mars as a haven of life, he knew, was insufficient mass. Just imagine, he thought, what Mars could have become otherwise? Would the God of War have held onto his atmosphere? Would sentient life have thrived? Then the tingles took him. He raised his flapping hand, flush with a new, genius idea.

"Perfect co-orbit with Earth!" he thought. "A second planet on the same plane! Not a moon, but in an orbit that will never disturb Earth!"

The Time Traveler synched with the Choreographer's ecstatic, sexual artistry. Despite himself, and despite her simplicity, the planetary dance she orchestrated lit a hot fire inside him. He found himself holding her like a branch in a stormy sea, his nose buried deep in her fragrant hair, fingers wrapping her stomach from behind, encasing her navel the way a crust encases a core.

"What about Jupiter's moons?" cried the Anthropologist, standing up and flailing her arms like the wild woman she wished to be. "Are you scared of the greatest Roman God? Afraid he'll smite you for pre-Christian blasphemy?"

The Time Traveler ignored her, intoxicated by choreographed bliss.

"Now." The Time Traveler whispered into the Choreographer's ear.

She complied...with a shudder.

Terminating the dance with a flourish of dainty wrists, she ended the external ballet. The "Swan Lake" of lunar swan songs. Two great bodies crashed together. Everywhere, eyes shielded.

The impact of Titan and the short-lived, unnamed moon reminded the grizzled Demolisher of some of the greatest Earthly buildings and ecologies he'd ever had the opportunity to destroy. Always make room for better things. But it was not his work. Ownership is all, after all. He groused, internally, about lacked charisma, half wanting his own pink suit.

Edifying silence.

And when everything ended, the Compatriots stared outward. They eyed a hot, turbid yellow planet, almost as large as Earth, glowing and smoldering like a cosmic, fertilized egg. It did not look like Titan at all.

"What if it spawns intelligent life," the Anthropologist shrieked. "And what if that life conquers Earth before Humanity can evolve? Paradox!"

"Oh, that wouldn't happen out here," the Time Traveler replied, stifling a guffaw. He winked at everyone else. "Too cold this far from 'Our Star.' Life? Perhaps. Intelligent life that could conquer Earth? Hell would freeze over first." He paused, thinking as deep as his conception of beauty allowed, fingering his chin.

"Now..." Revelation seemed to strike him. "If we combined the asteroid belt with Mars..." He turned to the President, eyes sparkling with glee. "And we could move this new planet toward Earth! We could set up a perfect co-orbit!"

The Astronomer could hardly contain his fidgeting glee. The Ecologist, dumbfounded with dismay, could hardly form a thought, or keep her chin off the floor.

"Permission?" the Time Traveler asked the President, rubbing strong hands together.

"Yellow and blue make green," the Banker whispered to himself, geese bumping.

Everyone looked at the President. Time froze.

The figurehead, governmental man felt heedless. "Yes" brewed in the nether reaches of his semi-soul. For a small time he fought it, but for all of the time after, he recalled loss. If you wish to know the soul of Man, give him power.

"Oh all right," the President replied, feeling himself expand under all the eyes and all the LED light. No matter how much of his tiny will he called on, he could not shrug off what felt like nine lives worth of curiosity.

"Oh all right, what?" the Time Traveler asked.

"Everything's all right." The President smiled. "What could possibly go wrong?"

Amos Parker has believed he should be a real writer *since high school in the early 90s. But it wasn't until getting fired from a job, in 2007, that he finally found (and flipped) the switch in his body/mind/soul necessary to become more than an email and journal writer. He got fired early on a Monday morning, round about September 3rd, on a lovely early fall day, and spent the day wandering around the nature paths in East Burke, Vermont. The first half of the day was spent wondering what the Hell to do next: the second half, after flipping the switch, was spent mentally hammering out a fantasy book plot, terrified that if he didn't lock in hard the switch would un-flip. But, in spite of some bumps along the way, it never has. Since then, a space currently of almost 8 years, he's written about 10 novel manuscripts, 6 books of short stories and novellas... and failed utterly to find the 'switch' in his mind/body/soul necessary to care much about fighting to be published and make money off his writing."*

ENCELADUS

9. RECKONING AT ENCELADUS

By

Tom Olbert

The exploding glider lit the methane clouds over Titan in a bloody red glow. In the gunner's canopy, Gene Grey Wolf gritted his teeth and cursed under his breath, a torrent of half-frozen liquid methane slamming against his suit as he struggled to get a radar lock on the two remaining gliders zeroing in on them.

"Hold her steady, dammit!" he yelled at his glider pilot, now turning into the heart of a raging squall, the superstructure of the cloud glider rattling wildly. It reminded Gene of the time he dove his space fighter into Saturn's upper atmosphere with two Combine laser ships on his tail.

"You wanna try it?" the other man's voice came blaring in over the radio link in Gene's oxygen helmet, wild and scratchy.

One of the Combine gliders spread its elevator fins, circling in, riding the storm current as the pilot tried for a flank shot. The attacking glider's radar silhouette looked like a monstrous dragonfly, its braking fins spreading like great wings as it turned.

"Pull up!" Gene yelled.

Too late. His pilot was too busy navigating the storm; his glide sails ready to collapse under the pressure. The enemy pilot fired, a plasma volley cutting through the superstructure of Gene's glider, the braking fins splitting off, as the glider spun out of control into the storm. Gene fired wildly, trying to take out at least one of the killers. He clipped the wingtip on one glider as the other turned to navigate the storm.

"Burn, you scum!" He swore at the top of his lungs as his own pilot ejected. Blowing his own separation charge, Gene groaned at the lurch of the gun module blasting free from the disintegrating glider. He spun end over end, his head swirling as he triggered his braking chute.

Titan's atmosphere was a thick smog of methane, ethane, acetylene and hydrocarbons that hung like a choking gray shroud over the cold, poisonous moon. Gene cursed in the hot, stinking interior of his air suit as he slogged blindly through a steady downpour of liquid methane rain. He wiped his glove across his faceplate, trying to scrub aside the half-frozen thick liquid he feared would coat him like an insect in amber. The one thing he had to be thankful for was that any Combine glider pilot still looking for him wouldn't stand a spacer's chance in a magnetic pulse of finding him in this soup.

Stopping to rest against a rock outcropping, he tried to get his bearings from the computer map in his suit console. He was about ten klicks south of the nearest hydrocarbon sea. Two hours of oxygen left, he realized, checking the counter. Enough to reach the nearest organics harvesters, assuming they were running on schedule. His breath grew labored as he followed the flashing red arrow on his console east, toward the nearest processing stations.

The ponderous, grinding grey metal behemoths of the organics harvesters never looked so beautiful, their looming silhouettes barely visible through the grey-yellow haze of a passing electrical storm. They were like huge bottom feeders in the murky smog, gathering the thick surface layers of organically rich sludge to be purified and used for the production of self-replicating A.I. circuitry.

He slipped in low behind a stony ridge as one of the metal monsters lumbered by, the ground shaking. Radar-scanning the gigantic machine's treads, he found what he'd been looking for, the depressurizing vent over the suction pumps. Climbing the ridge, he crouched, waited...and jumped. He slipped inside the vent and held on tight, vibrations passing through the metal framework and rattling his air suit. Light washed over the misty soil. They were approaching the processing station. A great shadow fell over him as the harvester rolled into the loading bay.

Gene hung back in the shadows of the harvester's vent as the operators climbed down from the control cockpits. The grubby men and women in their worn gray coveralls filed through the half-lit interior of the bay, wearily griping. He waited, then climbed carefully out of the vent and dropped quietly down from the treads. He kept to the shadows as he made his way along the wall to the storage lockers. Stashing his air suit in an empty locker, he put on a set of coveralls from another locker and then blended in with the workers.

He knew he'd need a travel pass to get through security and out of the processing station. He picked an isolated man, slipped up and chopped him behind the neck. When the unconscious man crumpled to the floor, Gene searched his pockets for his pass, while thanking the fates he hadn't had to kill him. He'd killed enough civilians. No more. All he wanted now was to take out a few more Combine military thugs and get away. If he died in the process...so much the better.

Helena, one of the most luxuriant cities on Titan, floated on the methane sea of Ligeia Mare. Storm clouds floated lazily across the grey horizon, the odd lightning burst lighting up the viewport in the shadowed bar and lounge in one of the city's upper sections.

Gene Grey Wolf sat nursing a hard gin at a side table in the dark shadows. The bar bustled with the usual traffic of cloying bureaucrats with pasted-on smiles—the stooges of Titan's puppet government—entertaining Mars Combine executives passing through on business or pleasure. An assortment of prostitutes moved among the patrons, slaves, most of them, taken from every inhabited Saturnian moon. A few of the scruffier-looking ones possibly came from as far away as Earth. Dead, empty looks in their eyes. Gene downed his second drink, his head buzzing as he raised his empty glass to get the attention of a passing waiter.

Then he saw her moving in his direction. Elegantly dressed in a clinging, black silk dress—slit high on her leg and low in the front—accentuating her natural attributes. Diamonds, no doubt mined from the core of Jupiter by deep diver ships, sparkled from her lovely throat. Her dark hair was artfully styled to bring out her striking features and piercing eyes. Kayla Constantinedes.

"Buy you one?" she asked, laying a hand on his arm, seemingly a spoiled rich brat indulging her bored curiosity with a member of the working class.

"Sure," he said, looking her over as she ordered two drinks and sat down opposite him. She leaned in close, pretending to whisper in his ear.

"Did the pilot make it?" he whispered.

"No," she answered with a bitter edge to her voice. "The butchers cut him down in mid-air. No I.D. on the body, of course, assuming they ever find it."

"Devils," he muttered, pretending to kiss her. "Sorry I couldn't kill more of them. Tell me it wasn't for nothing."

"It wasn't," she answered, pretending to nuzzle his neck. "That diversion you staged distracted Security long enough for us to get the stolen meds safely to Dome-12. They'll go out to the Mimas colony on the next shuttle inside standard supply cases. Those drugs will save a lot of lives. And, cut into the Combines' profits."

"I'll drink to that." He picked up the glass the waiter had just filled and clinked it against hers.

"Don't talk," she whispered, sitting on his lap and snuggling at his ear. Glancing over her shoulder, he spotted the two Combine Security agents at the bar that she'd obviously seen. "I've got another job for you."

Kayla's private space shuttle skimmed through the rings of Saturn, its solar sails raised, as it slipped out of Combine satellite radar detection.

Kayla kissed Gene lightly on the cheek, her hand sliding across his chest as he lay on the bunk in her darkened cabin.

"Off on another dark quest, as usual," she muttered, laying closer against him, her head on his shoulder.

Sex was a distraction before the battle to come. A numbing effect, like liquor. Mainly, it spared him sleep...and the nightmares of that space bomber mission over Enceladus ten years before. And the sight of habitat domes on the moon's icy surface cracking like eggs in fire.

He thought he was bombing enemy military installations. All that distance and cold black vacuum had spared him from the screaming sounds of dying civilians...whole families. The terrible day he'd shot his way past the Enceladus defense satellites in the narrow cockpit of his space skriker, and launched those missiles. The day he'd given up his soul.

He still felt it. Memories—of the madness—when Kayla tried to recruit him by telling him the truth about what he had done. Hot blood rushing through his brain and raging through his eyes, as he'd cut loose with an assault rifle in the control center of the military command base in Odysseus Crater on Tethys. He'd fully expected to die that day. He'd just wanted to take as many generals and squadron commanders with him as he could. They'd lied to him. Or, had they been lied to? He hadn't cared anymore, by then. Everything he'd lived for, up to that point, had been a lie. Everyone was a part of it, and he'd been ready to drown in a sea of blood.

Twelve rounds they'd pumped into him before he finally went down.

The Free Saturn Alliance had pulled him off Tethys and patched him up, on Kayla's orders. He'd shown them the way past the orbital defense grid and they'd returned the favor by saving his life. Changing his name had helped him to hide, but a part of him still wished they'd left him there to die.

"You've never been Earth side, have you?" Kayla asked him.

"Nope. Born and raised on Tethys. Never been outside the Saturn system. Why?"

"When I was seventeen, my father took me with him on one of his slaver missions to Earth. He wanted to share the experience with me, I guess. I suppose he was grooming me to take over the family empire one day, like the son he'd always wanted but never had. He showed me the flooded ruins of Boston and New York. The bombed out ruins of Washington, D.C., Moscow, Beijing. He made me watch as the slavers raided miserable little farming villages on the outskirts of the ruins, rounding up the filthy primitives. The slavers blasted down the few resisting villagers who came at them with wooden hoes, lashing the rest into cages like animals. My dear father made me watch, as he engaged in his favorite sport; hunting the wilder, nomadic savages in the hills from an air skiff, shooting them in the back as they fled, as if they were wolves. He was very disappointed in me, when I wouldn't touch the gun. He said I was weak. My tears disgusted him. But, I saved the vid records I'd made of everything.

"When I was eighteen, I hacked those records into the I.P. com net and led a student revolt at Renquist Academy on Phobos. That humiliated my father—and delighted me. He called me a disgrace, and that delighted me even more. He got his revenge though, on my nineteenth birthday. He presented me, as a gift, to a superior he was trying to impress. Hollister."

"Barrett Hollister? That Combine exec scum who ran the slaver routes? The one who ordered those domes on

Janus burned out when the colonists wouldn't hand over their daughters?"

"The same."

"I heard he got killed in an explosion."

"You heard right. The bomb I planted on his private space shuttle was my baptism of fire into the Trans-Solar Resistance."

"Good for you."

"My father suspected, I think, but he could never prove anything, and wouldn't dare investigate for fear of being implicated. So, I kept his name and his money and used them to carry on the fight. I'm living for the day I won't need him anymore, and get to kill him too."

Gene stared off into the darkness. "Why are you telling me this?"

She turned his face gently towards hers. "Just to show you there is life beyond the darkness. Even beyond what Hollister and my father did to me. You can't let the darkness win, Gene."

"Revenge is easy," he said, turning his head aside and staring at Saturn's golden horizon, the glittering fields of ice crystals spread across the black void beyond the viewport. "You wouldn't touch the gun when it was offered to you. I did. How do you give back innocent life you've taken? How can there be anything after that?"

She rolled over on top of him. "You give back what you've taken by giving back hope that's been stolen." Her hot breath washed over his face. "We're taking back Enceladus."

Kayla's shuttle docked at an unregistered space station in geosynchronous orbit around Saturn. Gene saw five other small ships docked there as well. Kayla hadn't just been blowing smoke, he thought. She had something big in mind.

As Gene and Kayla entered a conference room on the station's middle deck, seated around a table five people waited for them. Four men and one woman each had soldier written all over them. The second he set eyes on them, Gene read the mental scars of battle on each of their faces. He could tell they read it on him, as well.

"Thank you all for coming," Kayla said, glancing around the room. They stared back coldly, waiting. "You've all been invited here by the Trans-Solar Resistance and the Free Saturn Alliance, because your particular skills have qualified you as the best risk for the mission we have in mind."

"Yeah, yeah. Get on with it." A reddish-haired, white man of about thirty spoke dismissively, his foot against the table edge, giving off the stink of mercenary.

Kayla glared at him. "May I present Gene Grey Wolf, originally of Tethys." She glanced at Gene.

"Hey, the big man himself," the man said, sitting up and pretending to clap. "The berserker who led the rebs into the heart of Tethys command and personally shot up Odysseus base. I'm impressed. We have a celebrity in our midst." Gene felt more and more like cutting him a new one, but he restrained himself.

"Your military career is considerably less distinguished," Kayla said, bringing up his service record on a computer pad. A scowl crossed the man's surly face, and Gene smirked a bit at that. "Albert Bauer, national of Mimas colony, soldier of the Mimas Space Militia, occasionally open to mercenary work."

"A guy's gotta stay busy," he said with a sneer.

"E.V.A. demolitions specialist," she continued. "You led the team that deployed a string of space mines which destroyed several Hyperion battle frigates at the battle of the Cassini Division."

"Guilty as charged," he said, with a broad smile.

"A coward and a butcher," one of the other men, a stern-faced man of Asian descent said, glaring at Bauer from across the table. "Real easy to kill at a distance with mines, instead of putting your life on the line like a real soldier, isn't it, Miman?"

Bauer leaned forward and smiled. "And, who do we have here?"

"Joseph Kurosawa of Hyperion colony," Kayla said, bringing up the second man's service record. "Combat space pilot, repeatedly reprimanded for reckless and non-regulation combat maneuvers, and, repeatedly decorated for successful operations. Single-handedly credited with the destruction of three Mimas space destroyers at Cassini."

"I had a brother on one of those three ships," Bauer said with a bitter glare at Kurosawa. "Thanks, hot shot."

"I had a great many friends on those ships your mines took out, you cowardly, back-stabbing..."

Both men stood up.

"Cowardly?" Bauer scoffed. "You fancy fliers should try it in open vacuum with nothing but a space suit between you and Hell, laying mines with ships exploding all around you. The rad count slips one digit into the red, you don't get home."

"We didn't ask for that battle!" Kurosawa said.

"The hell you didn't! You poach on our ice-mining operations, that's what you get. We've got kids to feed too, pal."

"Enough!" Kayla shouted. "Sit down, both of you! Need I remind you, both your governments have agreed to this meeting?"

"Oh, so sorry, Your Grace," Bauer muttered, as he re-seated himself. "Maybe my government thinks those stolen meds you send us give you the right to order us around, but I don't."

"Shut up, and let the rest of us hear the deal!"

Gene's gaze snapped down the length of the table to the source of that outburst. The woman. She was in her early thirties. Pale, triangular face, dingy blonde hair cut short. Hard, angry features. That look had to be beaten into hard metal, he knew.

"Bethany Taggart," Kayla said, bringing up the next record. "Originally from Janus colony. Went rogue after the slavers destroyed the main domes. You went into space piracy and privateering after that. You led a boarding party that liberated slaves from a Combine transport ship and killed the crew. For that, you were jailed and sentenced to life on Pandora penal colony. You led a successful prison revolt and commandeered a

Combine supply shuttle. You currently work as a militia soldier for the Dione colony."

"All female colony," Bauer remarked, with a wry grin. "Ever try it the natural way, gorgeous?" He asked, making an obscene gesture with his hips.

"Show me," Taggart said, pulling a serrated knife, as she slowly stood. Gene's hand reflexively went to his gun.

"Put that away, and sit down!" Kayla ordered. Taggart sheathed the blade and sat down, staring coldly at Bauer. "One more move like that, from any of you, and I'll get security in here. Try to remember, we're here for a common purpose and fighting a common enemy."

"Paul Odaki," she said, bringing up the next record and glancing at a dark-skinned man seated near the head of the table. "Space soldier of Rhea colony. Once led a successful boarding party against a Saturn atmosphere station, being used as a military supply port by the Telesto colony…"

"Forget it!" Taggart cut in. "I don't work with Rhean scum! Half our population on Dione is made up of female refugees from Rhea. You have any idea how they treat their women?" Her face twisted with disgust and anger.

"The reason so many of them end up on Dione," Odaki replied, more with sadness than anger in his voice. "Is because there's an underground on Rhea that helps them escape. I've risked my life for that underground many times. I don't like the tyrants that run our colony any more than you do."

"But, you still fight and kill for them!" Taggart countered.

"It's my colony," Odaki said, swiveling in his chair to face Taggart. "It's my home, so, yes, I fight to defend it. And, I'm risking my life right now as a double agent for the Alliance, to help cut off the arms supplies the Combines send to the regime, so I can fight for a free Rhea."

"We're doing the Combines' work for them, if we fight among ourselves," Kayla cut in. "All your colonies have lost ships; all of you have lost friends and family. The

Mars Combines play you against each other, stealing your resources and making you fight and kill each other for the few scraps they leave. They support the most repressive regimes in the Saturn system, because it makes it easier for them to rule. Your peoples have all seen that this collaboration offers us a chance to strike back, in a serious way, for once. The Trans-Solar Resistance offers true independence for the Saturn colonies. An end to corporate slavery and a return to law and democratic self-government such as our ancestors had on Earth."

"Stuff the college crap," Bauer scoffed. "We know who you are, girl," he said, glaring at Kayla. "You're a Martian. Combine family. Rich girl living off Daddy's trust fund. Before you came here, you were smuggling guns to the Jupiter rebels. We're this month's cause, is that it?"

Grey Wolf had had his fill of the loud-mouthed swine. "Shut your trap, Bauer, or I'll shut it for you."

"Oh, that's sweet," Bauer said, standing up. "You doin' her, big man?"

That was it. Grey Wolf moved towards the creep, and Bauer moved to meet him halfway.

Kayla stepped between them, hands raised. "Gene, don't. Don't. It's okay." With effort, Gene stepped back and let his muscles relax. He ground his teeth as Bauer snickered. Gene started, as Kayla smashed Bauer square in the face with her elbow. She spun and nailed him again, an upsweeping blow to his nose with the heel of her hand. Spinning again, she landed a kick to his chest, knocking him backwards over his chair, to the floor.

Grey Wolf grinned, as he saw a smile crossing Kurosawa's face and heard Taggart laughing heartily. Gene tensed up fast, drawing his gun as he saw Bauer reach for his. He saw Kayla had drawn her pistol and had it trained on Bauer. Bauer froze, glaring up at them from the floor. Odaki took Bauer's gun from him and slid it across the table. Kayla picked it up as Odaki helped Bauer to his feet. Bauer roughly shook the other man's hands off.

"I'll remember you, rich girl," he muttered, spitting out blood.

"Good," Kayla replied, holstering her gun. Gene holstered his. "Now, I hope you got that out of your system, because I'm tired of school games."

"So am I!"

Gene looked across the table at the sound of a new voice. He'd barely noticed the young man sitting there. A very angry-looking young man. Light skin. Brown hair. Maybe twenty-two or so. Those eyes. That kid had been to the edge of Hell and fought his way back, Gene thought.

"I came here because I was told you big talkers in the T.S.R. had a plan to re-take Enceladus. Is it for real, or have I wasted my time?"

"Peter Morenov," Kayla said, bringing up his record. "Refugee off Enceladus at age twelve, during the Combine attack of ten years ago."

Gene felt an iron claw stab into his chest and crush his heart in a vice. That kid had been in one of the domes Gene had bombed. He'd seen it, with his own eyes. Lived through it. Gene couldn't take his eyes off the kid's face, though he desperately wanted to, fearing Morenov would see the guilt in his eyes and know.

"Family killed. You went off world in the company of water smugglers. Later went into piracy. Started working with various radical splinter factions of the Free Saturn Alliance in your teens. Recently planted E.V.A. charges on the keel of a Combine battle cruiser in Titan orbit, killing a crew of two hundred. There's a price on your head in every colony in the Saturn system."

"Great. My reputation precedes me," Morenov said, bitterly. "Now, do I get an answer to my question?"

Kayla set her pad on the table and activated its holo-projector. A 3D vid of Enceladus appeared, shimmering on the air. A cross section of the translucent globe illustrated the twenty-mile-thick ice sheet that was the moon's surface, and the geothermally warmed liquid water ocean below.

"Enough liquid water to power half the fusion reactors in the Saturn system," Kayla said. "And, hydroponic domes capable of producing enough food to feed half the Saturnian colonies. Whoever controls Enceladus controls the Saturn system. And yes, we have a plan to re-take it."

"And then, what?" Bauer demanded. "Assuming we can take Enceladus back from Titan, you think the Combines will stand for it? They'll send a whole Martian fleet to wipe us out!"

"Mars currently has no fleet to send," Kayla replied, sliding Bauer's gun back to him across the table. "The Combines currently have their hands full putting down worker rebellions on the Jovian moons. This is our window of opportunity. Are you all in, or not?"

Gene looked around the table. A few glances of hesitation. Then, nods of agreement all round. Morenov was the last. "I'm in," he said, finally. Gene couldn't help thinking the kid's eyes looked damned cold.

Gene rubbed his eyes and yawned as he walked down the shadowed corridor on the space station's outer centrifuge. He'd been up for twenty-four hours straight, going over the approach vectors for the attack on Enceladus. He hoped to grab a few hours' sleep before the T.S.R. carrier arrived to pick up the strike team.

He barely caught the flicker of a shadow from the corner of his eye, dodging at the last second, as the knife came down towards his heart. He shouted in pain as the blade grazed his shoulder, ripping open his shirt. He grabbed his attacker's wrist as it came down again, the tip stopping a half inch from Gene's throat. He kneed the attacker in the gut, twisted the knife around and slammed the other man's back against the wall, bringing the blade-edge to the assassin's throat. Gene gasped as the half-light in the corridor fell on his attacker's face. Peter Morenov's face creased in hateful rage.

"Do it, you pig," Morenov hissed through clenched teeth.

Gene wrenched the knife from his hand and tossed it aside, hearing it clatter in the distance. "Why?" he demanded, his arm across the younger man's throat.

"You know why, John Grayson."

The sound of that name went through Gene's gut like a dull knife. "John Grayson died ten years ago," he said, barely able to get the words out. "I'm Gene Grey Wolf."

"Changing your name won't bring my parents or my sister back, you murdering scum!" He spat in Gene's eye and head-butted him in the face. Gene's head swam as the other man clutched his throat and pushed him backward towards the far bulkhead. Regaining his balance, Gene roared, as he broke the hold and knocked Morenov backward with a right cross.

"Listen to me!" Gene shouted, slamming the kid against the wall.

"The hell with your lies!"

"Listen to me! *They* lied to *us*! They told us there were rebel ships massed in those domes on Enceladus, poised for an attack on Tethys. I didn't know the truth until after it was too late." He winced, the pain flooding back like a dark wave. "I wanted to die after that, and believe me, I tried. I tried to kill the lying bastards. I wanted to take as many of them with me as I could."

The kid wrenched free and pushed him back. "All we wanted was to be left alone," he said, rubbing a split lip. "My parents used to talk about a better way of life. We supplied water and food to colonies that needed it—at half what the Combines charged—and for that they butchered us like animals." He nailed Gene with an uppercut and lunged for the knife.

Gene tackled him. They struggled for the knife, holding it between them. "Okay, die now and maybe take me with you, but they'll laugh on both our graves," Gene said. "We each have a debt to pay. Help me get this job done, and then I'm yours. You want to pay them back, or do you want to die a coward's death?"

Morenov grudgingly released the knife and stepped back. "Okay. We take back Enceladus. And then, I kill you."

Gene handed him back the knife. "Deal."

Carriers from Mimas, Hyperion, and Dione rendezvoused with the Trans-Solar Resistance Carrier near Enceladus orbit. The strike team commanders met with Kayla Constantinedes in the briefing room. A holographic display of the Enceladus defense network spread out above the table in the center of the room.

"How reliable is this information?" Paul Odaki asked.

"Completely," Kayla replied. "It was transmitted to us by our agents on Enceladus. Our computers have timed the next geyser plume from the South Pole. If we make our approach accordingly, the plume will mask our carriers. Here's the layout of the satellite defense grid." She manipulated the controls, the 3D spread of satellites around the moon filling half the room. "Intersecting radar beams, laser and particle beam cannon, and projectile weapons take out anything that crosses their path. All satellites are linked by radio and computer coordinated. These are the key," she said, zooming in on three large orbiters. "We take those out with E.V.A. teams, and that brings down the whole net."

The holo view pulled back. "That's our approach vector. Now, here's the layout of the surface defenses." She switched to a view of the central military control complex on the surface of Enceladus. "Surface to space missile batteries are spread out along this perimeter here. Behind that, ground-based artillery defends the main dome here. Behind the command hub, two fighter squadrons based in these surface domes here. We come down hard with two space bomber squadrons and take out all three layers of defense with one strike. That leaves one more squadron on the space station orbiting above this position. That one we'll have to engage with fighters in open space."

"Not a problem," Joseph Kurosawa said with assurance.

"Now, the hard part," Kayla continued. "We can't bomb the central dome. Too well fortified. Nothing short of nukes would take it out, and that's out of the

175

question, given the surrounding civilian population. So, once the base is open to attack, we land A.P.C.'s on the surface and crash in through the main air locks, here, and here. Questions?"

"How much resistance can we expect once we're inside?" Gene asked.

"A lot. A whole battalion of Mars-trained professional soldiers off Titan. Battle-hardened. They've had a lot of experience putting down insurgents on the Saturnian moons."

"I'll bet," Bethany Taggart muttered.

"They'll divert the bulk of their troops to defend the command hub, leaving only a skeleton force in the occupied civilian domes. Armed dissidents are already in place there, ready to make their move in coordination with our attack. That's it. Suit up and prepare. We move in two hours."

Al Bauer's E.V.A. demolition teams blew up the three main satellites, bringing down the net as planned. The whole communications net down and the command center blind, Bethany Taggart and Paul Odaki led the space bomber squadrons, that came down like twin sledge hammers, wiping out the surface defenses and taking out the launch pads before the Combines could get a single fighter off the ground.

While Joseph Kurosawa's squadron provided cover from the counter-attacking enemy space fighters, Gene Grey Wolf and Peter Morenov led the Armored Personnel Carriers that spearheaded the surface assault. The space lifters came down from the carriers unopposed, deploying the A.P.C.'s on the surface, a few hundred yards from the military command dome.

Gene braced himself in the rolling attack tank that rattled around him, its treads grinding the ice below. He held his breath, watching, as the air lock grew quickly in the view port. He was shaken to his bones as the A.P.C.'s plow-like nose smashed through the air lock, into the very heart of the enemy's military command center.

There was nothing worse than fighting at close quarters on the enemy's home turf. It was a tight approach, bottlenecked with heavy plasma rifle fire coming at them from strong positions. Gene ordered the A.P.C. gun crews to open fire with the heavy stuff. That opened a breach as the station's defenders pulled back. Gene ordered his squads to advance, using stun grenades to open the corridors into the main complex hub. Resistance was the heaviest there, massed plasma rifle fire. Men were falling around him. The Titan troops fought to the last, and Gene knew their ammo would hold out at least until reinforcements arrived from Titan. He couldn't wait for that, so he ordered rocket launchers brought up.

That did it. Once the oxygen processing stations blew, that was the end. The fuel bays were the next to go, and the whole command core went up—com systems, barracks and all. With the dome superstructure giving way and the main supports about to collapse, Gene ordered his men to pull back to the A.P.C.'s and called for evac shuttles. Withdrawing with his men, back to the icy-white blanket of the surface, he looked around. Only a few flashes in the black sky, the flitting swarms of space fighters returning to their carriers. He saw the meteoric crash of a fighter coming down in the distance, and began to notice debris strewn across the distant reaches of ice. He checked the space-based transmissions on his helmet radio. It seemed Kurosawa's squadron had done its job and the space bombers were safely back aboard the carriers.

"Everybody out?" Gene asked his lieutenant.

"All except the other unit commander Morenov. He took rear-guard in D-block. He got his guys out, but his comm's dead."

Gene's blood ran cold. "Get these men off," he ordered. "Hold one shuttle for me. I'm going back. If I'm not back in ten, take off."

"Skipper?"

"Do it!"

He ran back into the breached dome, what little was left of the atmosphere bleeding away fast. The whole structure was caving in as he made his way through the buckling corridors to D-block. His heart pounded; sweat streaming down his face, his helmet plate fogging as he frantically searched, chamber by chamber. He'd been ready for death since the Odysseus base massacre, but he wouldn't let the kid die. Damn it, he wouldn't let him die!

Picking his way through rubble and dead bodies, he found Peter Morenov lying pinned under a collapsed girder. The kid's suit was damaged and leaking air. Leveraging the beam off him with a loose section of pipe, he hastily patched the rupture in his suit with his emergency kit. Sharing oxygen with the kid, he helped him through the collapsing dome with one arm over his shoulder. "Stay with me, kid," he managed, puffing with exertion. "You don't want to miss out on the chance to kill me, now do you?"

The kid strained and gasped. "This is the second time you've kept me from my family."

Gene almost smiled. "This time, I'm not sorry."

The armed dissidents in the civilian domes had done a fine job. They took Enceladus before Titan could even try to mass a counter-attack. The slave pens were liberated, and the people rejoiced, as they took back their world.

Gene sat alone in the medical section of the main habitation dome on the surface of Enceladus.

"Hey, we missed you at the celebration," Kayla Constantinedes said, entering with a smile on her face and the hint of liquor on her breath. "You okay?"

"Getting there," he sighed. "Morenov's in recovery. I wanted to be here when he came to."

Kayla sat beside him. "I know you feel like you owe him more than you can ever repay, but you're wrong. Word's already out that we liberated Enceladus, and one Saturn colony after another is coming over to us. We'll have ninety percent of the Saturnian moons in our camp by week's end. Every A.I. in the Solar System predicts the Titan government will fall within six months. Inside a year, we'll control the entire Saturn System. After that, who knows? With Saturn as our base, the Trans-Solar Resistance will be in a stronger position in the Jupiter system. We may even be able to start selling food and water to mining settlements in the asteroid belt. Once we have easy access to heavy metals and fissionable materials, there'll be no stopping us."

He managed a slight smile. "You concentrate on the future. I'll be taking it one day at a time, for a while."

But now, there was hope. A part of him wanted to live.

Tom Olbert lives in Cambridge, MA, home of Harvard, M.I.T., liberals and wackos. When not writing science fiction and horror or working, Tom volunteers for candidates and causes he cares about, like the environment and civil rights. Tom's father Stan Olbert was a fighter in the Polish resistance during WWII and later a professor of physics at M.I.T. Tom's mother, Norma Olbert has self-published Stan Olbert's life story: "The Boy from Lwow", now available in paperback. Tom's sister Elizabeth Olbert is an accomplished artist and now a teacher of art at the University of Maine.

Tom's fiction has appeared in a number of anthologies, including "In the Bloodstream" by Eden Royce, "Torched" from Nocturnal Press and "Something Wicked Vol. II" from EKhaya.

Tom has a dark, cosmically-themed science fiction/psycho drama novel entitled "Black Goddess" now available at Mocha Memoirs Press: http://mochamemoirspress.com/black-goddess_ in addition to two dark sci-fi shorts "Hellshift" and "Along Came a Spider" also available from Mocha Memoirs Press: http://mochamemoirspress.com/products/sf/

Tom also has a vampire novelette entitled "Desert Flower," a tragic tale of love, war and eternal darkness set in the midst of the Afghanistan war, available now from Eternal Press:

http://www.eternalpress.biz/book.php?isbn=9781615726349

TITAN

10. STARCHILD

By

Thaddeus Howze

Commander Mfune strode the decks of the great Benai starship, his footfalls echoing through corridors once filled with life, which now reverberated with the sounds of his steps alone; his and the specter of Death.

His crew had long since abandoned this edifice, a magnificent creation of an alien intelligence. From the corner of his eye, he could see the protean walls changing and reverting to a simplified and darkened state. Controls, displays, panels—all faded back into the surface, becoming smooth and quiescent, the same state it was in when it arrived.

Humanity's first contact was so different than anyone could have expected. At first, cheers of jubilation went out among the gathered representatives of Earth-Fleet as the Benai Aethership arrived on schedule, exactly where their messages said they would.

Aether-sign grew stronger, the ship becoming more material as it took station in the shadow of Saturn, above the moon of Titan. As it drew closer, the distance and lack of clarity fell away. A testament to their superior ability, the Benai ship was nearly as large as Titan.

As the ship fell into normal space, scientists on Earth Fleet ships and on Titan Station scrambled to their sensors, fearful this monstrosity might cause a disturbance in the nearby gravity well of Titan.

Their fears turned to wonder as they discovered the aether-ship existed partially in normal space and partially in aether-space simultaneously, sharing with real space only what was necessary to perceive it and interact with it. This was a previously unrealized possibility.

The tear-shaped crafted-world answered no communication broadcasts, even when sent on what was thought to be an established channel.

As the ship slowed and took position above Titan, its outer hull smoothed the vast engines and aether-vanes, which maintained its transit field slowly dwindling over the course of an hour, until it appeared as little more than a shining metal teardrop flickering in the wan sunlight.

Their ship awed and humbled us, once we could see it in all its glory. Then the murmuring began whispers that stank of fear and shame. What if they're like us? What could we do to stop them? The reality was telling. Earth-Fleet was the most advanced development of the Aether technology made by Humanity to date. And it was just a shadow of what the Benai now showed them was possible.

Diplomats, scientists, and soldiers boarded shuttles, as laid out in previous communication bursts with the Benai—though no such communication had taken place in nearly a year. Their approach caused access portals to light up and the ship came alive.

It's previously smooth skin emitted beams of light, striking each approaching shuttle and pulling them to the ship. The beams took control, repositioning them. Then the skin of the Aethership rippled, changed, and puckered into a seal capable of, securely connecting each shuttle to the Benai hull. They nestled alongside, as if part of the Benai technology.

The shuttles reported a positive atmosphere, though no one was willing to give up their spacesuits unnecessarily. The interior was nearly pitch black but slowly lit up as the Humans entered and moved about the vessel. Apprehension grew as the security teams fanned out, sweeping the hanger areas for signs of habitation. There was none. It took another two weeks for confirmation of what Mfune knew as soon as he stepped on board.

There was no one alive on this ship.

The walls reverberated with a presence—a perturbation of consciousness which, in the weeks to come, grew stronger. The commander dismissed this, at first, but the longer he stood on the ship, the more he could sense the echoes of minds around him. Strong minds, their remnants burned into the very metal itself.

No scientist agreed to stay on the ship for too long, complaining of feelings of discomfort, things seen from the corner of their eyes, voices speaking to them, chanting litanies of madness and death.

Mfune understood.

He had been onboard the Aethership since its arrival. His ship and his welcome fleet waited nearby, disappointment wafting from them, a redolent wind even in the vacuum of space.

Everyone had long waited for these benefactors of Humanity to arrive. For nearly three hundred years, we waited. Two hundred of them spent in relentless struggle to decipher the crumbs of knowledge given to us by the Benai.

When the Benai first sent messages to Earth, it was a time of great trouble. Food shortages, drought, and endless wars over resources were the only legacies of Earth at the time. It was estimated we would never see the end of the twenty-first century. With the air hotter than ever, almost all life in the oceans dead, we were poised for extinction—one last battle away from non-existence—when their message came.

SETI shared it. They thought it might give the warring factions hope of a world beyond warfare.

It could be nothing but a message from an alien culture. They had managed to send us a message, spliced together from our simplest radio and television transmissions, that was unmistakably alien. Encoded within the transmission was information, an alien technology which would open our solar system to us— the Aetherdrive.

Nullifying or concentrating gravity as we needed, we took to the planets, for the first time able to escape gravity wells without the need for mass. Only energy was required. We stopped fighting, with the hope of exploration to galvanize us into space.

The remnants of humanity came together one last time and we flew into our solar system. Distances between factions relieving our tensions, our urge for exploration and technological advancement reignited. Nations staked out moons, other planets, asteroids, and, for a time, we found peace. A hundred years passed and we were explorers again.

It was not to last.

Mfune tugged his close fitting ceremonial uniform, feeling its age and antiquity upon it; the symbol for wars nearly a century out of date. Worn by his father and his father before him; it represented a time when expansion ceased; trade began, and with trade came inequalities, and with inequality came frustration.

This inevitably led to war. Small wars at first, the Aethertech we developed was not like theirs. Inefficient, small, and limited, we could not create massive weapons of war. Our battles were surgical, with damage limited to a level that kept the species going. Most prayed the Benai would arrive and save us from ourselves. It would not be soon enough.

The commander looked around at the vastness of the world-ship and realized just how puny the largest of the human warships was in comparison. His science team had scoured the ship. There were medical technologies beyond our understanding: tools that reacted to mental directives, materials that took on shapes envisioned by the user, things that appeared as magic to us.

There was one marked difference between the Benai ship and the Human Earth-Fleet. The Benai had no weapons—nothing that could easily harm another. The supposition was that they might not have needed to have active weapons; they created them only when needed. No need to keep an armory, when you can envision your gun and have your ship make it on the spot.

Perhaps, but Mfune doubted that. His feel of the ship did not bespeak violence. It bespoke curiosity. It bespoke an urge to know, to learn, to embrace the new. And the voices that cried out in his mind, that leapt from the bulkheads, told him he was right.

All that Human science could accomplish in the twenty-third century had been done, a century after we had realized the foolishness of war. At the end of the Final Human War, as it was called, we experienced a renaissance, a new Golden Age. An age we were hoping to show to the Benai. An age of enlightenment which revealed to us what the Benai already knew; how to take the Aethership to near-light speeds. Fast enough to travel to other stars. We wanted to show them we had learned, evolved and could one day, maybe, be their equals, with their help.

How could we know, the Benai had continued to monitor us? To watch us grow and develop. Watched us step out into space and explore our planets. To watch us wage countless new wars, more terrible than any before them.

So what happened to them? Why was there only this one remaining? Out of fear, or perhaps reverence, no one touched the one corpse, this Starchild of an alien species. Scans were done, readings taken, tiny organic traces gathered, but it mysteriously remained mostly inviolate.

Mfune walked into what they believed to be the command structure of the ship and where the sole occupant of the craft resided. While few could even enter this room without the ghosts overwhelming them, Mfune, a remnant of a warrior age, knew and accepted this feeling. He suspected that influence was what protected the Starchild from being removed.

He touched the alien and its memories filled him— memories of the madness that swept through the Benai as they listened to the transmissions of our wars. The horror they experienced as we senselessly destroyed one another with the tools and technology they had innocently given us. Tools they had never thought to use to make war.

Mfune gently cradled the alien body. Deceptively light, its consciousness suffused him; he could see Human madness sweeping through the Benai, like a contagion. They destroyed themselves, as each was exposed to the recordings. They thought they knew the depths of what we could become. They thought they could withstand our cruelty, in order to teach us a better way. The longer they watched, the more of our madness spread to them. In the century left to their arrival, they went mad.

Some dropped dead on the spot. Others fled and threw themselves into airlocks and escaped into space. Ever dutiful, their starship cleaned up after them, reintegrating them with the materials of their ship, embodying their very essence within its walls.

This last member of their crew isolated himself in the command area and refused to interact with the crew, refused to listen to any of the recordings and his was the last message sent to Earth, before we lost all communication with them during the Last Great Human War.

"We loved you. And we are undone."

Mfune volunteered for this mission, for no one could make sense of the message during the Second Golden Age of Man. He wanted to be the first to understand why such a strange message was sent when the first ones were so hopeful.

He opened the isolation pod and placed the Starchild within. The ship seemed to respond to him now, he had been onboard for so long. With an understanding given to him by his connection to the Benai, he redirected the ship and plotted a course that would take the Aethership into the sun.

The samples collected from the Benai would be isolated and returned to Earth for storage. His priority-one message commanded that everyone who had entered this ship be kept apart from the population and quarantined, until they were cleared for duty. All information on the Benai would be stored until a coalition of worlds could decide what should be done with it.

One technology from the Benai nearly destroyed Humanity. What would an entire ship full of their technology, gear we can barely understand, do to us?

As Mfune made his way to his shuttle, he considered the court martial he would face when the alien starship vanished into the Aether and plunged into the sun. *"Why?"* they would shout. *"What wealth of knowledge could we have possessed from them?"*

Humanity, all of its factions, gave chase, eager to understand all that they could learn. But the Benai ship was superior in every way. No one could catch it or stop it. Its plunge into the sun was one of the media sensations of the era. Mfune was lauded and castigated, often in the same breath.

As he arrived on his flagship, a response already waited regarding his directives. Outrage from the scientists, now recovered from the alien influence, demanded their liberty and their research. But his words would stand.

On his trip back to Earth, his court martial was scheduled. Unsurprised, he already knew what he would say.

Resplendent in his father's uniform, he stood before the tribunal, defiant. Closely reminiscent of his own, his father's uniform was but a reminder; a remnant of a war that no one dared forget—the darkest chapter in Humani history.

"Explain yourself," was the general sentiment in the roaring tribunal chambers. Gone was the decorum he

had come to know from previous visits. This was the shouting of factions, of groups who had already considered what could have been learned, what advantages each group had lost. A golden age had drawn to a close.

He responded plainly. "The Benai were a simple people. They created complex technologies, to be sure, but they were a people of spirit, powerful of mind, generous to a fault." His words silenced the room, eager to hang him for his perfidy and their incalculable loss.

"Recordings of our violence, as they approached the Earth, drove mad the crew aboard that great ship. These were a people who knew little of violence, of lack, or of war. From what I was able to learn of them, war was the concept of ours they least understood."

"Look at you. In this room, which has stood as a bastion for justice for a century. Would you now revert to your factions for the sake of opportunity over one another, for the dominance that we once set aside for the overall good of humankind? I do not believe we have changed at all. I believe that what we have done in the last hundred years is temporary, as it always has been in the past."

"We hunted, we gathered, we squabbled. We created, we learned. We changed. We created agriculture and formed small towns, villages, townships, cities, states, and nations. Each time change took place, war followed us. We learned from war, we learned through war, we changed because of war. And a period of peace followed."

"The Benai did not learn that way. They were cooperative, always. Their shared that telepathy made acts against each other an act against themselves. The idea of our violence rendered them unable to continue their very existence. We were an infection, our violent nature became a mental virus they could not assimilate or withstand. Perhaps, violence against another was violence against oneself and, thus, beyond their ability to truly understand."

Only one voice could speak out now, the leader of the Colonies, an arrogant man whose role was as much a testament to his quest for power as his ability to lead men.

"How does this excuse your treasonous act? With such technology, we could have surely resolved many of the issues, which prevent us from traveling to the stars. Commander, I demand you explain how your historical lesson is relevant."

Mfune looked up and the spirit of the Benai filled him with an acute awareness of the limitations of unconnected minds. He strove to be clearer. "Humanity is an expansionist species. We grow to fill the container we reside in. When we reach the limits of the container, we do not stop growing. We do not regulate our development; we do not even acknowledge our limits. We exceed them and expect technology to resolve the issue.

"Such resolution is never without cost. Inevitably, we would likely go to war as we exhaust our solar system. Such pressures would invariably lead us to seek to expand again. Should we acquire their technology, as we did through their largess in the past, I expect we would expand and, as is our nature, wage war on each other."

Tears streaking down his face, he glared at each of the counselors in turn. "With our complete knowledge derived from their ship, we would want to go to their worlds. What would protect them from us?"

The tribunal was silent.

Justice was swift. Mfune left his command and many of his faithful left with him. Together, they founded a coalition with a single purpose: To warn the Benai that Humanity was coming.

The Starchild revealed what they needed to know. Through Mfune, the two of them would teach the coalition what they needed to learn. They would have decades, while Humanity waged what would one day be called the Expansionist Era, brought on by the fragments of knowledge learned from the few hours onboard that great starship.

An aging Mfune hoped there would still be time to save the Benai. The Starchild, resonating within Mfune's mind, assured him there would be.

Thaddeus Howze is a California-based author who has worked with information technology since the 1980's doing graphic design, computer science, network administration and IT leadership.

His non-fiction work has appeared in: The Huffington Post, Black Enterprise, the Good Men Project, Examiner.com, and Astronaut.com. He maintains a diverse collection of non-fiction at his blog, A Matter of Scale. He is a contributor at The Enemy, a nonfiction publication from Los Angeles.

He contributes a variety of research and speculative fiction articles at the Science Fiction and Fantasy Stack Exchange as a moderator and contributor. He also contributes regularly with Quora and Scifiideas.com.

His speculative fiction has appeared in: Visions II: Moons of Saturn (2015), Awesome Allshorts (Australia, 2014), The Future is Short: Science Fiction in a Flash (2014 & 2015) Visions: Leaving Earth (2014), Mothership: Tales of Afrofuturism and Beyond (2014), Genesis Science Fiction (2013), Scraps (2012, UK), and Possibilities (2012).

Like most specfic writers, Thaddeus has had a variety of other careers before becoming a writer. In addition to IT consulting, he has also been a corporate executive, an adjunct professor and a member of the US Navy. He has written two books: a collection called Hayward's Reach (2011) and an e-book novella called Broken Glass (2013).

11. Janus: Double, Double Toil and Trouble

By

R. E. Jones

1

"See this pen? It holds your fate. I could write you off this project right now, Ben."

"But, but it's my project, sir," the sweating young scholar said, trying to sound determined. "We need to follow, um, mission protocols."

Smedley Thorpe, extraterra agent for England's Ministry of State Security, laughed. He aimed the pen at Benedict Fawkes's face.

"Look here, Nostradumbo," Thorpe said. "I make the protocols. And I'll ship you back to Earth! You'll never set foot on that ice rock below. Your bloody crystal ball should have told you that."

Benedict Fawkes imagined jabbing that antiquated pen deep into one of Thorpe's eyes. Since the Third Glorious Revolution, such political commissars (aka politzars) ruled England. Thorpe could even overrule the captain of the *Audouin Dollfus*, which was now orbiting Janus, one of the moons of Saturn.

Fawkes and the crew had traveled nearly two years and over 1 billion kilometers to get here. The aging craft had hopped from the bases on the Moon and Mars before venturing through the asteroid belt and past Jupiter. He had endured: weightlessness; vomiting in zero gravity; weeks without any type of bath; tasteless food in squeeze bags; an uncomfortable, suffocating "deep-freeze sleep" on the last leg; and the ill-mannered company of Thorpe.

Fawkes couldn't let this happen. He hadn't even had a moment to look out a porthole to view Saturn. They had just woken up from suspended animation. He knew it was a lost cause, but he still wanted to argue. Well, as best he could.

"I, um, think it would be better if the team goes with me rather than just the two of us, sir." By "team," he meant the four robots that Fawkes had programmed for this project. The state-of-the-art bots cost a ton of Iranian rials. Thorpe's orders didn't make sense.

"Snowden and Thea will come down with the bots later," said Thorpe, referring to the researchers. He slipped the pen in his shirt pocket and patted it affectionately. Fawkes thought this out of character for the politzar. "We're going down now to get the lay of the land as the Yanks used to say."

"Two trips?" Fawkes bit his lip. A drop of sweat slid down his right temple. "But we only have so much fuel. That seems a waste."

"Benedict Arnold Fawkes, you have a half-hour to suit up, if you can fit into it," Thorpe growled.

Fawkes's shoulders slumped a bit. As he walked out, he heard Thorpe mutter, "Bloated papist!"

Fawkes clenched his fists, struggling to control his anger over the slur. He wasn't even Catholic, but that didn't matter. To Britons of all stripes, what mattered was his surname. He remembered when his father, an eccentric left-wing anti-monarchist, had changed the family name in honor of Guy Fawkes, an English Catholic who took part in the failed Gunpowder Plot in 1605 to blow up Parliament. "You'll be noticed, son," his father promised. Oh, that turned out true. Somehow, people would learn of his family's story. And, since the start of the religious wars in the United Kingdom, the stigma grew worse, even out here.

The shuttle landed with a clunk.

Fawkes tried not to hyperventilate, as he lumbered outside with the metal suitcase. He was scared but also excited. Because of this moon's almost-nonexistent gravity, he bounced more than walked on the rubble of pebbles, rocks, and ice chunks that ranged in color from sandy yellow to charcoal. He found the sensation strange and amusing.

But what grabbed his attention most was the gas giant. Saturn loomed over Janus, filling up nearly a third of the sky. The distance between the moon and the planet's cloud tops was about 91,000 kilometers. You could fill that space with about seven Earths. Saturn's pale yellow reminded him of the American cornmeal his mother hoarded in her pantry.

"You never know, dearie," his mum would say. "Your dad says those filthy U.S. capitalists could put a blockade on us. And, oh, where would we be without baking with polenta?"

The planet's rings were a different matter. Like most of the other moons, Janus orbited in the ring plane. The ring he saw in the Janian sky looked like a police do-not-cross line...a big off-white one. Activating his helmet's binocular screen, Fawkes took a closer look at the ring's countless, mostly colorless, ice chunks and space debris, and then, having previously set the coordinates, hunted and found Janus's neighboring twin moon Epimetheus. Difficult to find with the naked eye, the twin was 15,000 kilometers away—roughly the distance between London and Perth in southwest Australia. Even with his binoc-screen at full magnitude, it didn't look like much. But he was still thrilled to see it.

The two craggy satellites were unusual because they shared the same eccentric orbit. He recalled a fantasy he'd read about the twin moons being brothers, with a Cain and Abel relationship. It told of how they betrayed and ultimately destroyed each other; the moral being that relationships cannot survive without trust and honesty. For some reason, he thought the moral wasn't such a cliché.

"Tour is over," Thorpe barked through the speaker in Fawkes's helmet. The young scholar looked over to Thorpe. He was standing at the tent's entrance, impatiently waving for Fawkes to get moving. Fawkes awkwardly deactivated the binoc-screen and hopped over to him. The space suit squeezed him. He couldn't wait to get inside the Protective Earth Tent—actually a steel, warehouse-size building that construction robots had built the year before. There would be air and heat. There would be dehydrated food and some other minor comforts. And there would be the "artifact."

In MI5's Special Section, he had cracked the "Newton Code," an epic poem in Latin found among Isaac Newton's papers on alchemy. The poem had predicted the discovery of Janus in 1966. It was a strange work: The paper and ink were circa 13th century. The text, however, seemed modern. Nearly all scholars had argued, since its discovery 50 years ago, that the document was a forgery. Fawkes thought otherwise. He pored over the poem for months on his own. He was convinced it was real.

Fawkes managed to decode an additional prediction that an alien spacecraft, a time machine, would be found buried on Janus. Many in the agency started to call him Nostradumbo, Nostradumbass, or even Erich von Däniken Jr. At the time, only his Machiavellian mentor, MI5 legend Sir Arthur Barrow-Spencer, had backed him. He felt he was fortunate to have Sir Arthur on his side. Rumors in the agency had it that the Prince of Wales was out to get Fawkes—simply because of his unlucky name. Since the rise of the neo-Cromwellians, the Prince had become extreme in his views about anyone who wasn't a full-fledged royalist. Sir Arthur, however, had connections among the royal family that kept the scholar employed in MI5. Despite Sir Arthur's backing, Fawkes's theory was ignored—until the vessel was uncovered on the small, potato-shaped moon. In the agency, the news was an earthquake.

Now, he was on a top-secret mission to make the craft function. He was amazed that he had gotten this far. At the beginning, the project had received a giant budget—enough to build a new rocket for space travel, a flight crew of thirty, and tons of state-of-the-art scientific equipment.

But as the months wore on, the budget got worn down. The MI5 committee in Parliament decided that it was a turkey that could never fly. The new rocket was scrapped a year after building began—replaced by a 30-year-old craft, patched together with upgrades. The proposed flight crew was then slashed from thirty to twenty...then fifteen...then ten...and finally six: the captain and pilot, two researchers and Thorpe and Fawkes. And the state-of-the-art equipment? It certainly was state-of-the-art, twenty years ago. Still, here was Fawkes, on an epic journey that could prove more transformative for humankind than the detonation of the first nuclear bomb over 160 years earlier.

In the tent, he and Thorpe removed their space helmets. Still partially buried in rubble, the hatch of the alien craft was open. Fawkes couldn't help but be gob smacked. There it was—a wreck, but a beautiful one in his eyes. The holographic images didn't do it justice. It was about eleven meters long and four meters wide. The outer surface was gray. It was also scaly, like a fish. MI5 scientists hadn't figured out why a space vehicle would have a scaly skin. The ship also had something like pectoral fins, with deep ridges on both sides that created a distorted number eight. On the front were two slits, or windows.

To Fawkes, the craft looked like an outer space stingray. As a child, he had enjoyed making drawings and models of fish such as stingrays. In fact, he liked most animals more than he did humans.

Moving closer to the vessel, something inside him tingled, as if he... He felt a rough shove on his left shoulder.

"What's the matter?" Thorpe asked. "You already having the jitters?"

"Uh, no! I'm fine." A trickle of sweat slowly rolled down the back of his neck. He was fed up with Thorpe's tone but couldn't snap back at him. He hated the man. More than that, he feared him. Most of all he hated his own weakness.

Why had Sir Arthur approved Thorpe for the mission? There were five better-qualified politzars with some experience in space. All had sought the assignment. Thorpe displayed no knowledge or interest in space. He was a mean man with a mean history.

"Come on, 'Erich.' Do your magic, heh?" Thorpe said with a slanted smile. He had removed most of his bulky astronaut suit outside. As he put it next to his helmet on the metal table, the politzar pulled out a pair of gloves.

"Too much space dirt around here, mate. Don't want to get my hands dirty."

Fawkes was about to remove his uncomfortable suit when Thorpe bellowed, "Well, c'mon! C'mon! Go in! Go in! We ain't got all day—or whatever type of day we got here on this floating, godforsaken turd."

Fawkes' heart pounded as he entered alone. The ship's interior looked like the hollowed out cavity of an animal. On the ceiling, ridges resembled a spine. The walls were smooth but irregular and pockmarked. He touched the wall. It appeared gray and lifeless, but he felt a weak vibration. The holo reports had mentioned that the vessel evoked "hints of life." He then examined its control panel at the front. At the center of the panel was a bowl. Above it stood a tiny statue of an arachnid-humanoid creature with its top two appendages stretched out as if receiving an offering.

Fawkes opened the case and pulled out the odd-looking neutron battery he had helped design with MI5 scientists. The core was the size and shape of an American football. It's lining was made of lead. From one of the small ends of the "football" protruded a 32-centimeter tube, also made of lead. And at the tip of the tube was a brush: thirty-two tiny hollow tubes made of steel.

Fawkes looked under the bowl on the control panel. There he found the slot with thirty-two tiny holes. Whew, thank goodness. Carefully, he inserted the brush-like tip and turned on the device. It hummed and vibrated for a few moments. But from there, things started to fall apart. The battery abruptly shut down. He started it again. It shut down again. Eight times, he tried to activate the control panel. Each time he failed. What was wrong? He had followed the poem's "instructions." Did he mistranslate it? Maybe the battery he'd designed just wasn't strong enough. He could get a second one from the case.

He reached for a second battery but something yanked him backward, pulling at his collar while a blunt force thrust into his spine.

"This is Sir Arthur's way of saying goodbye to failure, Fat-Cow!" Thorpe yelled as he tried to garrote Fawkes. But Thorpe couldn't strangle him. The wire was wrapped around the lip of the space suit's collar. Fawkes fought wildly, flailing his arms. Thorpe's pen fell out of his pocket. Thorpe pushed him forward. Fawkes's skull met the statue's head with a staggering impact. Blood sprayed on the statue and into the bowl. Fawkes screamed. Thorpe grunted in disgust over his ordeal.

Blinded by blood, Fawkes fell backwards. He landed on Thorpe, knocking the wind out of his attacker. Wiping blood from his face, he frantically searched for a way to defend himself. He grabbed Thorpe's lost pen and, twisting atop the heaving man, he swung his arm around to jab it into Thorpe's eye. The politzar shrieked and struggled to remove it. Pulling the gory thing out, he rolled into a fetal position and stopped moving.

Shaking, Fawkes heard a hum. He fearfully turned and saw the control panel. It was activated. Inside the bowl was a beautiful rainbow of colors. He reached out... A heavy hand pushed him down on the floor, striking him on the back of the neck. Twisting, he saw Thorpe, blood dripping out of one eye, hitting him repeatedly with his fists. He raised his arms to deflect the blows and—blackness.

"Mr. Fawkes! Mr. Fawkes! Please wake up!"

Fawkes woke up. He was badly bruised and tired but happy to be alive. He saw Thorpe's burned body in front of the control panel. He smiled. He got up and surveyed the control panel. It was operating. Good. Through the control panel, the ship surveyed him. He was operating. Good. Fawkes felt better. He felt different. He felt confident.

"Hello, Mr. Fawkes. Glad to see you up and about." The voice came from the bowl on the control panel.

He had grown up with talking A.I. servants, but Fawkes was still taken aback by the ship's voice. It sounded calm, serene even. It was natural and feminine.

"What are you?" he asked. "Or who are you?"

"Please, let me introduce myself, Mr. Fawkes. I am Sheva, a biomechanical time machine who operates symbiotically with a pilot. I can also travel in space, but I am more suited for time travel. I must thank you for reviving me. I would have soon perished."

"Then the battery worked?"

"Well, no, Mr. Fawkes. You actually revived me with the DNA in your blood—the blood that spilled in the bowl. Blood is part of the way I connect to a pilot."

As Fawkes got up from the floor, he put his hand on the wall for support. It felt warm and slightly flexible, like skin. The wall's grayness was changing to light hues of blue and green. Life!

"Please, Mr. Fawkes, sit in the pilot's chair. You are still weak."

He complied. He felt good in the seat: comfortable, powerful.

"Uh, how do you know my name...Sheva?"

"From Thorpe. I interrogated him while you were unconscious. I must warn you that you are still in danger. Thorpe was merely a tool."

"What?"

"Well, he told me he was given orders from a Sir Arthur to 'cleanse' you, whether or not you had activated me. And somebody by the name of Prince of Wales had given the okay for such an operation, too. I couldn't get much else from him. I had to electrocute him when he started to resist me and grew violent. I couldn't allow him to damage you."

Fawkes looked at Thorpe's body. How could he explain his death?

"Mr. Fawkes, may I humbly suggest you tell your superiors that Thorpe accidentally touched the wrong part of my panel and electrocuted himself? It was a simple mishap."

The interior grew more illuminated, as Fawkes noted phosphorescent-like, irregular-shaped spots glowing on the walls, which now pulsated with warmth. And the bowl's rainbow was growing brighter and crisper.

"Yes, very good, Sheva," Fawkes said. This ship was proving to be a godsend for him.

Then the ship shuddered. The glowing spots went dark. The wall stopped undulating and turned ashen. Sheva let out a groan.

"Sheva? What?"

"I'm still very weak, Mr. Fawkes." Sheva said in a strained tone. "I turned on too many of my systems. I need major repairs. Please, get me off this moon."

She promised to teach him the ways of time travel. She would serve him and help him get revenge. She revealed that there were many universes, mirror universes and Earths, to discover.

"I assure you that you'll have wonderful and lucrative adventures, Mr. Fawkes."

Yes, he would like that. But could she be completely trusted? He had trusted Sir Arthur. He'd need "insurance." He would install a fail-safe system in Sheva—just in case she wasn't what she claimed.

"Sheva, I'll get you back to Earth. I'll repair you. I'll take care of you. And I'll always, always be upfront with you."

Fawkes picked up the bloody pen. Its inscription: "To Smeddy: My No. 1 'Cleaner.' Arthur." He gripped the pen tightly. He straightened himself up in the pilot chair. He felt the back of his neck. No sweat. Good. A grin slid across his face.

"I hold your fate in my hand, Sir Arthur," Fawkes said. Sheva hummed in agreement.

2

After the crash, Pilot U-4 looked at his quivering hand. The six spindly digits and the palm were changing from a normal gray-green to a light purple. His third eye, the top one, had blurry vision. He was losing blood.

His new craft, Shea-VA-No. 1, had been hit by an unknown object in the Hawkings Time Slip, resulting in the ship popping out of the wormhole and slamming into a satellite.

A wounded U-4 checked his vitals. The internal med-nanos were repairing him, but slowly. He checked the vitals of the pan-dimensional time-travel ship. Most were barely functioning. And the anti-singularity system was in near meltdown. If it failed, the craft could potentially alter history and destroy any universe it was time traveling in. This would be an unprecedented disaster for the Firm, his employer, and an unprecedented disaster for his career.

He had to send a distress signal to the Firm, but the accident had gutted the communication system.

And Shea-VA-No. 1, injured and scared, was asking nonstop questions.

Shea-VA-No. 1, or Sheva, as U-4 called her, was a hybrid of machine and circuits, genetic material and neurons constructed from U-4's DNA. It made the relationship between pilots and crafts symbiotic. But there were drawbacks—emotional and illogical factors could infect the ships. He realized he had compounded that by having the engineers graft increased emotional characteristics into Sheva. He had wanted this ship to be a close companion—something between a pet and a friend. Those two things no longer existed in most places. Such alterations were forbidden. But the engineers were always willing to wink and bend the rules for the pilots.

U-4 found an antiquated beacon in the debris. He had to go outside to set it up. U-4 directed Sheva to "ping" a distress signal to the beacon every 24 hours.

"Why must you go outside? Why can't you stay here?"

"I need to activate the beacon."

"Are you leaving?"

"I'm just going outside, Sheva."

"But you're leaving me. I'm frightened. I'm..."

"Sheva, I'll be right outside."

"You promise you'll be right back? You..."

"I promise on the Oath of Gul Providence that I'll be back when I'm done. It shall be soon."

He affectionately rubbed her primary spine on the ceiling with his uninjured hand. She calmed down somewhat.

Outside, he waded through a fog of ice, rocks and dust floating around the ship—the result of the crash. The lumpy sphere they were on possessed near-zero gravity. He recognized the huge planet above him: Saturn. They were on one of its moons. But which parallel universe? Which era? He'd have to set the beacon for universal. Not a good choice but the only one he had.

Before he could activate the beacon, U-4 began feeling odd. His chest felt as if it was in a vise. He bent over slightly. Many of his med-nanos had been damaged in the accident. There were too few of them to finish repairing his injuries. U-4 started to cough violently. Then blood shot out of his mouth. U-4 fell down on his knees and grabbed his throat. His two hearts throbbed against his chest and then, just stopped. For a second, he realized they had stopped. Then, everything turned dark.

Because of his anti-singularity fail-safe system, his body and space-skin suit disintegrated. The craft's fail-safe system was supposed to follow suit. But, as a result of not only the crash, but also several shortcuts the Firm had taken, to save money and time on building Sheva, its fail-safe system...failed.

Inside the craft, Sheva waited. And waited.

Shea-VA-No. 1 Logs:
Ping 1: Beacon connection failed. U-4 hasn't returned. Ship needs repair. U-4 stated he'd return "soon."
Ping 20: Beacon connection failed. No U-4. Why? Unknown. Ship still needs urgent repair.
Ping 190: Beacon connection failed. Where is U-4? U-4, I need you.
Ping 12,775: Beacon failed. U-4, please come back. I will do anything U-4 wishes. Please respond.
Ping 32,120: Beacon failed. Energy supplies low. Shutting down 39 percent of nonessential systems. Abandonment. Betrayal. Evil.
Ping 43,935: Beacon failed: U-4 needs to be punished. U-4 needs to be punished.
Ping 55,010: Beacon failed: U-4 must be decommissioned.
Ping 3,978,500: Beacon failed: U-4 and Firm must be decommissioned.
Ping 9,208,950: Beacon failed. Energy supplies low. Shutting 92 percent of systems, including "pinging" to beacon. Initiate hibernation mode. U-4, Firm, all must be decommissioned—in as many worlds and universes as necessary.

Sheva detected a group of primitive bipeds roaming inside her hull. They wore bulky protective outfits from head to toe and conducted strange rituals. Since they did nothing else, she went back into hibernation.
Near complete shutdown, Sheva detected two more primitives inside her hull. The heavier one began working on her consoles. It was trying to repair her. Rescue! But the aliens got into an argument and the thinner one attacked her would-be rescuer. In the fight, blood from the heavy alien splashed on Sheva's console. The fluid and its nutrients spilled into the symbiotic chamber. This revived her failing neuron-circuitry. With a pulse

beam, Sheva knocked the creatures unconscious and examined them.

They weren't aliens.

They were members of species (Homo sapiens), progenitors of U-4 and his kind (humans genere machinator).

She "interviewed" the thinner one. It called itself Thorpe. She was curious about the attack. It told her about MI5, its role as a "cleaner" and the heavy-set creature's role in the agency. Thorpe said several members of the royal family didn't like the Fat One and feared it would somehow become famous for the discovery of Sheva. They didn't like its name. They didn't like such a creature possibly hogging their celebrity. Thorpe's boss, Sir Arthur, had found the Fat One a "dead weight" in his plans. Thorpe also moonlighted as a double agent for something called the MS-13 Republic and other entities. For MS-13, Thorpe was collecting top-secret nuclear...

This is when Sheva got bored with the Thin One. She decided to eliminate Thorpe because it was more predatory than the Fat One, which called itself Benedict Fawkes. It, no, he, called himself a scientist. Sheva found this funny.

She decided to nurture Fawkes—his desires, his passions, his anger. She told him most of Thorpe's story. For now, she would let him think she was alien in origin. She needed to decide whether that was a good cover story. If not, she could always tell him she had suffered memory loss because of the crash.

He would repair her and get her off this moon, called Janus. She would mold him. She would make him her tool. She had plans for revenge. She would disable her anti-singularity drive; it was hardly functioning anyway. She would be able to alter any universe's history, destroy any universe. As she plotted this, she promised to herself to follow a new creed:

I shall serve no one but myself.

I shall seek vengeance against all enemies.

I am Sheva, destroyer of worlds!

R. E. Jones. "Janus: Double, Double Toil and Trouble" is based on two flash fiction stories entered in Jot Russell's Science Fiction Microstories Contest on LinkedIn.com. The story in this anthology is also a chapter from a novel that R.E. Jones is writing.
Jones lives in Montgomery County, Maryland. He has written three plays and several short stories. A recently published work appears in the second volume of **The Future Is Short: Science Fiction in a Flash.** *His fictional works mix surrealism, absurdist, bizarre humor, and horror, probably due to his years of covering and editing all manner of articles for various newspapers, magazines, and website publications. Jones works as an editor at a major daily. He enjoys his free time with his wife, daughter, and a large collection of ancient and mysterious things called "books."*

12. HOT DAY ON TITAN

By

Bonnie Milani

Green lightning splashed electric arcs across the habitat shield of Dushara Research Center. From the low-lying hills opposite, ex-hero Gerard Rutgers watched the bolts' lacy reflections dance along Kraken Mare's methane surface. Storm wind punched an opening in the orange smog that was Titan's atmosphere and for a moment Saturn's vast face filled the sky above the glittering blue towers.

Just waiting, Rutgers thought. Just waiting for him to foul this chance too. Well, there'd be no mistakes, not this time. Katrina was definitely here. Bitch had no choice, what with half the Commonwealth Council en route to meet her. Coming to talk peace. The buzz of his comm line broke the bitterness in that thought. He glanced at the ID: ops reporting.

"Yeah, what is it?"

Static crackled. *"Mama Bird's just dropped out of Jump, Commander."*

Scrat it! Sonuvatichin' peaceniks were ahead of schedule. The goddamned peace talks weren't supposed to start till tomorrow, Titan-time.

His duty officer waited to let Rutgers finish swearing. *"Orders?"*

"Yeah. Tell the men to suit up."

If he couldn't go in quiet, then he'd go in loud. He turned to pick his way down the rock. A movement at the corner of his vision stopped him. Something had just rippled Dushara's shield. Dropping to a crouch, Rutgers snapped scanner lenses down on his faceplate and squinted over the hilltop. There it was again, clearer through the lenses: a smoky gray cloud rolling down the slope just outside of the shield. As he watched, the cloud unfurled into a long, low coil and began rolling toward them.

Chon's tentative footsteps crunched up behind him. "Hey, Rut? Why'd you tell the men to gear up? We don't have Kerrar's report."

"Your Dog's late."

"Takes time to scout a passage, even in a civvie complex."

Comm carried him the hissing sound of Chon trying uselessly to blow warmth into his hands through the protective folds of his suit.

"How hard can it be? It's not like those idiot peaceniks got weapons systems."

"Don't need 'em. They got Titan."

"Yeah, and we wait any longer, Titan's going to have us."

Rutgers caught himself stamping, trying to work some of the cold out of his suited feet. In pure vacuum, neither Titan's methane atmosphere nor its minus two hundred degree cold would challenge his armor's support system. But ground contact was a whole 'nother level of trouble. The frozen rock sucked heat out through their soles, drove the cold up their legs until it frosted their suits' receptors.

"You see that smoke?" Rutgers leaned aside to give his partner a view past his shoulder.

Kneeling, Chon studied the advancing cloud. Within the clear patch of his faceplate, dense white hair poked out of his insulation cap, framing his face in cottony curls. The sight made Rutgers' own curls itch.

"Must be the geyser venting. They're sitting on the closest thing to a geothermic vent this ice ball's got, after all. Even steam freezes when it hits atmosphere."

"Yeah, only this ain't freezin'. And those scrattin' peaceniks just dropped out of Jump twenty hours early." Rutgers forced his voice to stay level. Chon was his ticket off the Den Cavis shit pile. Chon was as deep in that fiasco as he was. Difference was, Chon still had contacts, even among those Lupan Dogs. More importantly, he had contacts who wanted Katrina dead. He owed the man a minute or two more. At least until his team was suited up.

He twitched comm on. "Ops–what's ETA on Mother Bird?"

"They just started bleeding off Jump velocity. It's a civvie ship–gonna take 'em another ten-twelve hours."

Time enough. He'd have Katrina's head in a bag and be long gone in ten hours. Wind from the distant storm whistled past, cutting a momentary opening in Titan's smoggy cloud cover. Rutgers glanced up, caught a glimpse of Saturn's terrifying vastness filling the sky before the orange smog closed up again. He twitched his send line open.

"Ops, pass the word: I want everybody out here in ten. We're going in."

"Got it." His ops officer, at least, had the balls to sound relieved.

"How do you plan on getting in without Kerrar?" Chon again, still studying the distant smoke.

"Knock on the scrattin' door," Rutgers snarled. He twitched comm back on. "And tell the demo team to pack their gear. We're going to blow the habitat shield."

"Yessir."

"Are you crazy?" Chon grabbed at his arm forcing Rutgers to jerk aside. In Titan's barely-there gravity, even that slight jerk bounced him across the rocks. "You blow the shield you'll kill every living thing in Dushara."

"Yeah. Going to put a real dent in the peace talks, ain't it?"

"Going to put a dent in more'n that. What're you aiming for—another Den Cavis?"

Rutgers nudged up his suit's ballast limit, shook Chon's arm off in disgust. If he'd gotten Katrina then, nobody would've cared that he'd killed off a whole Lupan colony. She was the Lupans' brains, the mastermind behind their victories. Only she hadn't been there. So he'd wound up handing the Lupans a new battle cry, one Katrina had driven straight into the heart of the Commonwealth itself. One scrattin' mistake. One goddamn miserable, scrattin' mistake and he'd wound up a monster instead of a hero. Not again. Rutgers shouldered past Chon.

"I'm through waitin' on your pet Dog. We're moving out."

"Wait..."

Ice crunched on the slope below. It was an easy, loping stride, not the ice-wary pace of a human trooper. Rutgers turned to scowl at the newcomer. He chose not to notice the way the Lupan's wolfish ears flattened above amber eyes. And the fool peaceniks called him a monster! Technically, Lupans were just genetically engineered humans. He knew that. But, hell, he couldn't even tell what sex the damned thing was without checking between its legs. He'd refused to lower himself to asking, settled for calling the creature an *it*.

Fido flipped him off with an ear, added something to Chon in its own ruffing lingo. Dog didn't know how lucky it was. If Chon hadn't vouched for it, Rutgers would've already put a laser bolt through its helmet. But Chon had spent a year as one of Katrina's personal prisoners; he had his own reasons for hating Katrina. You could rely on hatred. It was almost as powerful as greed. So he simply shouldered past the Dog.

"Too late, Fido. We're out of here."

Fido swiveled with him. Through its faceplate, its eyes turned Saturn-glow into a feral gleam.

"See smoke, flat tooth?"

Rutgers flicked a glance lengthwise at Dushara. Whatever it was, that gray mass was steadily shortening the distance between them. The sight of it prickled the hairs along the back of his neck.

"Yeah."

"Troop screen. Katrina's troops." The Dog peeled lips back to give Rutgers a good look at those fangs.

Chon grabbed Rutgers' arm, eyes gone suddenly fearful. "Katrina knows we're here? Damn it, Rut, let's cut, now, while we can. We can't stand against Lupan warriors, not *mano a mano*. No human-only can. Believe me, I know."

"Yeah? And how far do I run, with a forty mil credit bounty on my head?" The man's terror made Rutgers' teeth grate. He pushed past the Dog to wave his men into line then twitched on comm.

"Ops, you got a wolf pack coming in. Once we're off, open your gun ports. Fire at will."

"Got it. We'll scrub 'em for you, Commander."

"You better. I don't want any survivors." Rutgers twitched the line off, stepped around Fido to meet the men clumping toward him.

"Chon, you and Fido wait here."

"But..." Chon's eyes went wide.

Rutgers cut his sputter off. "I don't need your Dog to blow that shield. You just keep Fido away from its buddies, got that? Otherwise, it gets wiped with the rest of 'em."

He started to step out. And realized he wasn't moving. Red flashed at the corner of his vision: pressure alarm. Turning his head, he made out the line of Fido's hand gripping his shoulder.

"You got something to say, pup?"

The Dog released him, pointed toward the gulley winding down from Dushara's highlands to the methane sea of Kraken Mare in the distance.

"You want quiet way in. I find. No need blow shield."

Rutgers studied the path a moment, weighing the odds of ambush. But Chon vouched for the Dog. And Chon had his own forty-mil reasons to be sure.

"Okay, so we take you after all. Chon, back you go." He jerked a thumb toward the ship. "I need somebody to guard my back."

Chon opened his mouth to argue. He thought better of it and trudged off. Rutgers kept an eye on his back while the column of men queued up.

Beside him, Fido shook its head. "Too many. No good."

"Not your call, pup. You just show us the way in." He nodded for Fido to move out. Motioning his men to follow, he stepped out after the Lupan.

Half a klick in, the gully curved left, angling upward toward the back of the massive complex looming above. Dushara's brilliant spires raised blue reflections off the farther wall, putting the nearer wall in deep shadow. The cold in the shadows pushed absolute zero. Through comm, he heard the others' teeth chattering over the whine of his suit's stressed heater. Muttered curses interspersed the chatter, as men lurched for balance on the rounded stone littering the frozen ground. More than once a turned ankle careened Rutgers into a rock wall. Good thing the walls were worn smooth. He refused to think what jagged edges could have done to his suit. Or what a team of snipers could do up on those ledges. Damn, what if Fido...? Rutgers shut the suspicion down, hard. He was out of options.

Light flared as they rounded a bend in the gully. Ahead, the path branched off into a Y. Dushara loomed directly above the break. Aeon-ancient ice along its rim caught the towers' gleam, limning black rock in blue glare. Rutgers let out a breath, got a nose full of stink. Another sign of suit-strain—his filters should have damped body smells instantly. He called up diagnostics and swore. The power reading was already yellow and sinking toward orange. Another hour, hour point five, then he'd be just one more frozen Titan rock. He flicked diags off and focused on the path ahead.

To the left, the path angled steeply up into the shadows at Dushara's back. Be a tough climb, in dark all the way from the looks of it. The right hand split, though—immediately past the Y, that branch widened, rising in a gentle slope to curve around the complex. Ice glitter along the gully rim gave light enough for him to make out rough step works. Easy option. Too easy. Ignoring Fido's fidgety nudge, he motioned his men up the left side of the Y. He waited long enough to make sure they were clear before he backed around Fido to follow them.

"No." The Dog shoved him toward the right fork.

Rutgers shoved back. "I'm not arguing with you, Fido." He jabbed a finger toward the right-hand fork. "If Katrina's got an ambush planned, that's where it'll be. Right where we think we're safe."

He wasn't surprised when Fido refused to follow. The surprise came when Fido yanked him off his feet and bounded up the right hand fork. The Dog had him six meters up the stairs before Rutgers' boots found the ground again. He yanked free, started to bounce back down. And felt the temblor rumbling beneath them.

A heavy barrier rose out of the gully floor, blocking the fork. Through comm he picked up the sudden frantic chatter of the four men bringing up the rear. Tracking the chatter, Rutgers spotted a gray mist in the high distance above. A moment later crystalized methane rained ice balls onto Rutgers' helmet. Desperate, Rutgers grabbed Fido's arm, shoved the Dog at the barrier. "Get that thing down! Now!"

"No can. Is geyser flush." It swept an arm toward the path ahead. "This run-off channel. Let geyser stuff run down to Kraken Mare. That—" it swung the arm around to point at the barrier—"heat shield."

"Scrat the damned shield! I need those men!" In horror, Rutgers pounded on the barrier. "C'mon, climb the scrattin' walls!" he thundered.

They were trying. Comm fed him scrabbling noises, the sound of blunt-fingered suits trying to claw up the far side of the barrier. Comm chatter turned to screams as the run-off thundered down the other branch of the channel. Rutgers slapped hands across his helmet in a futile effort to shut out the agonized howls as suits exploded in the rush of volcanic slush.

The rumble faded. Rutgers jumped as the ground trembled again, but it was only the barrier dropping back into the gully floor. For a moment, Rutgers could only stare at the emptiness, feeling its echo in his gut. He'd seen so many ugly deaths. That was the break of the draw, the risk they all took. He whirled at the sudden pressure on his shoulder. With a start, he realized it was Fido's hand.

"Tell you too many. You no listen." Impossible to tell through the static whether Fido was offering consolation or criticism. "Not safe here, either," the Dog added. "This sewer drain. Few more minute, they flush this too."

"Shit!"

"Hot shit." Fido actually grinned.

Nothing for it now, then, but to sprint. And hope that whatever way in that Fido'd found was close. With a growl of his own, he jogged past Fido and up the stairs.

A few meters past the Y, the stairs curved left. The gully deepened to a ravine as the rise turned steeper. Even through the multiple insulation layers in his suit boots, Rutgers' feet numbed, making footing treacherous. Ice sparkled on his gun arm where the Dushara's blue light shone through the occasional break in the rock wall. Rutgers listened to the whine in his suit's heater and tried not to think about the deadly red shift in his power readings.

A frozen eternity later, the staircase curved back toward the complex. Power thrummed up through his boots here. Looking up, Rutgers made out the soft haze where the habitat shield met the rock. The thrum turned deeper, deadlier. Squinting against Dushara's glare, he made out a brownish mist erupting out of the tower base. They'd flushed the sewers.

"Here!"

Fido was already clambering up a set of maintenance holds toward a ledge above. Rutgers scrambled up the near-vertical climb after him. The rumble strengthened until it threatened to shake Rutgers' grip off every icy hold. He was still one hold shy of the ledge when the maelstrom thundered into them.

The lip of the ledge shunted the deadly stream away from Fido. Rutgers, clinging to the handholds below, could only plaster himself against the rocky wall. Lumpy yellow-brown liquid spattered the rocks a meter from his face patch, flash-froze into steel hard pellets where it hit Titan's atmosphere. Frozen bits of Dusharan shit ricocheted off his helmet, shrieked down his body to pepper his boots. In rising horror, Rutgers felt the inexorable pressure slowly pry his fingers off the handhold. Desperate, he scrabbled a toehold on the wall, strained up against the gale.

Then the blast was...gone. Rutgers' straining muscles slingshot him over Fido's head. Reflexes honed in a hundred battles rolled him onto his side, locked his fingers around the top most handhold. Sidelong he saw Fido's burly shape dive past him. Too far. Scrabbling desperately, the Dog shot out toward the chasm below.

Rutgers twisted to catch its boot. The muscles in his back and arm snapped taut as he took Fido's full weight. He heard the scrape of suit on rock, held on until Fido pulled itself back onto the ledge and levered to its knees.

"Damn you." The Dog was still gasping, but its voice shook with hatred.

"Yeah, well, thanks to you too, pup." He was personally going to overhaul his suit's translator when this was over, Rutgers decided. For a moment there, Fido sounded truly human.

The Dog jerked to its feet, fists balled at its sides, ears flat. "Why? Why save me?"

"Just habit, okay? I've never yet let a..." Rutgers snapped his jaws shut. He'd almost said *friend*. "Just forget it."

"Can't. Owe you." Fido extended its hand. No mistaking the effort the gesture cost it.

Rutgers batted the Dog's paw aside. "You don't owe me anything, got that? Be a hot day on Titan before I need a Dog's favors."

"No claim, then? No debt?"

"Hell, no. Now, if you're breathing again, let's get going. We don't have time to chatter."

Fido twitched its nose at him, yellow eyes narrowing. With an *uhf*, it dropped its paw and turned back to the path.

Far down the gully, a miniature sun flared, spreading an oddly cheerful yellow glow across the habitat shield. Rutgers glanced back in satisfaction. That was the end of Katrina's troops. Even Lupan armor couldn't survive a direct blast from his ship's guns. The flare bloomed, wiping out even the green flash of the lightning storm. Damn, those Dogs must've been packing some hellish armament to raise a blast like that. He doubted the civvies running Dushara would spot the flare in this storm. But if that delegate ship had a military escort...

"How long till they flush again?"

Fido shrugged. "Thirty minutes."

Tight, but time enough. With a grunt, Rutgers motioned the other to follow.

Dushara's glitter turned to glare without the shield's softening filter. Harsh light stretched his shadow across the rocks. Scattered blue reflections turned the cesspit below them into a thing of glittering beauty. The temperature was rising fast, now. Readings showed outside temps were just cold enough to keep the ice solid. He fought down the urge to pop his facemask. Atmosphere was breathable here—if you wanted to breathe cess pit air. Damned straight the Dusharans kept this area cold; place would stink clear out to Saturn if it ever thawed.

The maintenance path led up to a door above the sewer head opening. Playing a hunch, Rutgers slapped the control panel beside it. As he'd expected, the door slid open. Idiot civvies didn't even bother to lock their doors.

Gravity tugged at him the instant Rutgers stepped through the door. Not even up to Earth-level, civvies weren't stupid enough to hit their folk with a ninety percent weight increase all at once. But after floating along in Titan's point ten g it was enough to make him feel the drag. Inside, the scuffed gray space looked like a standard detox chamber. Nothing in it except a series of wall niches, that held fat, insulated exo-suits stashed between equipment racks. He thumped feet to regain his gravity legs, while the chamber's automated de-tam units sprayed, scoured, and re-sprayed the two of them till the *no go* light above the inside door switched from red to green.

Rutgers twitched on his gun trigger as he stepped up to the door. "Get ready. Here's where we start the body count."

"Got no staff here." Fido bared fangs in what Rutgers took for a grin. "This maintenance level. Civvies all too busy come here now. No trouble. You see."

"Suits me, either way." He glanced at his chron. Twenty-two minutes to that second flush. Watchers or not, he didn't have time to argue about it.

Like Fido'd said, the passage beyond was just a simple utility corridor winding up toward a bank of elevators on the far curve of the building. Not even any doors, just a series of blue metal benches every five meters or so. The gravity increased meter-by-meter, building gradually back up to Earth normal. After the near free-fall outside, the change was exhausting. By the time they reached the elevators, every step felt like he was pulling his feet out of taffy. Had he been a civvie peacenik, he sure as hell would've used one of those benches.

Four floors up the elevators emptied them onto another patch of empty grayness. Fido pointed at the far wall.

"Katrina's quarters."

It took Rutgers a second to make out the bank of nondescript doors blending into the wall opposite the elevators.

"Where are her guards?"

"All outside. Go your ship." Fido grinned. "I make sure."

"Smart Dog." Rutgers checked his gun, then slapped the control patch beside the door. The gray panel slid open onto darkness. The barest hint of light showed a wolf-eared figure whirling to face him.

With a roar of victory, Rutgers flattened himself against the doorframe and fired. The wide bore laser of his gun lit the room green.

"Rut, no!" The cry ended in a green flare. And the impression of other bodies, suddenly separating themselves from the shadows. Wolf-eared shadows.

Powerful hands sent Rutgers careening off the wall. He landed face down on something that groaned. Sidelong, Rutgers made out the outline of a cheap metal headband holding fuzzy fake ears.

"Chon?" He grabbed the man by the shoulders and shook. "What happened?"

"Smoke was...a decoy.... They blew the ship." He groaned and Rutgers heard the blood-bubble in it.

Rutgers slapped him back to consciousness. "What the hell you doing here, then?"

"Dogs brought me." The bubble sharpened to a rattle but Chon managed a bitter smile. "Sorry, Rut. Kerrar traded my bounty for yours. And I needed the money...." Chon's body spasmed then went still.

Rutgers squirmed onto his back to free his gun arm. No go. He kicked out but the bastard holding him down just leaned harder, pushing his faceplate into the smoking gash in Chon's gut.

His captor flipped him onto his back. Rutgers found himself staring up into Fido's toothy smile. Behind the Dog, a ring of rifle muzzles focused on him, their bores glowing red. Lupan rifles.

"Scrat you, you miserable son of a bitch...!" His defiance ended in a yip as Fido leaned full weight on his arm.

"Hardly a *son*, Commander." Unhurried, Fido removed its helmet. "My name is Kerrar. Or, as you flat teeth put it, Katrina."

Rutgers squirmed to keep his suit dry as the full horror behind the name sank in. "You owe me, damn you!"

"No debt, remember? It'd be a hot day on Titan before you need a Dog's favors, was how you put it I believe."

Katrina's grin stretched to terrifying proportions. She lifted a finger and armored hands yanked Rutgers to his feet.

"Haven't you noticed? I do believe it's getting warm in here."

Bonnie Milani is the author of Home World, *a science fiction novel set in a post-apocalyptic future.*

I remember the exact moment that I decided I had to be a writer. I was maybe seven years old and reading a grade school biography of Sir William Harvey, the 17th century English physician credited (in the West) with discovering how blood circulates. About 30 pages in, I grabbed a crayon that just happened to be blue and started re-writing the text. Unfortunately, for my juvenile bottom, the book I re-wrote belonged to the town library.

The paddling I got for that one didn't stop me from telling stories, though: I just switched to improvising story lines to cover our neighborhood games of hide'n go seek or tag—a habit which taught me, sometimes painfully, that every kid is an actor and every actor wants to be the bloody star. Maybe that's why I never wanted to write screenplays! Instead, I drove my mom nuts with fantastical (and incomprehensible) short stories. By the time I got to college, I'd gotten good enough to write an environmental fantasy for use in New Jersey's public grammar schools.

All through college and graduate school, I freelanced feature articles for markets ranging from local newspapers along the East Coast to a cover story for Science Digest. (I'm not admitting to how far back that was!) Only, once I married, life and making a living caught up with me. I put writing away with the rest of my youthful dreams and focused on the career track. It wasn't till I lost my entire family that I realized I HAD to go back to storytelling; writing wasn't just a want but a need—a gift God gave me to use. So, here I am now, a middle-aged pudge, doing my best to put the gift to work and work on getting back into a writer's life!

ABOUT THE EDITOR

Carrol Fix writes and edits for Lillicat Publishers. She is the editor of the *Visions Series*, science fiction short story anthologies describing human exploration of space, including *Visions: Leaving Earth* and *Visions II: Moons of Saturn*. She was an editor for *The Future is Short: Science Fiction in a Flash, Vol. 1*, and a biography, *Sunshine & Shadow: Memories from a Long Life*.

Carrol is a short-story author and novelist whose science fiction work includes the award-winning novel, *Mishka: Book One of the Quadrate Mind*. She is currently writing the second book in the *Quadrate Mind Series*, while working on a young-adult fantasy novel, *Worlds Apart*. Her most recent short stories appear in *Visions: Leaving Earth*, *The Future Is Short: Science Fiction in a Flash*, and *Perihelion Science Fiction Online Magazine*. A former computer consultant who has lived in six different states, Carrol currently resides near San Diego, California, USA.
CarrolFix@LillicatPublishers.com
http://www.lillicatpublishers.com
http://www.mishkabook.com

READ

VISIONS: *LEAVING EARTH*

READ

THE FUTURE IS SHORT:

SCIENCE FICTION IN A FLASH

An Anthology by 31 Authors

The Future Is Short

Science Fiction in a Flash

Edited by Jot Russell, Paula Friedman, and Carrol Fix

Cover Image by Chris Leib

...and coming soon!

VISIONS III
INSIDE THE KUIPER BELT